Smugglers!

Ralph intended to ⬚ ⬚ ⬚ ⬚ arrived with their b⬚ ⬚ ⬚ ⬚ ⬚ them on his land. There had been no sign of them but he had seen the boy making his way furtively along the path towards the shore and he had followed.

Only it was not a boy but the girl who was constantly in his thoughts. He had believed her assertion she knew nothing about the smugglers because he had wanted to believe it, but how could he deny the evidence of his own eyes?

He supposed she had warned them off and there would be no landing tonight.

Ralph stirred his cramped limbs and went home, furious with Lydia for frustrating him. Lydia Fostyn, young, beautiful, contrary, defiant, a thorn in his flesh so deeply embedded he did not know how to rid himself of it. Having her arrested with all the others might serve. He knew, even as the thought entered his head, he could not do it. Somehow he must make sure she was safe before he made a move.

Born in Singapore, **Mary Nichols** came to England when she was three, and has spent most of her life in different parts of East Anglia. She has been a radiographer, school secretary, information officer and industrial editor, as well as a writer. She has three grown-up children, and four grandchildren.

Recent titles by the same author:

THE WESTMERE LEGACY
THE RELUCTANT ESCORT

THE HONOURABLE EARL

Mary Nichols

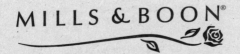
MILLS & BOON®

*First published in Great Britain 2001
Harlequin Mills & Boon Limited,
Eton House, 18-24 Paradise Road, Richmond, Surrey TW9 1SR*

© Mary Nichols 2001

ISBN 0 263 82738 0

*Set in Times Roman 10½ on 12 pt.
04-0701-86581*

*Printed and bound in Spain
by Litografia Rosés S.A., Barcelona*

Prologue

1753

The rambling old vicarage was eerily quiet, but then it was five o'clock in the morning and eight-year-old Lydia, watching by the window, saw the first flush of pink on the horizon above the marshes and knew it would soon be dawn. There was a thick mist above the ground and the trees in the coppice on her left appeared to be growing in the air and the rooftops in the village of Colston to her right seemed to be floating without walls to support them. Nearer the house the stables were solid enough and the ground beneath her window, though damp, was becoming more visible as the light strengthened.

Perhaps he would not go. Perhaps friendship had prevailed and nothing untoward would happen. Perhaps Freddie, her beloved brother, and his great friend, Lord Ralph Latimer, had made up their quarrel and there would be no duel. She could not imagine anything terrible enough to make the two young men hate each other. And yet, earlier that evening when she had found Freddie in the book-

room, cleaning their father's pistols, and had asked him
what he was doing, he had been grim and angry.

'It is time you were in bed and asleep, Lydia,' he had
said. 'I must do what I must do.'

'But what must you do?'

'Nothing. Go to bed. If Father catches you here, he will
be angry.'

'He will be angry if he sees you with those pistols. You
know he never allows anyone to touch them.'

'They will be back in their case before he misses them.'
He had paused to peer into her face. 'Unless you tell him.'

'Oh, no, Freddie, I would never do that. But why are
you so angry?'

'I am not angry. At least, I am not angry with you, but
I shall be if you do not go upstairs this minute and forget
you ever saw me.'

'But guns are dangerous things, you might be killed.'

'So if I am, honour will be satisfied.'

It was then she realised that he meant to fight a duel.
Mistress Grey, her teacher and mentor, was a great reader
of romantic fiction in which duels frequently featured and
she often left her books lying about. Lydia had devoured
them as she did all manner of reading matter, her curiosity
about everything insatiable. Sometimes there were reports
of duels in the newspapers which she had been forbidden
to read. But forbidding Lydia to do something was tan-
tamount to an invitation and she read them clandestinely
after they had been sent to the kitchen to be used to light
the fires.

'But who has doubted your honour?'

'Ralph,' he had said morosely.

'But he is your best friend. You have always done everything together— you are even together at Cambridge.
How can you fight him?'

'I have no choice. He has insulted me. And...' He stopped, as if remembering his listener was only an eight-year-old. 'Now go to bed and not a word to anyone or I'll have your hide.' And when she smiled at this empty threat, had added, 'I mean it, Lydia. It is not a jest.'

She had crept to her room and undressed, slipping into bed beside the five-year-old Annabelle, but she could not sleep. She knew that Freddie was impulsive and head-strong, as she was herself, or so Mistress Grey told her often enough, but surely he would not put his life at risk or shoot Ralph? Ralph was the son of the Earl of Black-water; there would be a terrible outcry if anything happened to him. She would not even begin to think of the possibility that it might be Freddie who came off worse. And duelling had been outlawed, hadn't it? She must do something. But what? Freddie had forbidden her to tell their father and, in any case, she would do nothing that would get him into trouble. She could tell Susan or Margaret, her older sisters, but they would certainly go to their father with the tale, and she could not worry her mother with it. After all, the two young men might come to their senses if someone were to jolt them into seeing the fool-ishness of their ways. And, lying sleepless in her bed, it seemed to her that she was the only one who could do it.

She had dressed in the dimity dress she had worn that day, tied her thick brown hair back with a ribbon and seated herself on the deep window ledge of her bedroom to wait for Freddie to make a move, praying that he would not, but fearing the worst.

She heard a sound below her window and looked down to see Robert Dent, another of Freddie's friends, riding up to the house. He stopped beneath her brother's window and threw a handful of gravel at it. A moment later Freddie's head appeared in the aperture. 'I'll be down in a minute,' he hissed. 'Go round to the stable.'

In less than a minute she heard the door of her brother's room being opened and shut very softly. She crept to her own door and, as soon as she heard the front door open and close, grabbed a cloak from her closet and hurried downstairs. She had never saddled her pony herself, but she had watched the groom do it often enough and felt sure she could manage it. She had to be quick because she was not exactly sure where the duel was to take place.

In her haste she stumbled over her father's walking stick which he had propped against the wall in the hall. She stopped to pick it up and replace it, then reached for the door latch.

'Lydia! Where do you think you are going?'

She froze as her father, with a dressing gown over his nightshirt and his grey hair awry, came down the stairs behind her. Slowly she turned to face him. 'I...I thought...I thought I heard a fox in the hen run.'

'I hear nothing. And you are dressed.' He grabbed her arm and almost dragged her into the room he used for a study, where he kept his books and composed his sermons. 'Now, you will come in here and tell me what this is all about.'

'But I can't,' she wailed. 'It is not my secret.'

'Oh, then it must be Freddie's. Only Frederick would be irresponsible enough to drag you into one of his scrapes.'

'He didn't drag me in—'

'Where is he?'

She hung her head and did not answer.

'He has left the house, hasn't he? I was sure it was the sound of horses that woke me. Where has he gone? It is only just after five o'clock.'

She looked up at him, her eyes filled with tears. 'Papa, I must go to him, I really must. Please do not ask me why.'

Her reply in no way reassured him and he looked about him as if the contents of the book-lined room would give him his answer. She suddenly became aware that Freddie had left the cupboard open where the pistols were usually kept and the empty shelf seemed to stare out at them accusingly. She tried to move across to shut the cupboard door at the same moment her father saw it.

'My God! What has the silly fool been up to?' He swung round to Lydia. 'You know, don't you? You know where he has gone?'

She was truly frightened by the steely look in his eye and backed away a little. 'No, Papa, that was why I wanted to follow him. To stop him. Now it is too late. He is gone. Oh, Papa, he is going to fight Ralph Latimer.'

'Back to bed,' he commanded. 'I will deal with this.'

'But you don't know where he has gone.'

'I can guess. Now back to bed. We will talk about it when I return.'

She turned wearily to go back to her room, knowing that when he did come back she would be in for a scolding and probably punishment; her father could be very severe when he chose, but that would be nothing to what would happen to Freddie. Papa was always scolding Freddie over something or other and threatening to take him away from University and send him into the army 'to make a man of him', he said. Mama had always argued him out of it, but now... Losing her beloved brother was something she did not dare think about.

She curled up in her bed beside the still-sleeping Annabelle, and waited.

* * *

She must have fallen asleep because it was bright day when she woke and five-year-old Annabelle was gone. The house was silent as the grave; she could not hear even the servants going about their business. Nor had Janet, the maid who looked after all the girls, brought her hot water as she usually did. She rose and went to the window. The sun was high and Partridge, who was both groom and driver when they took the carriage out, was leading her father's cob into the stable. And Freddie's horse stood nearby, still saddled.

She dressed hurriedly without bothering to wash and dashed down the stairs. At the entrance to the morning room she stopped suddenly. Her mother and two older sisters were sitting in a group, looking up at Freddie. The two girls were weeping loudly and Freddie looked as though he had seen a ghost. His face was almost transparent and his blue eyes, usually so bright with mischief, were dull and lifeless. She turned from her siblings to her mother and drew in her breath in shock. Her mother was staring up at her brother as if she did not recognise her son. Her face was chalky white with two high spots of colour on her cheeks and her hands were kneading a lace handkerchief, tearing it to shreds.

'What has happened?' Lydia asked.

'Lydia. Come here.' Her mother held out one hand to her and she went to kneel at her mother's feet and put her head in her lap. 'Lydia, you must be very brave. We have lost our prop, the centrepiece of our lives, our dearest, most faithful...' She paused, as if wondering how to put what had happened into words, and then, deciding there was no way to soften the blow, added, 'Lydia, your poor papa is dead.'

Lydia tilted her head up to her mother. 'I don't understand. I don't. I thought it was Lord Latimer...' She swung round to her brother. 'You said...'

'Papa came,' he said. 'Ralph shot him.'

Lydia scrambled angrily to her feet and faced her brother. 'Then why didn't you shoot him back? I'll do it if you won't. Papa...' She collapsed in a heap, sobbing out her grief. 'It's my fault. I told him and he went after you. I let him go.'

'You could not have stopped him, any more than you could have stopped me.'

'And this is what your wickedness has brought us to,' her mother said bitterly, addressing Freddie. 'You have been going wild for months, you and that young man from the Hall, and this is the result. I dread to think what his lordship will have to say on the matter—'

'He has no cause for complaint,' Freddie said heatedly. 'It was his son who fired the shot, not me. It is not his family cast into mourning.'

'Will he be prosecuted?' Margaret stopped crying and scrubbed at her eyes with her handkerchief.

'Who is there to prosecute him?' her mother put in bitterly. 'His father is the Lord of the Manor and a justice. It will be hushed up as an accident and it were better it were, because duelling is illegal and Freddie was not blameless in the matter—'

'Mama!' Freddie protested.

'Oh, what is to become of us?' her mother wailed. 'Without your papa...'

'Mama, I think you should lie down and I will send for Dr Dunsden to give you something to help you sleep,' Susan said, taking charge of the situation. 'Later, there will be arrangements to make.'

At that moment, they heard a horse galloping up to the house and then a loud knocking on the door. Lydia, only half aware of what was going on around her, heard the maid go to the door and a few moments later came to announce the Earl of Blackwater.

'God, he wasted no time,' Freddie muttered, as the Earl made his way into the room, dressed in a riding coat and buckskin breeches tucked into polished riding boots. He was wearing a short brown wig and, except for his drawn countenance and bleak eyes, anyone would think he was out for a morning hack. He stopped just inside the door and surveyed the tableau.

'Anne, we must talk.'

'Yes,' she answered dully while the girls looked from one to the other taken aback by his familiar mode of addressing her. 'But can it not wait? My husband is hardly—'

'I know. I am sorry, but send the girls away. There are things to resolve…'

'Like this living—'

'God! Do you take me for an unfeeling monster? I did not mean that and you know it. Duelling is illegal. The boys have broken the law and as a result a man has been killed, and he not one of the protagonists, which might have made it excusable.'

'Do you think I don't know that?' she cried. 'How can you come here, when your son has deprived me of my husband…?' And she began to weep, losing all the dignity she had been trying so hard to maintain. Lydia went to her and threw her arms about her. 'Mama, Mama, don't cry.' And she too burst into noisy tears.

'Susan, take your sisters away,' his lordship said. 'Your mother and I and Freddie will decide what is to be done.'

Susan prised Lydia from her mother. 'Come, Lydia, we must find Annabelle and John. Goodness knows what mischief they will be up to while we have been in here. They are both too young to understand, but we must try and explain.' She led her away, followed by the still-tearful Margaret.

Lydia never knew what was said by the three who were left behind. The only thing her mind fastened on was that on the day she lost her papa, she also lost her beloved older brother. He did not even wait for the funeral, but was gone that night.

'It is for the best,' her mother told her when she asked why. 'His lordship cannot ignore the fact that the law was broken—'

'By his son,' Lydia put in. 'Not Freddie.'

'They were both at fault and Ralph has been banished too. His lordship has sent his only son and heir into exile. And now we must both go on with our lives without them.'

'You sound as if you are sorry for the Earl.'

'I am. It was not his fault.' She took Lydia's hand and tried to draw her closer, but Lydia resisted, too angry to draw comfort from her mother. Or give it either.

'No, it was his Ralph's. Freddie didn't want to fight him, I know he didn't.'

'Now, Lydia,' her mother said patiently. 'We will have no more talk of fault or blame or anything else of that nature, do you understand?'

She nodded, but she did not understand. She might say nothing in front of her mother, but she would never forgive Ralph Latimer for what he had done. Never. Never. Never.

Chapter One

March 1763

The Victory Ball, to celebrate the end of the seven years of war which had been waged between half the countries of Europe and which had now come to an end, was going to be the biggest occasion the little port and market town of Malden had seen for years, even though there were many who said it was not a victory but a shameful compromise. Anne had decided she would attend with her daughters, Lydia and Annabelle. Finding suitable gowns for all three was going to be a problem, but Anne found an old trunk in the attic, which contained gowns she had worn years before in their more affluent days, and brought it down to her boudoir.

From it she drew a sack-backed pale pink silk which had yards and yards of good material in it. 'The colour will suit Annabelle,' she said, pulling it from its protective covering of thin cotton. 'And here is another that will remake.' She delved into the trunk again and pulled out a yellow watered silk with panels of darker figured brocade. She held it up against Lydia's slim figure. 'Yes, perfect for your dark colouring. I wore it when I was your age, the first time I met your papa. It has kept very well, though it is very out of fashion. We will remake them both.'

'What about you, Mama?' Lydia asked.

'Oh, my grey and lilac stripe will do very nicely. After all, I am only going to escort you and at my age it would not do to go looking like a peacock, would it?'

Anne was by no means old and she was still very beautiful in Lydia's eyes. If it had not been for her large family and lack of wealth she might have remarried, except that she always said she had no wish to do so. 'I am content as I am,' she said, when anyone suggested such a thing. Lydia wondered how true that might be but knew it would do no good to question her. Instead she smiled and spoke about how they would remake the gowns.

Annabelle could hardly contain her excitement as she and Lydia set to work unpicking the old garments while their mother searched through copies of the *Ladies' Magazine* for suitable patterns. 'Oh, I am so looking forward to it,' she said, eyes shining. 'My first ball. I cannot wait.'

Lydia smiled indulgently. 'No doubt you expect every young man there to fall at your feet.'

'Oh, do you think they will? Oh, Lydia, would it not be wonderful if we could both find husbands there?'

'There is plenty of time for that. And we are unlikely to meet anyone of consequence. It is only the Assembly Rooms after all, and everyone knows everyone hereabouts.'

'There might be someone new to the town—surely, now the war is over, the officers will be coming back home.'

'You are too impatient, Annabelle,' Lydia said. 'Why, you are only fifteen.'

'Sixteen next month,' her sister corrected her. 'And you are eighteen. It is time you thought about marriage, for you should marry before me.'

'I am in no hurry.'

'You may not be,' their mother put in, as they sat side by side over their needlework, their dark heads almost touching. 'But most young ladies are married by nineteen. To delay longer will make everyone think you too partic- ular or that there is something wrong with you. And I will not have that. You are comely and intelligent and I have brought you up to your proper duties. It is time to be thinking seriously of whom you might marry.'

'I have not met anyone I think I should like, Mama, and I would rather earn my living than jump too hastily into marriage.'

'Earn your living! My goodness, I never heard anything so outlandish. Why, your grandfather was a baronet and he would turn in his grave, if he could hear you. We are not of that class, Lydia, even if we are poor...'

'Are we poor?' Lydia asked, in surprise.

Her mother sighed. 'I had hoped it would not come to this, but now I think I must tell you.'

'Tell me what, Mama? Oh, do not look so stern. Have I done something wrong?'

'No, dearest. But we have been living off the income from investments ever since your papa was taken from us so suddenly. There was never a great deal, but stocks have gone down and I have had to encroach on the capital. It is dwindling at an alarming rate. There will be no dowry for you, I am afraid. You must make as good a marriage as you can without one. It is not what I had hoped for you...'

Lydia was shocked; she had not known things were as bad as that. Her mother was always so cheerful and practical, though she abhorred what she called extravagance. It was no wonder, if they had so little money. And yet she had never stinted her children of anything they really needed. What a struggle it must have been for her!

'Oh, Mama, why did you not say? We could have recouped, eaten a little more cheaply, bought fewer ribbons and lace. Done without the chaise.'

'And have everyone pointing the finger and ruining your chances of finding any sort of marriage where you might be comfortable. Poverty is not something to advertise, Lydia. It gives quite the wrong impression.'

'You mean I must find a husband soon?'

Anne sighed. 'I am afraid so. A professional gentleman perhaps, or a younger son, or someone like Sir Arthur Thomas-Smith, who has been married before and is looking for a second wife and would not be particular as to a dowry.'

'Oh, Mama!' Lydia was horrified at the thought. 'He is old. And fat. And he has three daughters already.'

'But he is rich enough to indulge you in anything you might want. He might be persuaded to give Annabelle a dowry and help with John's schooling...'

'Mama, surely things are not as bad as that?'

'Dearest, I am afraid it is beginning to look very bleak indeed. We are fortunate that his lordship has allowed us to live here...'

Ever since the tragedy, when a new incumbent had been appointed and moved into the rectory, they had lived in the dower house on the Earl's estate, which had been standing empty since his mother died a year or two before. Lydia's feelings on accepting help from the Earl of Blackwater were ambivalent. Her pride against taking charity from the father of the man who had killed her beloved papa did battle with the conviction that he should be made to pay and anything they had from him was little enough compensation for their loss. Her mother saw it differently. She was grateful. Grateful!

Lydia's hate had not diminished over the years but she had learned to control it, to put on a cheerful face and live in the same small village without exploding every time someone mentioned his lordship's name, or she saw him smiling and chatting to the congregation after church on a Sunday. He was well liked and some even sympathised with him at the loss of his son and the protracted illness of his wife brought on, so it was said, by the tragedy. As if his loss was the greater.

Why, he could send his son funds to keep him in luxury wherever he was, but she had lost her papa and her brother might as well be dead as well for all the news they had of him. They certainly could not afford to send him money. Ten long years he had been gone and she still missed him. She missed her older sisters too.

At the time of the tragedy, Susan had been betrothed to the son of the recently knighted Sir Godfrey Mallard who lived in Lancashire, where the family had interests in cotton spinning. The marriage contract had already been signed by both fathers, otherwise the groom might very well have backed out of it, but on the grounds that Lancashire was a long way from Essex and news of the duel was unlikely to reach there, Sir Godfrey had allowed the wedding to go ahead a year later, though he discouraged his new daughter-in-law from visiting her old home more often than was absolutely necessary for appearances' sake.

As for Margaret, she had been betrothed to a young captain in the Hussars, but when he had been killed in the war, had eschewed marriage to anyone else and had gone to Hertfordshire to be schoolmistress to the children of the Duke of Grafton. Somehow working for the duke was acceptable employment in her mother's eyes. It meant Lydia was the eldest still at home and now they had become so poor she must sacrifice herself for the sake of the rest of the family and marry money. But Sir Arthur…!

'He has not been long in the district,' her mother said. 'He is not acquainted with the past.'

'Someone will soon tell him, you can be sure.'

'Then you must engage his attention and make him see the advantages of the match before he has time to listen…'

'Oh, Mama, that is surely deceitful.'

'No, he will take no heed of gossip when he gets to know you and realises what an excellent wife you will make.'

'Wife *and* mother,' Lydia added bitterly. 'Don't forget his daughters.'

'Oh, my dear child, I am so very sorry it has come to this but I cannot see any other way out. If your father had lived or even if Freddie…' She could not bring herself to go on. The absence of her elder son seemed to be an even greater cross for her to bear than the death of her husband.

'Can I not wait? Someone else might come along.'

'If you are harbouring romantic notions about falling in love, Lydia, I should caution you against allowing them free rein. Life is not like that. And especially our life.'

'No, I suppose not.' Lydia sighed heavily. She could not upset her mother by saying what was in her heart: the anger and despair, the black hate which she had pushed into the background but which now returned full force.

'If you do not care for Sir Arthur, there is Robert Dent,' her mother said. 'He is still single and will come into his father's wealth, even if it has been got by industry.'

'He is a rake and a gambler,' Lydia put in. 'Living with

him would be like twisting the knife in a wound which will not heal. He could have stopped that duel long before Papa ever got there. He should have refused to be Freddie's second.'

'Freddie would have found someone else to do it. But you are right, Robert Dent's reputation is a little tarnished and I would not want my daughter to be made unhappy by a profligate husband, however rich.'

'There is always the Comte de Carlemont,' Annabelle put in with a giggle. 'Such a dandy, but very polite. He would not care about the gossip. He would carry you away to the French court now that the war is ended. He might even find positions there for Mama and me.'

'I have no wish to go to France,' Lydia said and refused to say another word on the subject. She tried not to think about it, to look forward to the ball as Annabelle was doing and dream of finding a husband who lived up to her very high ideals. He must be handsome and strong but, more than that, he must be kind and attentive and not given to gambling. He would love her devotedly and not even think about taking a mistress because they would be so happy together, he would never see the need. And he might restore Freddie to them…

She sighed. What was the good of dreaming? They had no idea where her brother was. He had written soon after he left, telling them that he had enlisted but then nothing. They did not even know if he were alive or dead.

They were about to set aside their sewing and have dinner when Janet came to say one of the grooms from Colston Hall was in the kitchen, with a message for Mrs Fostyn. Lydia and Annabelle looked as each other as their mother rose to go to speak with the man.

'What can he want?' Lydia mused, after Anne had left

the room. 'I cannot understand why Mama continues to bow down to that man.'

'You mean the Earl? He has done nothing wrong.'

'What do you know of it? You were not there.'

'I heard what happened. Everyone did. It was his son who shot Papa, not him.'

'He sent Freddie away. He took our home from us.'

'He had to. We couldn't have gone on living in the Rectory when the new rector came, could we? And he lets us live here.'

'That's no reason for Mama to hurry over there whenever the Countess throws a fit.'

Their mother returned before they could continue the conversation. 'His lordship has had a fall,' she said. 'They need me at the Hall.'

'Why, Mama? His lordship has servants in plenty if he needs a nurse. I do not know why you have to go.'

'I must. Lydia, look after everything while I am away. Do not wait dinner for me. I will be back as soon as I can.'

Janet fetched her cloak for her and she flung it over her shoulders, lifted the hood over her curls and left with the servant from the Hall.

Mrs Fostyn did not return until nearly dawn the next morning. Lydia, who had been sleeping fitfully, heard her step on the stair and hurried out in her nightgown to meet her. She looked pale and tired and her eyes, though dark-rimmed, were bright with tears. 'Mama, what has happened? Why have you been so long?'

'He is dead, Lydia,' she said flatly. 'The Earl of Blackwater is dead.'

'Oh.' She could not bring herself to say she was sorry. 'How did it happen?'

'I will tell you all about it later. I am tired. I must rest.'

'Of course. I'll wake Janet to help you.'

'No, I can manage. Go back to bed or you will disturb everyone. Later we will talk.' She turned from Lydia and went into her own room, shutting the door softly behind her, shutting her daughter out. Hurt and feeling somewhat resentful, Lydia returned to her own room.

It was nearly noon before her mother put in an appearance in the drawing room, but by then she looked more like her normal self. She smiled at the girls who, for want of anything else to do and to keep their fingers busy, were continuing their needlework. 'Let me see how much you have done,' she said, taking Lydia's from her and inspecting the stitches. 'Very good, very good indeed, though I am not sure we shall be able to go now, what with the Earl—'

'Oh, Mama, surely you will not cancel going because he has died?' Annabelle wailed. 'He is not a relative. We do not have to go into mourning for him.'

'No, but the organisers may well decide not to hold the ball in view of the fact that his lordship was one of its main sponsors.'

'Oh, no.' It seemed to Lydia that every bad thing that had happened to them, every disappointment, could be laid at the door of the Earl.

In the event the ball was not to be cancelled, simply postponed until after funeral, when his lordship's heir might decide whether it should take place or not. His heir. Lord Ralph Latimer was new Earl of Blackwater, though it seemed no one knew where he was to be found. 'I was told by his lordship's valet that there has been no contact between him and the family since…since it happened,' their mother told them. 'I thought they corresponded; that his lordship knew where he was, but if he did, he died without saying. I believe the lawyers are looking into it.'

'How did his lordship die, Mama?' Lydia asked. 'You said it was an accident.'

'Yes, he fell down the stairs from the upper floor to the gallery.' She gulped hard and went on. 'The doctor said his back was broken.'

'But he was conscious. He asked for you?'

'Yes.'

'Why you? Why not his wife?'

'She was not well… Oh, this is so difficult. His wife has never been the same since Ralph went away. She has not always been in her right mind. Sometimes she raves, sometimes she is quite violent towards him. I believe he went to her room to visit her. She…you must promise not to say a word of this to anyone…' They nodded and she went on, 'She attacked him. It is why he fell. They have had to restrain her.'

'You mean she pushed him?'

'I believe so.'

'Poor lady,' Lydia said, for the first time feeling some sympathy for her.

'Yes. But you see why she would have been no use to his lordship.'

'But you were.'

'Yes. We have…we have a strong bond. We have both lost those nearest to us by a cruel blow…'

'Is that how you see it? How can you be so forgiving? And if Lord Latimer—I mean, the new Earl comes home, how will you greet him? With a curtsy and a smile?'

'I do not know,' her mother answered. 'We shall have to wait and see.'

The funeral could not be delayed when no one knew if the new Earl had even been informed of the tragedy.

Some said he had died of a fever in the tropics; some said he had served as a common soldier and died in battle. Others said he was alive, but would never dare show his face. Others, who sympathised, said he would see the Fostyns off his land as soon as he came, which was no more than they deserved.

The day before the funeral, a second tragedy struck. The Countess escaped those employed to look after her and threw herself from the roof of the Hall. Grief, everyone said, grief and the fact that her husband had turned to Mrs Fostyn when he lay dying and not to his wife. Lydia was furious on her mother's behalf and was all for making public what her mother told her about the Countess's state of mind, but Anne refused to countenance such a thing and said the Earl and Countess should be allowed to lie in peace.

There were two funerals instead of one and still the speculation went on about the new Earl and what was to happen to the Hall if he could not be found. And no one speculated more than the Fostyn family. They lived in the dower house only by courtesy of the dead man. Where would they go if they were turned out? How would they live?

'We must hold our heads up, pretend nothing is wrong,' their mother said, though Lydia was not sure how much of the gossip she had heard. 'We will finish these gowns. If there is no Victory Ball, there will be others.'

Which was how Lydia and Anne came to be in Chelmsford a month after the funeral, searching for pink velvet ribbon for Annabelle's gown and braid to match the brocade of Lydia's. Anne wanted to visit an old friend and Lydia suspected she needed someone to confide in, someone to whom she could tell her troubles; talking to her daughters was not the same thing at all.

'You look for the ribbon, Lydia, and meet me in the lending library.' She smiled suddenly. 'I do not know how long I shall be but, if you are surrounded by books, you will not mind waiting.'

They parted in the street. Lydia watched her mother go with an ache in her heart, wishing she would confide in her more than she had. But when she had spoken of her problems, the day before the Earl's death, Lydia admitted she had not taken her as seriously as she should have done. And now her mother had shut her out, taken control of herself, and was determined to look after her brood no matter what. Lydia sighed. She had to do something to help and the only thing she could do was to consider marriage.

She pulled herself together and went into a tiny haberdashery shop where she found the pink ribbon, but there was no match for the braid. She tried other establishments to no avail and was just leaving the last shop when it started to rain heavily. She stood in the doorway, waiting for it to ease, when she was joined by a young man with an umbrella. The doorway was narrow and the rain was pouring off the overhanging roof on to her shoulders.

'Allow me,' he said, holding the umbrella over her. 'It is big enough for both of us if we stand closer.'

'Thank you,' she said primly, but declined to move nearer to him. He was already too close for her peace of mind.

Her first impression of him was his height and the breadth of his shoulders as he stood beside her. The second was the fineness of his clothes. He was wearing a coat of a fine worsted cloth lined with red silk. The collar and cuffs of the sleeve were faced with the same silk embroidered with gold and silver thread. It was an expensive coat, but he wore it casually as if it was of no importance to him that it was being spotted with rain. She tilted her head up so see his face and was taken aback to find him scrutinising her as if he meant to memorise every detail.

For a moment she continued to look up at him, noticing that his features were even, his nose long, almost haughty, and his skin was tanned and crinkled round his mouth as if he were more used to laughter than frowns. He wore a dark wig dressed away from his face with long side curls and the back tied with a narrow grey ribbon. His dark eyes were looking at her with a slightly mocking expression and she realised that she, too, had been staring and cast her eyes down.

She was met with the sight of an embroidered brocade waistcoat with a row of silver buttons from the neck, where a lace cravat frothed, down to his narrow waist. His long legs were clad in knee-length fitted breeches tucked into shining boots, which emphasised his muscular calves. Embarrassed, she turned to stare out at the rain-sodden street where puddles were gathering and filling the gutter.

'I never thought an article like an umbrella would stand me in such good stead,' he said with a chuckle. 'I was in a mind not to bring it out today, but I am glad that I did.'

She was aware of the undercurrent of meaning he put behind the words and felt the colour flare in her face. 'Indeed, sir, you would have been very wet else.' She risked a glance up into his face and smiled. 'As it is, I do believe you are already very damp. Pray, hold it over yourself and not me. I have my cloak.'

'I do not mind the rain. I am used to it. Where I come from, the monsoon is a hundred times more wet.'

She laughed. 'Wet is wet, sir, how can one rain be wetter than another?'

'Oh, I assure you it is. Have you ever been to India? No, I will wager you have not, but if you had, you would know exactly what I mean.'

India, she mused. Then he was a nabob, grown rich on trade and made bold by it. But the strange thing was that she was not repelled as she should have been. She found herself drawn to him, as if there was something from him to her, a fine but strong thread, pulling her to him. 'I should like to travel some day.' she said. 'But you are right. I have never been away from England in my life.'

'Not even to London?'

'Once I went, a long time ago, but not since—' She stopped suddenly and then went on. 'Not since I was a child.'

He detected the wistfulness in her voice and wondered what had caused it. He looked down at her. She was slight; the top of her head hardly reached his shoulder, but he sensed an inner strength, a steely determination. She was no wilting violet. Her eyes, looking up at him without fear, were hazel, but they had golden lights in them that glowed when she smiled like the tiny lights of the will o' the wisp that twinkled over the marshes on dark nights. Her hair was thick and a glorious russet brown. The cloak which covered her gown was a plain grey broadcloth tied at the neck with matching ribbon, not the garment of a young lady from a wealthy family, but not poverty-stricken either. 'Then I hope you have your wish, my lady.'

'Thank you, but I am not entitled to be called lady.'

'You are in my book,' he said softly. 'For want of a name.'

She ignored his hint to provide her name and turned

from him. 'I do believe the rain is easing and I shall venture forth.'

'Must you? I was just beginning to enjoy myself.'

'I have arranged to meet my mother at the library. She will be waiting for me.'

'Then allow me to escort you. The rain has not quite stopped and you will need my umbrella.'

'It is but a short step, sir. I would not put you to the trouble…'

'It is no trouble, it is a pleasure.' He fell into step beside her, carefully holding the umbrella over her. 'Do you come often to Chelmsford?'

'Occasionally when I need something I cannot buy in the village.'

'Which village?'

'Oh, it is such a small place, you would not have heard of it, I am sure.' He was flirting with her, she knew, and she ought not to be talking to him at all, but they were unlikely to meet again, so where was the harm? And keeping him guessing was all part of the fun. She stopped at the door of the library. 'Here we are. I said it was only a step, did I not? Thank you for your escort, sir.'

He made her a sweeping leg, which was not easy considering he was holding an umbrella, and it made her laugh. 'You should laugh all the time,' he said softly. 'Laughter lights up your eyes, brings them to life.'

'Sir, you are too forward.'

He sighed. 'It was ever thus with me. But one must seize opportunities when and where they occur, don't you think? Take the bull by the horns. Shall we meet again?'

'That, sir, is in the hands of Providence.'

'Then I hope Providence will be kind to me.'

She smiled as he left her, striding away down the street, his umbrella bobbing up and down as he lifted it clear of

other walkers who were venturing out after the downpour.
She supposed it would be the last she ever saw of him.
She rarely came to Chelmsford and, even if she did, the
chances of bumping into him again were slight.

She turned to go into the library, still smiling. He had
been so handsome and evidently wealthy, though without
pretensions to grandeur and certainly not over-proud, exactly the sort of man her mother said she should look for
as a husband. But you did not pick up husbands in the
street, did you? And she knew nothing about him—he
might be married, or disreputable. And even if he were
not, he would not think of her as a wife. Sensible men
did not pick up wives in the street either. Mistresses, perhaps, someone with whom to have a short-lived dalliance.
He must have thought she was that kind of girl. But he
had called her 'my lady'. His idea of a jest, no doubt. She
was glad she had not told him her name or where she
lived.

Her mother had not yet arrived and Lydia spent the next
half-hour browsing among the books, though they came
to Chelmsford too infrequently for her to think of taking
out a subscription. She smiled. If she did, it would be an
excuse to come again. But then she sobered immediately;
it would be what her mother called an unnecessary extravagance and, since her revelation about their finances,
she must consider every penny carefully before spending
it. Even ribbons and braid were luxuries.

'Ah, there you are, Lydia.' She heard her mother's
voice behind her. 'I am sorry I am late. I stayed until the
rain stopped. Did you get wet?'

'No, I sheltered in a doorway.' She did not know why
she said nothing about the young man and his umbrella.
Perhaps because she was determined to forget him and
that strange pull he had over her. She had spoken to him

for only a few minutes and yet he had left an emptiness behind, a promise unfulfilled, a glimpse of sunshine even in the rain, and she felt sad. And isolated.

They walked out to where their only outdoor servant, the ancient Joshua Partridge, who had been groom and driver to her father, waited with the old coach and elderly horse. As they trotted through the now-crowded streets towards home, Lydia looked about her for the sight of a bobbing umbrella. But he had gone, disappeared as if he had never been.

Ralph Latimer, fourth Earl of Blackwater, returned to his carriage which he had left at an inn on the outskirts of town, climbed in and directed his coachman to take him home to Colston Hall. Home! How often, in the heat and red dust of India, had he dreamed of coming home to the cool green of England, of being restored to the bosom of his family and taking his place beside his father, learning to take over the running of the estate, the welfare of the villagers, of hunting and fishing and sailing as he had done as a boy.

Thinking of his boyish pursuits made him think of Freddie Fostyn. They had been almost inseparable, sharing their lessons in the schoolroom at the Hall, getting into mischief as boys always do, vying with each other on the sports field, riding and gambling and talking about women.

It was women that had been their undoing or, to be more precise, one young lady they had met on picnic on the banks of the Cam one day soon after Freddie had joined him at Cambridge. The picnic had been arranged by Mrs Henrietta Gordon, a plump matron who had what was laughingly called an Academy for Young Ladies, supposedly a school for the education of the daughters of the middling classes. Everyone except the most naïve, and that apparently included Freddie, knew the girls were no such thing and their mission in life was of an entirely different kind.

Ralph had found one of the girls very much to his liking and had enjoyed flirting with her, unaware that Freddie had fallen head over heels in love with her. It was only later, when they had returned home for the summer vacation that he had told his friend, laughing the while, that a certain young lady had been more than receptive to his advances and he had invited her to stay in rooms he had taken in a house in Malden, so that they might continue their dalliance during the vacation. In a year or two he would have to settle down, but until then he would allow himself to dip his toe in the waters of sexual experience just as every other young man of his acquaintance did. He had hoped Freddie would not mind forgoing their planned sailing trip around the coast to Worthing.

Freddie had appeared surprised and reminded him in tones that sounded just like his strait-laced mama that he was promised to the Duke of Colchester's daughter, Juliette. 'Not yet,' he had said. 'The parents are still haggling over the dowry and marriage contract, and while they do, I intend to have my fun.'

'And who is this *fille de joie* and where did you meet her?'

Freddie was two years younger than Ralph and, a rung or two lower down the social scale; though that had never meant a thing as far as Ralph and their friendship was concerned, Freddie was decidedly touchy about it, especially when it came to women. Ralph had a way with them, a flattering manner and, besides that, he was wealthy enough to give them expensive trinkets.

'At Mrs Gordon's picnic. Her name is Fanny.'

'Fanny?' Freddie had repeated, giving every appearance of being shocked. 'You are speaking of Miss Fanny Glissop?'

He should have been warned by the fierce look in his friend's eye, the way his jaw began to work, the clenching of the fists, that all was not well. But he was busy casting a rod into the sluggish waters of the River Crouch, which bordered his father's estate, and did not look at him. Instead he said, 'If that's her name, yes, I never enquired the rest of it.'

'How could you insult her so?'

'Insult her? I did not insult her, rather I flattered her, for I am very particular as to where I lay my head.' He had laughed with the exuberance of youth. 'And my body. And I shall enjoy an hour or two amusing myself discovering more of hers—'

Freddie's blow was so unexpected and delivered with such force it toppled him into the river. He came up spluttering and began to clamber out, holding out his hand to be helped up the bank. Freddie ignored the hand and glared at him with pure venom in his eyes.

'What's the matter with you, man?' Ralph had demanded. 'Take my hand and help me out. You will have your little jest, but for the life of me I cannot think what brought it on.'

'Can't you? Can't you? You insult a lady, a young and innocent lady, a pure flower who has known nothing but her parents' love, and talk of defiling her!' His voice reached a shriek of outrage. 'You are an abomination…'

He had climbed out without help and stood facing his friend, dripping water from his fine kerseymere coat and buckskin breeches, ready to grasp him by the shoulders and smile away his fury. 'Freddie, my old friend, you know she is nothing of the sort. Why, she would not be at Mrs Gordon's establishment if that were so…'

Even then, Freddie did not understand and pushed him away. 'You are a monster, a spoiler of women, a pervert,' he yelled.

Instead of continuing to try to placate him, Ralph had lost his own temper and advanced on his friend with fists raised. 'You will take that back, Freddie Fostyn, and apologise.'

'I will not. Never.'

'Then I will have to fight you and you know I can best you.'

'Call me out, then.'

Such a thing had never crossed his mind. All he wanted was to teach Freddie a lesson, show him that he could not be insulted with impunity, and fisticuffs was what he had meant. 'Don't be a fool.'

It was almost the worst thing he could have said. It put Freddie in his place, poured scorn on him, laughed at him. And Freddie could not take it. With a roar of rage, he took a step towards Ralph and, for want of a glove, slapped his face, first with the palm and then the back of his hand. 'My representatives with call upon you,' he said and strode away.

Ralph had watched him go, rubbing his stinging cheek and laughing. He was still chuckling to himself when he picked up the rods and fishing tackle and went home. His laughter stopped abruptly when Robert Dent arrived that evening with another of their friends and told him Mr Frederick Fostyn demanded satisfaction.

He could not believe it and sent them back with a message that he hoped Freddie would think again before taking a step that was not only illegal but might end in the death of one or the other of them. For the sake of their

friendship, he hoped Freddie would come to his senses.
They returned half an hour later and told him that their
principal had said if his lordship refused the challenge he
would let it be known that he was a coward.

Ralph had had no choice. It was all Freddie's fault, all
of it. Robert had asked him for his choice of weapons and
his confused mind had chosen pistols, though later he realised that if he had said rapiers, the subsequent tragedy
could not have happened.

Pistols at dawn! How laughable and how tragic! Neither
of them owned pistols and his father's were locked up
where he could not get at them. Knowing that the Reverend Fostyn had a matched pair bequeathed to him by
his father, Ralph had suggested they use those. It might
give Freddie a tiny advantage, though why he should consider his erstwhile friend and now sworn enemy, he did
not know.

The mist had been so heavy that dreadful morning, they
could hardly see more than a few yards and he had begun
to hope they might both miss their target and that would
be an end of the affair. It was like some macabre play as
they paced out the ground in a clearing in a copse of trees
on the edge of his father's land. There were few stands
of trees in the area and the little wood was the only one
for miles, the land being on the edge of the marshes which
led to the sea. It was a place that had been used before
for such a purpose, far from any habitation, where a body
could be heaved into the soggy bog and never be seen
again. But whose body? Could he refuse to fire? Could
he stand and take whatever was coming to him without
trying to defend himself?

They reached the end of the slow walk being counted
out by one of his seconds and turned. Ralph raised his
gun at the shadowing figure twenty paces away but he

could not bring himself to fire. And then he heard a click and an oath and realised that Freddie's pistol had misfired. 'Go on,' his second said quietly. 'You've got him now.'

Instead, he had deliberately fired away. He had been so absorbed in his dilemma, he had not heard the horse cantering over the fallen leaves beneath the trees, nor did he see the shadowy figure fling himself from the saddle and run towards them. He only knew he had hit something when he heard a harsh cry and felt, rather than saw, the body hit the ground, almost at his feet. After that there was pandemonium. In a dumb daze he watched Freddie fly to his father, saw everyone looking at each other in horror, heard someone mount a horse and gallop off to fetch a doctor. He simply stood there, the gun still in his almost lifeless fingers.

Robert took it from him, while Freddie sobbed, yelling at him, accusing him, as if he had meant to do it. He felt sick. And then his father had come. His father, a notable Justice of the Peace, should have had them both taken up and sent to gaol for duelling, let alone killing an innocent man, but instead had sent him into exile. He had never seen him or his mother again.

Ten long years he had been gone, ten years in which he had matured in body and mind, had learned to control his anger and subdue his softness, to deal straight with all men, and take his pleasures where he found them, never letting anyone see his vulnerability. In truth, he thought he had been so clever at concealing it, there was now nothing left to hide; he had become a hard man inside and out. Oh, he could be charming when he chose and there was many a young lady in that over-hot subcontinent who could vouch for that, but it was never more than skin deep.

Now he had to pick up the pieces, decide if he should

stay in England, stay at Colston Hall and face those who decried him as a murderer. But why should he not stay? He was the Earl of Blackwater, an honourable man, and he would treat every man fairly; if he should come upon Freddie Fostyn, he would ignore him, ignore the whole Fostyn family for they had brought him nothing but grief. They had probably gone from the village because his father had had to appoint a new rector and the house went with the living.

As the coach rattled towards Colston Hall, his thoughts drifted to the young lady he had met in Chelmsford, a much more pleasant subject than the past which still had the power to torment him. She was a beauty with those classic features, that lustrous hair and those oh-so-expressive hazel eyes. She had been composed and ready to answer him without simpering or fluttering her eyelashes at him as some young ladies had been known to do under his scrutiny. She was a cool one, but under that he sensed a fire waiting to be kindled into life. He would have liked the opportunity to be the one to set the blaze going.

He wished now he had been more insistent on learning her name or the name of that village she mentioned. He could have amused himself with a little dalliance between the bouts of serious exchanges with his lawyer. According to that gentleman, there was much to be done, so many things which had been neglected in and around the Hall: tenants' homes needing repair, walls broken, ditches and drains overgrown, estate roads full of potholes.

'How did it come to this?' he had asked.

'My lord, his lordship was not himself, worried, you know, about…'

'About what? Out with it, man.'

'The Countess's health, my lord. She never got over it, you know.'

He did not need to ask what 'it' was. It was one more thing to lay at the door of Freddie Fostyn. He hoped he would never meet him again.

He discovered he had been wrong about the Fostyn family leaving the village the very next afternoon, when his lawyer called to go over the tenancies of the estate and he discovered they were living in the dower house, not a quarter of a mile away.

'How did this come about?' he demanded, angrily.

'His lordship, your father, allowed it, my lord. I think he felt sorry for them when they had to leave the rectory.'

'Sorry for them!' he repeated bitterly. 'And how much rent do they pay?'

'Why, none, my lord. The dower house has never brought in rent. After your grandmother died, it stood empty and—'

'Well, things are about to change,' he said. 'Write to Mrs Fostyn and tell her to remove herself from the house. Give her a week—'

'My lord, she can hardly make other arrangements in a week and his lordship said Mrs Fostyn might stay there as long as she wished to.'

'My father is dead, Falconer,' he said. 'And I am master here now. But I will not be unfair. Give them a month.'

'Yes, my lord.'

He might not have been so harsh, he realised later, if he had not spent the journey from Chelmsford going over the past, and in doing so resurrected all his bitterness and resentment. Let Mr Frederick Fostyn look to his mother; after all, he was the one who had got off scot free. His years in exile, far from mellowing him, had only served to harden him.

Chapter Two

The girls were putting the finishing touches to their ball gowns, although no decision had been reached about whether the ball was going to take place. Rumours were flying about the village that the new Earl had arrived, but no one had seen him.

'I saw a grand carriage turn into the gates of the Hall earlier today,' John said over supper the previous evening. 'It wasn't the old Earl's because everyone knows that was falling to bits. This was much newer and it had four matched bays and two postilions.'

'Did you see anyone in it?' Annabelle had demanded.

'No. Whoever it was was sitting back in the shadows.'

'That doesn't mean it was the Earl,' Lydia said, hoping that it wasn't. She didn't want to see him, ever again. 'It could have been Mr Falconer, his lawyer. They say he is staying at the Hall, for there is so much to be done, especially if the Earl is not coming home.'

'I doubt there will be a ball now,' Annabelle said, snipping off her thread and looking at her beautiful pink gown with her head on one side. 'And I did so want to wear this and dance the latest dances. How am I to find a hus-

band if we never go anywhere? Caroline Brotherton is to
have the Season in London.'

'Caroline Brotherton is the daughter of a marquis, Annabelle,' their mother said gently. 'We cannot aspire to
such things.'

Annabelle had met Caroline at the school for young
ladies they had both attended in Chelmsford and had sub-
sequently been invited to a birthday celebration at her
home when both girls, their education supposedly complete, had left school for good. She had talked of little
else ever since and Lydia suspected that was where all
this talk of husbands had come from.

'I don't see why not. Susan is going to London for the
Season.' Annabelle pouted. 'I could stay with her.' Susan
had written to say she and her husband were going to stay
in town for the summer months and she was looking forward to attending a few of the Season's social occasions.

'Dearest, even if you stayed with your sister, I could
not buy all the gowns and frippery you would need. And
besides…' She paused, wondering how to go on. 'We are
not aristocracy, my love, and though you are very pretty,
you would not be considered. We must keep to our station
in life, for otherwise lies misery, believe me.'

She spoke so firmly and with such conviction, it made
Lydia look up from her work in surprise, wondering what
had caused such strength of feeling. She came to the conclusion her mother was thinking of the friendship between
Freddie and Ralph Latimer and what it had brought them
to.

'We are not common people,' Annabelle said. 'Papa's
family is one of the oldest in the kingdom, Grandpapa
used to say so at every opportunity. He had a title—'

'It was only a minor one as you very well know, child.
And in any case, ever since…' Anne paused. The old man

had died six years ago, only a year after his wife. His older son and heir, her dead husband's brother, had declined to do anything to help them and rarely communicated. She smiled, knowing how disappointed her youngest daughter was. 'You may go with Lydia to the lecture tomorrow evening at the Assembly Rooms in Malden. I must confess I am feeling too tired to accompany her and you may use my ticket.'

'A lecture! What would I want with a lecture? I am given far too many of them at home to want to go to Malden to hear one.'

Anne sighed. She had expected Lydia to be difficult, but not Annabelle. 'Go, for Lydia's sake. She cannot go unaccompanied and you would not deprive her of an outing, would you?'

'Oh, very well. But no doubt I shall be bored to death.' She turned to Lydia. 'What is it about?'

'The title is "With Clive in India". The lecturer has just come home from there after many years with the East India Company. I think it might be vastly interesting.'

She did not go on to explain why she thought it might be interesting, but ever since she had met the young man in Chelmsford, she had been wondering if he might be the speaker; it was surely no coincidence that he had arrived in the area just before the lecture. And she had to confess to a desire to see him again, if only to confirm or deny the original impression she had had of him.

Unwilling to admit why, even to herself, she dressed with especial care the following evening. Her gown was of a fashionable mustard yellow silk; the narrow boned bodice had a wide décolletage infilled with lace, gathered into a knot in the cleft of her bosom. The back was pleated from the neck to the floor and the sleeves had wide em-

broidered cuffs. Like so many of her gowns, she had made
it herself with the help of her mother and it meant she
could appear far more richly dressed than they could really afford.

Janet arranged her hair in a thick coil at the back of
her neck and decorated it with two curling white feathers
which were all the rage. She had a fan of chicken feathers
which had been brought out of her mother's trunk at the
same time as the old gowns. She knew she looked well
and smiled at herself in her dressing mirror as Janet put
the finishing touches to her toilette and then bent to slip
her feet into tan leather shoes. She would have liked shoes
to match her gown, with embroidered toes and painted
heels, but that was not to be and she hoped, in the crush,
no one would notice her serviceable footwear.

Partridge harnessed the cob to the battered chaise and
drove them to the Assembly Rooms. 'I hope he does not
mean to take us right up to the door,' Annabelle whispered to her sister. 'It would be too mortifying to be seen
arriving in this.'

'Why?' Lydia asked, amused. 'Everyone knows us and
they know our circumstances. Why pretend to be something we are not?'

'We do not have to advertise it. And supposing the Earl
is there?'

Lydia laughed. 'Of course he will not be there. Why
should he interest himself in a country lecture?'

'Then why have you dressed yourself in your best
gown? I thought—'

'Good heavens, Annabelle, I would certainly not dress
to impress that fiend. How could you think it? I hate him
and all he stands for. You know that.'

'Oh. Then why? Have you got a beau?'

'Annabelle,' she said impatiently. 'You know very well
I have not.'

'What about Sir Arthur?'

'What about him?'

'Mama thinks you should set your cap at him.'

'What a vulgar expression! And I shall do no such
thing. Now, may we drop the subject?'

They had arrived at the meeting rooms and Partridge
drew up behind the carriages already standing in line,
waiting to discharge their occupants. Others of the audi-
ence had walked from houses nearby and were jostling
their way into the building. Lydia and Annabelle followed
them in and found their seats. There was a great deal of
noise in the hall as friend greeted friend and exchanged
news and gossip, but when the town mayor, who was
acting as master of ceremonies, walked on to the stage
followed by two or three other dignitaries who took seats
arranged behind the lectern, everyone became silent and
turned to listen.

Lydia, who had been holding her breath for this moment, let it out in a sigh of disappointment. The speaker,
when he was introduced and stood to begin his talk, was
not the young gentleman she had been hoping for, but a
middle-aged man with a red, bewhiskered face and a huge
stomach which threatened to burst the buttons off his
black waistcoat. There was nothing she could do but appear interested in what he had to say, but appearances
were deceptive because her mind was miles away, in a
rainy street in Chelmsford.

Oh, why had she not provided her name when asked
for it? Even the name of her village would have been
enough if he had meant it when he said he hoped to see
her again. But had he meant it? He was doing no more
than enjoy a little harmless flirtation with a young woman.

Not a lady, for all he called her one, for he would never have presumed to speak so familiarly to anyone highborn. But would anyone highborn have been standing in the rain and not a carriage or servant in sight? She was becoming more than a little desperate if one chance encounter could set her mind in such confusion.

She was being very foolish. Her future was already mapped out for her: a sensible marriage to provide for her mother in her old age, furnish Annabelle with a dowry and send John to public school, now that he was becoming too old for the day school he attended in Burnham, all things her father would have done, but for that devil up at the Hall. And there was no one she knew of who might do that except Sir Arthur Thomas-Smith.

What would it be like married to him? Oh, she could guess. Humdrum, that's what it would be. A daily grind of looking after his house and his daughters, acting as hostess at boring suppers and card games, looking forward with an inordinate amount of pleasure to attending meetings like this, lectures, readings, with the occasional country dance to liven things up. As for the marriage bed... But as she knew nothing whatever about that piece of furniture and what happened in it, her imagination failed her.

She was startled to hear those about her applauding and realised the lecture had come to the halfway stage and she had not heard a single word. She forced herself back to the present and clapped politely.

'There are refreshments in the next room,' Annabelle said, as everyone stood up and made a beeline for the door. 'I am very thirsty and I saw Sir Arthur go in there a moment ago.'

Lydia's heart sank. 'So? The man may come to a lecture, may he not?'

'Yes, but now's your chance. You could speak to him.'

'And what am I to say? Am I to throw myself at his feet and beg him to marry me?'

Annabelle laughed. 'No, you goose, but you could make yourself agreeable. Oh, look, here he comes.'

Sir Arthur, his waistcoat straining across his front and his ill-fitting wig slightly lopsided, was bowing over her. 'Miss Fostyn, may I have the pleasure of escorting you into the supper room?' For a big man his voice was extraordinarily high, almost effete.

Smiling, she lifted her hand, and allowed him to take it and raise her to her feet. 'Thank you, sir.'

'Mrs Fostyn is not here tonight?'

'No, she is a little fatigued. I brought my sister instead. May I present Annabelle to you?'

'Miss Annabelle.' He bowed towards her with exaggerated civility which made the young lady stifle a laugh behind her fan.

Together they walked into the next room where a cold collation and large bowls of punch and cordial were set on a long table at one end of the room and left for everyone to help themselves and take to small tables arranged in the body of the room. Sir Arthur found seats for them and went to fight his way through the throng to obtain food for them.

'Lydia, there is Peregrine Baverstock,' Annabelle hissed, nodding in the direction of a young man in a pink satin suit and red high-heeled shoes who was standing on the periphery of a group on other side of the room.

'Baverstock?' Lydia queried. 'You mean Lord Baverstock's son?'

'Yes. Who else should I mean?'

'How did you come to meet him?'

'At Lady Brotherton's, when I went to Caroline's birthday celebration. He was one of the guests. Oh, I do believe he has spotted me.'

The young man had indeed seen her, for he made his way through the crowd and bowed before them. 'Miss Annabelle.'

'Good evening, Mr Baverstock,' Annabelle said, laughing at his formality. 'I did not expect you here.'

'Had to come. Parents insisted. Glad I did now.' His face was fiery red.

'May I present you to my sister?'

'Miss Fostyn, your obedient. May I take Miss Annabelle to be presented to my parents?'

Annabelle looked at Lydia. 'May I go?'

'Of course.'

Annabelle was gone in an instant. Who could blame her for preferring the enlivening company of a young man nearer her own age than Sir Arthur? Lydia asked herself.

She certainly would.

'Why, if it isn't my little water nymph.'

Startled, she looked up and found herself gazing into the brown eyes of the man from Chelmsford. He was soberly dressed in a plain black coat and matching breeches with a white waistcoat and stockings. 'Sir,' she managed, though her heart was beating so fast she was almost too breathless to speak. 'What are you doing here?'

'I was about to ask you the same question. Are you interested in India?'

'Oh, very,' she said.

'Would you like me to introduce you to the speaker? I have known him for some time. We both served under Lord Clive.'

'Oh, I had forgot you came from that continent,' she lied.

'There is no reason why you should have remembered a chance remark,' he said. 'Nor remembered me.'

'No.' She was so tongue-tied her usual easy manner quite deserted her.

'But you did? You knew me as soon as I spoke.'

'You remembered me.'

'How could I forget?' he said softly. 'One minute the shop doorway was empty and the next it contained an apparition of such exquisite beauty I was transfixed. Did you come safely home?'

'Yes, thank you.' She felt the warmth creep up her cheeks and wished she could control it, knowing he could not fail to see it, so closely was he studying her. It was most disconcerting.

'And you took no harm from your wetting?'

'I did not get wet, sir, but you did. I hope you did not catch cold. After India, the climate here must be very trying...'

'Not a bit of it. It is wonderful. The rain is so gentle, the wind but a zephyr breeze, the trees so green, the flowers so delicate and their perfume heady. I am drunk with it.'

'La, sir,' she said, laughing. 'Are you sure it is not the punch? I believe it is an Indian concoction made up in honour of the subject and can be very potent.'

'Indeed, yes. In India, where I first sampled it, the spirit it contained was arrack, but I imagine that has been substituted in this case with brandy. May I fetch you some? The lime and spices in it make it a refreshing drink.'

'No, thank you, I am being looked after.'

'Of course,' he said, suddenly serious. 'You would not be here alone, how silly of me.'

'There you are, my dear. Such a dreadful crush.' Sir Arthur was approaching, balancing three plates precariously in two hands. Seeing the young man with Lydia, he stopped, his mouth half open. Someone, who had not realised he had come to a sudden halt, jolted his elbow and the whole lot tipped over his waistcoat and down his breeches. In the ensuing confusion, while servants came to clear up the mess and he was led away to have his clothes cleaned, the young man from Chelmsford disappeared. Lydia, who wanted desperately to laugh at the sight of Sir Arthur with broken pigeon pie and bits of chicken leg, not to mention fruit tartlets, clinging to the satin and brocade of his suit, was almost reduced to tears when she realised the young man had gone.

He had been so handsome and attentive. He made her legs weak and her hands shake and she realised that the thread was still there, stronger than ever, so why had Fate denied her the opportunity to further their acquaintance? Wealthy and not likely from a background where lineage and blood counted for much, he would have fitted the bill as a husband very well. She would not have minded being married to him. And Sir Arthur had spoiled it all, spoiled her evening. It just wasn't fair.

The bell went for the end of the intermission, Annabelle returned to her and they resumed their seats for the second half of the lecture, most of it of a political nature and very boring indeed. Annabelle, too, was bored, and could hardly wait for the polite applause which signalled the end of the lecture to tell Lydia all about her interview with Perry's parents, who had been most gracious towards her. 'He is the one,' she told Lydia. 'He is the one I am going to marry. I can feel it. Here.' And she put her hand on her heart.

Lydia resisted the temptation to laugh. 'Oh, Annabelle, it is too soon.'

'No, it is not. If we are to find husbands, then we must

do it quickly, you know that.' She paused. 'The only difficulty I can see is my lack of a dowry. Lord Baverstock
would expect one, wouldn't he?'

'Yes, I think he would.'

'Then the sooner you marry Sir Arthur the better.
Mama said—'

'I know what Mama said,' Lydia interrupted her, as
they made their way to the exit, standing in the crush
while everyone waited for their carriages to be brought
up to the door. In the euphoria of meeting the young man
again she did not want to be reminded of her duty.

'Ah, Miss Fostyn.'

Lydia turned to find Sir Arthur at her elbow and wondered if he could possibly have heard Annabelle's remarks. He was wearing a long overcoat which he had
buttoned from neck almost to hem to hide his stained suit.
It looked as though he had borrowed it from his coachman.

'Sir Arthur. I am sorry for your mishap.'

'Oh, 'twas nothing. I am only sorry you were deprived
of your supper. May I escort you home?'

'No, thank you, sir. We have our own coach.'

'Then may I call and pay my respects to your mama in
the near future?'

'I am sure she will be pleased to receive you, sir.'

The crowd had thinned while they had been talking and
Lydia was suddenly aware of her umbrella man watching
her, watching them both with a look on his face which
was both quizzical and disapproving. He stepped forward
and bowed. 'Goodnight, my lady.'

She found herself dipping a small curtsy and smiling.
'Goodnight, my lord.'

'Who was that?' Annabelle demanded, when they were
settled in the chaise and were trotting towards Colston.

'I have no idea.'

'But you called him "my lord".'

'He called me "my lady", so why not?'

'Who does he think you are, then?'

'I don't know that either. We are perfect strangers.'

'It didn't look like that to me. Is that why you are wearing your best gown? You expected him to be here. Oh, what will Mama say?'

'She will say nothing, because you are not to tell her.'

'Oh, a secret. Have you an assignation with him? Oh, Lydia, he is so handsome, but supposing he is a mountebank?'

'I am sure he is nothing of the kind. And I do not have an assignation with him. Whatever gave you that idea? We spoke half a dozen words while you were busy fluttering your eyelashes at Peregrine Baverstock…'

'At least I was doing it to some purpose. You seem to have gained nothing. But there, I suppose we should hold to the maxim that a bird in the hand is worth two in the bush.'

'Whatever do you mean?'

'Sir Arthur. He is going to call, is he not? He would not do that if he were not serious.'

'Annabelle, if you mention Sir Arthur just once more, I shall slap your face, really I will. Let it be, will you?'

'Oh, if you are going to fly into a temper, then I shall say no more. But if you want me to keep your secret from Mama, then you will have to find a way of persuading me.'

'Oh, Annabelle,' Lydia said, laughing, 'you are such a mischievous child…'

'Not so much of the child, if you please. I am old enough to fall in love.'

'Are you, indeed?'

'Yes, indeed. And do not tell me you do not know what it feels like, for I am persuaded that you do. I saw the look you had for the handsome stranger. Who is he, Lydia?'

'I told you, I do not know the gentleman.'

'So what are you going to do about it?'

'The stranger? Why, nothing. Why should I?'

'No, I meant about persuading me to hold my tongue.'

'You can have my silk fan, the one Grandmama gave me.'

'Can I? Oh, can I?' her sister said eagerly, then laughed. 'You must love him very much to part with that.'

'Don't be silly. I have been thinking of giving it to you ever since we made that pink gown up. It matches it exactly and would certainly not go with my yellow brocade.'

'Oh, you are a darling!' And Annabelle flung her arms about her sister in the rocking vehicle, making it sway more than ever. 'The best sister anyone could have.'

They continued in silence for a few minutes, but Annabelle was still bubbling over and could not keep quiet. 'Do you think the Earl will allow the ball to go ahead?' she asked.

'I don't know, nor do I care very much.'

'Oh, Lydia, do not be such a misery. If we go to the ball I shall see Perry there and, who knows, your fine gentleman might attend.'

And what good would that do? Lydia asked herself. Annabelle had said a bird in the hand was worth two in the bush. She knew nothing whatever about the handsome young man, not even his name, but she knew all she wanted to know about Sir Arthur Thomas-Smith. Tears pricked at her eyes and she was thankful that the darkness in the coach hid them from her sister's eyes.

Their mother had not waited up for them so, as soon

as they arrived home, Lydia pleaded tiredness and went to her own room, thankful that now her older sisters no longer lived at home she had a room to herself. She could not bear another minute of Annabelle's excited chatter, her bubbling optimism which hinged on Lydia marrying Sir Arthur in order to smooth the way for her own marriage. He was a respectable gentleman who had done nothing wrong; in truth, had done everything right, at least in her mother's eyes, but she did not want to marry him.

Oh, she knew perfectly well that most young ladies bowed to the superior knowledge and experience of their parents in the matter of matrimony and usually married the men chosen for them. Sometimes, it worked very well; if it did not, both discreetly took lovers. She did not think she could bring herself to do that. But if someone like her man from Chelmsford came along… Oh, no she could not commit that sin, not even with him; she believed in the sanctity of marriage and if she married Sir Arthur she would be faithful to him. If… Had she any choice?

She tossed and turned and fell asleep at last.

Next morning Lydia rose bleary-eyed and not in the least prepared for the bombshell her mother delivered at the breakfast table.

'The Earl is back,' Mrs Fostyn said, picking up a sheet of paper which lay beside her plate. 'I have had a letter from him, or, more precisely, from Mr George Falconer, his lawyer.'

'What about?'

'Our tenure of this house. It appears he wishes us gone.'

'Gone?' Lydia repeated.

'Yes, read it for yourself.' She handed the letter to Lydia, who read it through quickly.

'One month to leave,' she said, her face white with

fury. 'He has given us a month's notice. The fiend! The
indescribable charlatan! I have always hated him and I
was right to do so. He cannot bear to have us on his land
because it reminds him of his guilt. I knew this would
happen as soon as he came back. You thought so too,
didn't you? That's why you spoke to me about marrying.'

'I thought it might. You see, if...' She paused, then
went on. 'If the old Earl did not correspond with his son,
then he would not know our circumstances—'

'It would have made no difference if he had. He is
entirely selfish. He could have exonerated Freddie, accepted the blame. But no, he must drag us all down with
him. Only he is not down, but on top, and he means to
grind us into the dirt.'

'Lydia, pray do not be so melodramatic,' Anne said
gently. 'The house is his to do with as he likes and he
says he needs it, though why I do not know. If the Countess had lived and he had a wife and family, then of course
he would expect his mother to live here, but as it is...'

'Do you think he has a wife, then?' Annabelle put in.

'He is twenty-nine years old, so it is more than possible.'

'Then I feel sorry for her,' Lydia said sharply. 'I wonder if she knows what happened? I wonder if he knows
what people are saying about him?'

'What are they saying?'

'Oh, you know,' Lydia said vaguely. 'About him murdering Papa.'

'I am sure they are saying nothing of the sort,' her
mother protested. 'And I wish you would not speak of
him in that fashion.'

'Why not? It is the truth, isn't it? Papa was unarmed
and he was only trying to stop him firing—'

'Lydia, you would not spread calumny about him,

surely?' her mother said, horrified at the violence of her daughter's feelings. 'That is deceitful and unjust.'

'Which is exactly what he is. He allowed Freddie to take the blame for something that was entirely his fault. Freddie was always under his sway, even when they were boys.'

'I do not think that is quite the case, dearest, and I beg you to curb your excessive feelings. It can only do you harm. Your papa preached forgiveness, remember.'

'If he had lived, do you think even he could have forgiven Ralph Latimer for what he did?'

'I like to think he would.'

'But he did not live, did he? And we are in this coil because of what that…that devil did.' She left her chair suddenly. 'I am going to see him. I am going to tell him exactly what I think of him.'

Anne reached out and seized Lydia by the wrist as she passed her. 'No, child, you will do no such thing. He is within his rights. If you provoke him, he might not even allow us a month.'

Lydia made no attempt to pull herself away, but stood passively, looking down at her mother. 'You mean you are going to buckle under and leave without one word of protest?'

'No.' Anne smiled wanly. 'We have nowhere to go. I will speak to him myself, he may not know our circumstances….'

'Mama, you are never going to beg?'

'No, but we need a little more time, Lydia. And I shall make a reasonable request for that.'

'Time?'

'Time to bring our family fortunes on to a more even keel.'

'How? Oh, I see. When I have captured Sir Arthur. I

am to be punished for what that man did ten years ago,
just as Freddie was punished and you have been punished.
It goes on and on. If I could think of a way to make him
pay, then I would. I would see him rot in hell.'

'Lydia!' her mother cried. This battling daughter of hers
was so consumed by her hate, it was threatening to destroy her. 'You must not say such things. It is wicked.'
She paused. 'Sit down again, Lydia, and calm yourself.
You know, you frighten me when you talk like that. Hate
is a dreadful emotion, and you should remember that vengeance is for God, not man. We are none of us guiltless.'

Lydia sank back into her chair. 'Oh, Mama, there is no
one more innocent than you. How have you borne it all
these years? How have you found the fortitude?'

'Through my faith, child. The faith your father
preached. Now, I want you to promise me one thing—
that you will not attempt to see or speak to his lordship.'

Lydia smiled wanly. 'That is an easy promise to make,
for he is the last man in the world I should want to have
any discourse with.'

'Good. Now, tell me, dearest, would it be so very bad
to marry Sir Arthur? He is not an ogre, he is a pleasant,
respectable man who is very fond of you. I am not thinking only of our circumstances, but your happiness. He will
look after you…'

Lydia gave a cracked laugh. 'And curb my fiery temper,
you think?'

Her mother smiled and patted her hand. 'He might. And
living at his home in Southminster, with other things to
occupy you, might bring you peace of mind, the strength
to accept what we cannot change.' She paused and added
gently. 'At least, say you will consider it.'

Lydia sighed. She really had no choice. 'Very well. I
met him last night and he asked if he might call. You may

intimate to him when he comes that I shall look favourably on his suit.' She smiled suddenly. 'But do not make me sound too eager, will you?' Her mother released her hand and she rose to leave. 'I am going to Malden—I need a book from the lending library. Is there anything you need?'

'No, I do not think so, thank you.'

Partridge was busy in the garden and, rather than take him from his work, she decided to walk the three miles into the little town which stood at the confluence of the Chelmer and Blackwater rivers. It was a spring fine day and Malden Water, though grey, was calm and several fishing boats could be seen either coming up from the sea or heading out towards it. Inland there were lambs in the fields, and the mare Farmer Carter kept in his meadow was proudly showing off a new foal which frisked about on its spindly legs, obviously pleased with life. It was the sort of day to raise the spirits and Lydia would have enjoyed the walk if her thoughts had not been occupied with her dilemma.

It was all very well for Mama to say hate was a dreadful emotion, she knew it was, but she could not help herself. How could she be calm about the prospect of marrying a man old enough to be her father when there were men like her umbrella man in the vicinity? If she had never met the handsome stranger, would she have been content to marry as her mother directed? He had set her heart beating and fired her into longing for something she could only guess at: a passion, perhaps, that transcended everything.

She did not need to know his name, or his circumstances, or anything about him in order to know that he could ignite in her an overpowering desire. It was wicked of her, wicked and almost depraved. She had not been brought up to feel like that, had not, until a week before, realised that such feelings existed, certainly not in young ladies with any pretensions of decency. She must squash such thoughts and feelings, cut them out of her life altogether, forget the young man and his dangerously compelling eyes.

Ralph had spent most of the previous evening in the library at Colston Hall with a glass of brandy at his elbow, pouring over accounts and maps and reports from his general factotum about the condition of the estate, and what he read had appalled him. Today he had decided to see for himself and that could only be done on foot.

Donning leather breeches and topboots, he had thrown on a brown worsted coat and visited all the farms on his domain, talking to the tenants and finding out what was needed. New thatch on the roofs, new glass in windows, new clunch on the pigsty walls, he was told when they got over their surprise at seeing him thus clad and being convinced he meant business. The ditches needed clearing, too, or come the winter there would be an inundation from the marshes.

He was thankful he had come back home a wealthy man, or such a catalogue would have sent him bankrupt. He was doubly thankful when he realised that the fabric of the ancient church needed repair and that half the pews had woodworm and only he had the means to remedy it. After that, it was a quart of best ale in the village inn and back home via the old Roman road, now only a track, which ran alongside the marshes and the copse of trees where game was reared. Game birds were rare in this part of the world, which had few trees, except those planted in the gardens of the wealthy, who were following the latest trend for landscaping. His great-grandfather had planted this wood and his father had taken on a man who called himself a gamekeeper and who was skilled in breeding and rearing the birds simply for the sport. The woodland was his particular domain.

It was also the domain of a very different breed, he realised, as he picked his way through a tangle of under-growth which had spread out over the path. A man could hide there for weeks without being found. The path itself was well-worn and some of the bushes alongside it had been broken recently, as if something wide and heavy had travelled along it. Curious, he moved forward cautiously.

He came to a small clearing in the middle of which was a tumble-down hovel which had once been inhabited by a woodsman. He smiled, remembering how he and Freddie used to play round it as boys, pretending it was a fort and one was attacker and one defender. Its windows were broken and the ivy which clambered round it was invading the inside. Deserted it looked, almost ready to fall in on itself and return to nature.

But that was how it was meant to look, he realised, as he noticed the thatch on the roof had been repaired and so had the stout door, which was securely locked. Someone was either living here on his land or using it for some secret purpose. He looked up at the chimney. There was no smoke. Did that mean there was no one there now? He went to the door and knocked. There was no reply. He walked all round it. The path at the rear led down to the marshes where there was an old boat house, as he very well knew; and here there were signs of a cart and hoofmarks in the mud.

He returned to the house and peered into the windows, cupping his hands about his face. As his eyes became accustomed to the gloom, he noticed a pile of sacks and a barrel on the floor and a table with a pair of scales.

There was a bottle beside them and the remains of an oilskin wrapping. Smugglers! This was a hideout for smugglers.

He was inclined to be amused, since nearly everyone tolerated free-traders, as they preferred to be called; half the tobacco, tea, wine and spirits consumed in the country was contraband. His father may even have condoned it in exchange for the odd barrel. But only two days ago, he had learned from Robert Dent that there was going to be a concerted effort by the revenue men to stamp out smuggling and extra patrols were to be sent out. 'There wasn't so much of it during the war,' Robert had said. 'But now it has grown again and we do not want to return to the days of the vicious gangs who plied the trade openly and thought nothing of murdering anyone who got in their way.'

He would keep watch and find out who these men were. Depending who they turned out to be, he would hand them over to the justices or warn them off.

Leaving everything exactly as he found it, he returned home to find Mrs Fostyn waiting for him. The servants, accustomed to admitting her, had had no reason to change their habits and she had been conducted to the drawing room to await his return.

'Madam, your obedient,' he said, sweeping her a low bow. 'You find me somewhat dishevelled. I was not expecting company.'

'It is no matter, my lord. I had to come.'

'Oh.' He had always liked Freddie's mother and could not bring himself to be rude to her. What had happened had certainly not been her fault and she must have suffered greatly at the loss of her husband. 'Pray, go on.'

'It is the matter of the letter I received from your lawyer. I assume it was written at your dictation.'

'It was.'

'I know you have every right to ask us to leave and I do not dispute that, but a month is so little time to find somewhere else to live. Could you not find it in your heart to extend that? Your father, the late Earl, said we could stay as long as we wished.'

'My father is no more.'

'Yes. I should have offered my condolences. Forgive me.'

She was almost grovelling and it pained him to see it.

'You see,' she went on when his only reply was a slight inclination of the head, 'I have two daughters as well as a young son of twelve still at home and I must find some way of supporting them.'

'You support them? Why not Freddie? Surely it is up to him?'

'Freddie?' She looked astonished. 'Freddie left home at the same time as you did and we have not seen or heard from him since. Did you not know?'

It was his turn to be surprised. 'No, I did not. I assumed—'

'Your father thought it would be for the best. He came to see me. He told me that, as a magistrate, he was duty bound to arrest anyone breaking the law, but he couldn't bring himself to have you arrested and was determined to send you away. He said the Countess was bowed down with grief and it would not do for her to see my son about the village after you had gone. He was determined Freddie must be sent away too. Besides, Freddie himself was so distraught, blaming himself for what happened, that he was eager to be gone.'

'I am sorry,' he said softly. So his father had threatened them with the law. 'I knew none of this.'

'But the late Earl was a kind and generous man and he

knew I had no means of support except my husband's investments, which were by no means large enough to allow us to find a new home and keep us in comfort. He offered me the dower house and, for the sake of my children, I agreed. Except that we did not know whether Freddie was alive or dead, we have been happy there and…'

'Have you not seen your son in all that time?'

'No, my lord. Oh, I knew from the beginning we could not stay forever. Sooner or later you would come home and everything would change. But I hoped it would not be until after my daughters were safely wed. Susan married Sir Godfrey Mallard's son some time ago and Margaret has decided to devote her life to other people's children—she is governess to the Duke of Grafton's children. But Lydia and Annabelle are still at home…'

'Lydia,' he said, smiling faintly. 'She's the one with the russet hair and the mischievous smile, isn't she?'

Anne smiled back, realising that he was not such an ogre and was civil enough to listen to her. But then, if he was his father's son, he would be. 'Yes, she is eighteen now and, though perhaps I should not say it, or even think it, she is the most comely of my children and…' this with a little deprecating laugh '…the most stubborn and independent.'

'Yes, I remember,' he said. 'She used to follow me and Freddie about and try to do everything we did. We tried to shake her off and she would disappear for a little while, but then, when we least expected it, she would be back, dogging our footsteps.'

'She is past all that, my lord, and ripe for marriage. I think, in a very little time, I shall be able to announce her engagement to Sir Arthur Thomas-Smith.'

'Sir Arthur!' he exclaimed, his sympathy going out to the child he had once known in spite of who she was.

The brief glimpse he had had of the gentleman the previous evening had struck a chord in his memory. He had
met him somewhere before but, for the life of him, he
could not recall where. He certainly could not place the
name, nor that high-pitched voice. Thomas-Smith, not an
aristocratic name, not a memorable name, but the face,
that was different. He never forgot a face. 'I believe I met
Sir Arthur last evening, a portly gentleman of middle
years.'

'Yes. He is devoted to Lydia and will curb her exuberance, you may be sure. And he has the means to support her. Annabelle, who is very pretty and biddable, will
soon find a suitor, especially as Sir Arthur has indicated
he will provide her with a small dowry...'

'I understand.' He understood very well. Lydia was to
be sacrificed. When he had last seen her, she had been no
more than a child, a nuisance to two young men bent on
enjoying themselves. But even then there had been something about her that was different. Independent, her
mother had described her. Would such a one marry a man
old enough to be her father? Well, it was not his business.

'Then you will give us a little more time?' she asked,
watching his face.

He looked at the woman sitting so still on his drawing
room sofa and, though he could not even begin to forgive
her son for forcing him into that duel, and he was equally
certain she did not forgive him for what he had done, he
could afford to be magnanimous, especially as Freddie
was not at home. Somehow, the knowledge that his erstwhile friend had suffered the same fate as he had in some
measure mitigated his raw hatred, though he would not
go so far as to say it had disappeared totally. You could
not harbour the resentment he had for over ten years and
lose it in the space of a short interview with a plausible

woman. But she was a mother, and knowing what his own mother had suffered set him thinking. 'Very well. You may stay until Lydia is married. And I hope she may be happy.'

'Do you mean that?'

'I am not in the habit of saying things I do not mean, madam.' He had done what he could, given the circumstances, and he would take care to avoid the path that led to the dower house until they had gone.

She rose and curtsied. 'Then I thank you and I shall convey your good wishes to Lydia and Annabelle.' He bowed in response and a moment later she had glided noiselessly from the room and he was alone once more.

He must be going soft, he told himself as he strode upstairs to change into something more suitable for a visit to Chelmsford. He had been told there was a builder there who could do the repairs to his tenants' houses at a reasonable price, and the sooner they were put in hand the better. Even if he decided not to stay in the village, he could not lease or sell the estate as it was.

Was he going to stay? he asked himself as his well-sprung coach took him through the lanes of Colston where the leaves were just appearing on the trees and the air was balmy with the promise of spring. It was not the family coach, which like everything else had been neglected, but the one he had bought in London when he landed from India. Could he pick up his life where he had left it ten years before, and carry on as if nothing had happened? But how could he?

For a start, he could no longer expect to marry a duke's daughter. He had been sufficiently in touch with the London gossip, even on the other side of the world, to know of the advantageous marriage Juliette had made only a year after his exile began. But he ought to marry or what was the point of coming home? Who would have him, given that the scandal seemed not to have died? He was immensely rich, he could take his pick. He smiled. That unknown beauty he had met in Chelmsford, perhaps. She had been with Sir Arthur last night—his daughter, no doubt. No, he contradicted himself at once. If he were to marry her, it might make Lydia Fostyn his mother-in-law and the idea of that was laughable

His business done, he was almost home when he be-came aware that it was raining again, spattering on the roof, and reminding him of the girl he had met in Chelms-ford. Why did his mind keep returning to her? Why, even in the middle of talking bricks and mortar and broken walls, had she kept invading his thoughts, stirring his body into a tingle of desire? He had even been fool enough to take a stroll round the streets of Chelmsford, hoping he might meet her again.

At the junction where the road separated, one arm going to Malden and the other to Southminster and Colston, the coach passed the entrance to Sir Arthur Thomas-Smith's new mansion, which set him wondering about the man all over again. Two minutes later they slowed to pass a woman in a grey cloak, who stood aside to let it overtake her. Glancing casually from the window, he realised she was his nymph! He banged on the roof to tell the coach-man to stop.

Chapter Three

Lydia had spent a long time in the library, trying to find some suitable uplifting book which might make her calmer, more in control of emotions and, having found a volume of sermons which she thought might fit the bill, set out for home.

On the outskirts of the town, she had to pass the gate of Sir Arthur's newly built mansion. It stood in about two acres of land, shielded from the crossroad by a high wall. She stopped to peer along the drive through the ornamental gates. It was a large building, but box-like, with a central door and tall portico on Corinthian columns. Either side were evenly spaced long-sash windows. Because it was so new, no creeper grew up the walls to peep in at the windows, no moss had invaded its roof. The gardens, in the latest landscape design which had yet to mature, had no flower beds and no large trees, though some saplings had been planted here and there. It was a house without character, unlike the dower house which was even more ancient than the Hall itself.

She shook herself; how could she regret leaving the house she now lived in, so close to Colston Hall and its detested occupant? She should be glad. She might enjoy adding her own touches to this place, making a home from bricks and mortar. Slowly she pushed open the gate and began walking towards it, not even thinking what she might say if Sir Arthur or a servant were to see her and ask what she was doing there.

There was no sign of life, no open windows, no children or dogs. It was silent as the grave. She turned away from the front door with its lion's head knocker and went round the side of the building. Here was a long low wing at right angles to the main building and a separate stable block in the same brick as the house. A horse snickered and she heard men talking in low voices and it was enough to bring her to her senses. Hurriedly she turned to go back the way she had come.

'Miss Fostyn.' The voice behind her was undoubtedly Sir Arthur's. She turned to face him, her face on fire with embarrassment. He was dressed in a brown cloth coat, buckskin breeches and riding boots.

'I...I went to the front of the house. No one came to the door.' That was true, no need to tell him she had not even knocked.

'Then I am sorry for that. My sister who keeps house for me is out and no doubt the servants were busy in the kitchen and did not hear you arrive. Where is your mama? Have you left her in the carriage?'

'No, Sir Arthur, I am alone and I walked.'

His eyebrows shot up in surprise, but he did not comment. 'Then, please come in.'

She could do nothing but retrieve her scattered dignity and follow him into the marble-floored hall with its intricately carved oak staircase, where he summoned a servant to take her cloak and fetch refreshments before turning back to her with a polite smile and escorting her into a drawing room where he invited her to be seated, standing himself with his back to the new Adam fireplace.

'I was not expecting you, Miss Fostyn, or I would have been better prepared to entertain you.'

She sat on the edge of a chair, surveying the room and searching her mind for an excuse for visiting him alone. The doors and most of the furniture were in the new red mahogany wood which was so fashionable. The ceilings were intricately carved and gilded, the soft furnishings of damask and the ornaments oriental in design. It smelled of recently applied paint and everything—wood inlay tables, ornaments and pictures—shone, but time had not yet dulled any of it, had not added the ambience of it having been lived in and used, of being loved. It was all too perfect. And cold.

'I am sorry to arrive unannounced,' she said. 'I was in Malden, changing my library book.' She raised the book she carried so that he might see its uplifting title, which might help to alleviate the poor impression she had obviously made on him. 'I had to pass here and as you said you would call on my mother...'

'So I did.'

'I was not sure which day it might be and Mama will not be at home on Wednesday and Friday, so it came to my mind I should leave a message with your butler to that effect. I thought it would save you a wasted journey.'

'Indeed, that was thoughtful in you. Ah, here comes our tea.' They watched as a servant put the tea tray on low table between them and withdrew. 'Would you like to do the honours?'

She forced herself to smile at this little bit of domesticity as she lifted the teapot, hoping that he would not notice how much her hands were shaking, and praying fervently she would not rattle the cup in the saucer when she handed it to him. Would she soon be doing this as a matter of course?

'I understand the reason for your visit,' he said, sipping tea. 'But perhaps it was a little unwise of you to arrive unaccompanied and unannounced? I and my daughters are newcomers to the district and anxious to be accepted among its inhabitants. I would not like our name to be sullied by gossip.'

'Oh, Sir Arthur, I am very sorry, if you think it would,' she said, mortified that he had managed to put her down, as if she were a naughty schoolgirl. 'Our family is well known and respected and we are used to being seen out and about. I would not for the world embarrass you.'

'No matter. If, as I sincerely hope, our two families are soon to be joined, there will be no harm done.'

'I believe you have already spoken to my mama on the subject,' she said, deciding she might as well jump in with both feet.

'Yes. Two weeks ago, when I was introduced to her at a Missionary Society meeting. I mentioned that I was looking for a lady to share my life and I had been led to believe you were chaste and modest and dutiful, and I asked Mrs Fostyn how she would view an overture from me.'

'And what did she say?'

'She said it would be entirely up to you, which I thought a very evasive answer, for who would be so fool-ish as to allow a young lady to please herself on such an important matter?'

His answer annoyed her; for two pins she would walk out, but doing that would ruin her sister's chances and her brother's education, not to mention failing her beloved mama, who still fostered the hope that Freddie might be restored to them. All this depended on her finding favour with Sir Arthur. She had to play her part.

She managed a smile. 'Why? Did you think I might refuse you?'

He smiled briefly. 'No man likes to have his best intentions thrown back into his teeth. I would need to feel more sure of your answer before I ventured the question.'

She suppressed the laugh which bubbled up at this pomposity. 'Do you not find the prize worthy of the chase, sir?'

'Chase, ma'am? Do I appear to you as a man who would chase a lady?'

'No, Sir Arthur, I was attempting humour. I beg your pardon.'

He smiled thinly. 'Are you saying you would welcome an offer?'

'Let us say I would not be averse to becoming better acquainted,' she said, putting down her teacup and rising to leave. 'It is not a decision to be taken lightly.'

'No, to be sure,' he said. 'We must both give it careful consideration.'

When she politely refused the offer of his carriage to convey her home, he insisted on accompanying her to the door himself. 'I am sorry the children are not at home to meet you,' he said. 'They are visiting their grandmother for a few weeks until I have everything as it should be and have engaged a new governess for them. The one they have now has declined to move with us. Such a pity, she was excellent.'

'I look forward to meeting them another time,' she said, smiling and holding out her hand.

He took it and raised the back of it to his lips. 'I shall call on Mrs Fostyn very soon.'

She left him, her skin crawling with distaste, and yet

she did not know why. He had done nothing untoward, in fact had been the perfect gentleman, except for his air of disapproval, which she supposed was justified. It was she who had behaved disgracefully and she dreaded to think what her mother would say. And she would have to be told, because he was sure to mention her visit when he called.

She walked down the drive and out of the gates, fighting back tears. Why had fate been so unkind to her? Why, if she must marry for money, could it not be someone young and handsome? And now, to add to her misery, it had started to rain again. She pulled the hood of her cloak over her head and plodded on, moving to the side of the road when she heard a carriage coming up behind her. She was unprepared for it to stop.

'My lady, you should procure yourself an umbrella or at least refrain from going out when the sky threatens rain.'

She whipped round at the sound of his voice and a smile lit her face, making it come brilliantly alive. But then she remembered her predicament and the smile faded. 'Oh, you again.'

'Yes, me again.' There was something very wrong, he realised. She was not the cheerful girl who had laughed at the rain in Chelmsford, nor the elegantly clad young lady he had spoken to at the assembly rooms at Malden the night before. Her grey cloak was bedraggled and her shoes mud-spattered, and even that lovely hair seemed not so vibrant. And it wasn't only caused by the rain. 'Get in, my lady, or we shall both be soaked, while I hold the door open.'

She climbed in and sat beside him, acutely aware of his nearness and the strength of him and that he was again surveying her from head to foot. 'Thank you,' she said, inching away to sit as far away from him as she could, which was difficult in the confines of the coach.

He called out to his postilion to find somewhere to turn the vehicle round and her breath caught in her throat. He was going to abduct her! How could she have been so foolish as to come out alone and then climb willingly into his carriage?

'Where are you taking me?' she asked in alarm as the coachman jumped down and went to the head of the horses to wheel them round in a convenient gateway.

'Home,' he said. 'You will become very wet if you continue with your walk.'

'H…home? Sir, I have no wish to go home with you, wherever that might be. I cannot think why you think I would.'

He threw back his head and laughed aloud. 'My dear young lady, I did not mean my home. I am not a seducer of women, whatever you may think. I meant your home.'

'But you are turning us round.'

'So I am. That is Sir Arthur's house behind us, is it not?'

'Yes,' she said. 'But why should you take me there?'

'It is where you live, is it not?'

'No, it is not. Whatever gave you that idea?' She paused, horrified to think that he had seen her leave there. 'Oh, I see, you took me for one of his servants with whom you might have a little dalliance.'

'No, I did not.' He sounded suddenly angry. 'Anyone less like a servant would be hard to imagine. I assumed you were Sir Arthur's daughter, especially after seeing you together last night.'

'His daughter?' she repeated. Was Sir Arthur really old enough to have a daughter of her age?

'I have it!' he cried, not noticing the query in her voice

and assuming she was confirming his supposition. 'You are married and no longer live at home. Forgive me. Tell me your direction and I will have you home in a twinkling.'

'I am not married and I am not Sir Arthur's daughter. I was simply paying a visit.'

'Not married?'

'No.'

'Then I beg your pardon.' There was no disguising his pleasure at this piece of news as he put his head out of the door and bade the postilion to turn the coach round again, just as he had got it facing the way they had come. Three times he had seen her and on each occasion they had been nearer Colston, and surely it was an omen that they were destined to know each other better. The prospect filled him with pleasurable anticipation. He knew nothing about her except that she was beautiful, had a captivating smile and eyes alight with mischief, or they had been on the two previous occasions he had spoken to her. Today, the shimmer was of tears she was trying to suppress.

'What is wrong?' he asked.

'Nothing. Why did you think there was?'

He reached out and ran the back of his finger along her lower eyelid, making her shiver. A tiny glistening teardrop transferred itself to his finger. 'Tears?' he queried.

'No, sir, raindrops.' She surprised herself with the swiftness of her response. How could she possibly tell him that he was the embodiment of all her dreams, but those dreams had all been shattered by the man who seemed to have sway over their lives whether they willed it or not. The man who lived at Colston Hall.

He smiled. 'As you say, raindrops. Now, tell me where you live and I promise to deliver you safely to your door.

Or would your papa come after me with a blunderbuss for so presuming?'

'He cannot do that. He is dead.'

'Oh, I am truly sorry for it. I have recently lost both my beloved parents and know how you feel. Allow me to offer condolences.'

'Thank you, sir. It happened a long time ago, but is no less difficult to accept.'

They were nearing Colston and just beyond the village were the gates of the Hall, where he would normally turn off the road, and she had still not given him her direction. 'We could continue this delightful ride forever,' he said. 'We could ride on and on, over hills and down dale, on and on into the sunset…'

She laughed. 'The horses would tire long before that.'

'Oh, no, for they are magic horses and this is a magic coach. In it we could ride into eternity, discover the secrets of the universe, learn all there is to know about each other, our likes and dislikes. I am very partial to plum pie and gooseberry tart and I dislike hypocrisy and false pride. What about you?'

'You are talking nonsense,' she said, though she was smiling.

'Yes, but it is worth it to see you smile.' He turned towards her and took her chin in his hand, forcing her to look into his dark eyes. They were deep pools, drawing her in, drowning her. 'You have a smile to enchant, a smile to make a man forget himself…'

She trembled, knowing he was going to kiss her and not caring, wanting him to, holding her breath. She shut her eyes, unable to bear the intensity of his gaze, and she felt his lips touch hers and it was no more than the pressure a butterfly might make. Then he released her and she came to her senses with a suddenness that left her gasping.

'How could you? I thought you were a gentleman or I would never have entered your coach…'

He laughed. 'Would you not? I think I would have been less of a gentleman if I had refused your kind invitation to kiss you.'

'Invitation? Oh, no.'

'Oh, yes. Flagrant it was. And you did not find it repugnant, did you?'

'N…no.'

'You do not sound too sure. Do you want to sample it again?'

'You are making fun of me.'

He was suddenly serious, the smile gone from his lips. 'No, my dear, fun with you, perhaps, not of you. But you know, we will ride straight into the sea unless you tell me where you live.'

She could not take him home. What would her mother and sister say, when she arrived in a coach with an unknown man, especially after she had bribed Annabelle not to say a word about him to her mother? Life was difficult and complicated enough without having to explain away a strange man, especially one who had somehow captured her heart. While their meetings were by chance and ephemeral they were the stuff of dreams. She did not want reality to intrude. 'You may stop here. I am going to visit someone close by.'

He called out for the coach to pull up and pulled his umbrella from under the seat. 'Here, my lady, take this, if you will not let me take you to the door.'

'How will I return it?'

'Oh, I have no doubt we shall meet again, it is written in the stars. You may give it to me then.'

She took it and stood in the road, watching the coach disappear round the bend at the end of the village, going she knew not where. Who was he and where did he live? Would they meet again? Perhaps she should have told him that she was to marry Sir Arthur. He would not have been so sanguine about things being written in stars if he knew that, would he? Did she want to see him again? She did. Oh, she did.

She turned down the lane that led to the dower house, carrying the umbrella above her head, though it did little to keep her skirts dry. But she hardly noticed; she was dreaming of the young man with his deep, dark eyes and smiling mouth, a mouth that had touched hers, ever so briefly.

Once indoors, she put the umbrella down and leaned it against the wall in the hall while she took off her cloak and hung it up. Her mother, hearing her, came out of the drawing room to meet her. 'Lydia, where have you been? And where did you get that?' She pointed at the umbrella. 'You surely did not buy it?'

'No, Mama, I did not buy it, I borrowed it. And I have been to the library as I said I would. And I met Sir Arthur. He invited me into his house and gave me tea. He has those new teacups with handles, much better than dishes. They save you from burning your fingers.'

Her mother refused to be sidetracked by talk of teacups. 'Alone, Lydia?'

'Why not?' She led the way into the parlour and threw herself on to the sofa. 'I was on his driveway. Oh, do not look so cross, I saw the gates and curiosity overcame me. The place looked deserted and I thought he was from home…'

'And he found you? Lydia, whatever did he think?'

'Nothing, why should he? I said I had come with a message from you about when you would be at home to receive him.'

Her mother sat down beside her and took her hand. 'Oh, does that mean…?'

Lydia sighed. 'I have no choice, have I? Thanks to that man.'

'You mean the Earl?'

'Of course I mean the Earl.'

'I have been to the Hall and spoken to his lordship.'

'And no doubt he gave you short shrift. I could tell by the tone of that letter he would not change his mind.'

'He was most condescending. He agreed to let us stay until you are married.'

'And what about you and Annabelle and John?'

'If all goes according to plan, we will be looked after. I told you, it will be written into the marriage contract. Sir Arthur intimated he was prepared to negotiate.'

'Then I suppose the sooner it comes about the better, for I do not wish to be in that man's debt for a single minute.'

'Lydia, he was charming, just like his father when he was young, and I do believe he has suffered greatly—'

'So have we.' She was on the point of saying that it seemed she was to continue to do so, but stopped herself in time; it would only upset her mother. She must accept her fate as cheerfully as she could, but so soon after that difficult interview with Sir Arthur and her last encounter with her handsome stranger, who did not seem like a stranger at all, it was doubly difficult.

'He asked me to wish you happy.'

'He did that?' She was astonished.

'Yes.'

'He did not mean it.'

'Why should he not? He is an honourable man and a gentleman. He did not even know Freddie had been sent away too. I thought they might have corresponded, even met, but it seems not.'

'Oh, Mama, you were surely not hoping that he knew where Freddie is…?'

'Why not?' Anne admitted. 'They were always the best of friends. I thought that if he knew, he might tell us. If he can return without anyone seizing him for what happened all those years ago, then I do not see why Freddie should not do so too.'

'No, but then I never saw a reason for him to leave in the first place. It was all Ralph Latimer's fault, all of it. And just because you have prostrated yourself to him for a few weeks' grace to find a home when it was because of him we lost the first one, do not expect me to feel grateful. I hate him as much as ever and nothing in the world will make me change my mind.'

The carriage pulled up at the front door of Colston Hall and Ralph climbed out and ran up the steps to the entrance, leaving the postilions to take the equipage round to the stables and see to the horses. His butler had the door open before he reached it and took his hat. 'My lord, have you lost your umbrella?'

'No, I lent it. I shall have it back one day.'

He smiled to himself as he made his way to the drawing room and flung himself into a chair, throwing one leg over the arm. He still did not know who the young lady was, nor anything of her background. Perhaps she was a servant after all, but he did not think so. She had too much spirit, too much hauteur, but she could have learned that from a mistress. She could even be someone's mistress. Sir Arthur's? If she was not his daughter and not his servant, but went to visit him at his house without escort or chaperon, then it stood to reason she was not a respectable, well-raised young lady. The thought sobered him for a moment, but not for long. Mistresses could easily be persuaded to change their loyalties.

Did Miss Fostyn know of a rival's existence? Oh, that would set the cat among the pigeons if she found out! Could she actually be Miss Fostyn? No, he told himself, she would not have visited Sir Arthur without her mama and he could see nothing in that beautiful countenance to remind him of the freckle-faced child he had known ten years before. Besides, he would surely not be such a fool as not to know a mortal enemy when he met one, even if she was a pretty girl who had taken his fancy. And she must know who he was, everyone did. Last night she had called him 'my lord', though today she had been careful not to repeat that slip of the tongue. Perhaps she was as ready for dalliance as he was. But oh, she had a marvellously original way of going about getting what she wanted.

The idea of a mystery intrigued him. But it would not be a mystery for long; the village was small, everyone knew everyone else and he would soon learn who she was. He would tell the mayor to go ahead with the Victory Ball. If she lived nearby or had relatives in the village, she would be bound to attend.

'The ball is to go ahead a week from now,' Annabelle announced at supper two nights later. 'Caroline Brotherton heard it from his lordship himself. She is all agog. His lordship, she said, is very handsome and has the nicest manners....'

'I shall not go,' Lydia said. 'If that man is there, I cannot promise to be responsible for my actions.'

'Lydia, he has a name and a title,' their mother put in. 'Do not, pray, refer to him as "that man".'

'It is how I think of him, when I think of him at all, which is as little as possible.'

'But you must go. Sir Arthur will be there and you never know, he might make his offer.'

Lydia could hardly suppress the shudder which shook her. 'So soon?'

'You said the sooner the better.'

'So I did, but I did not mean with indecent haste.'

'Lydia, have you changed your mind? If so, you must say so now and I will do what I can to retrieve the situation, though how, I do not know.'

Lydia took a deep breath and pulled herself together. 'No, I have not changed my mind. We will go.'

'Good,' her mother said, then noticing the untouched food on Lydia's plate. 'Finish your supper, child, Janet is waiting to clear the table.'

Lydia pushed her plate away. 'I am not hungry.'

Annabelle giggled. 'Lydia is in love, Mama.' And as Lydia shot her a venomous look, added, 'With Sir Arthur, I mean, of course.'

It was so palpably untrue, that their troubled mother looked from one to the other in puzzlement. 'One doesn't need to be in love to make a contented marriage, Annabelle. Lydia knows that, and it is unkind of you to tease.'

'Well, I shall marry for love.'

Anne smiled indulgently. 'Is that so, dear?'

'Yes. Lydia is not the only one who might receive a proposal at the ball. You know it will be the same day as my sixteenth birthday and I am expecting Perry to speak to you.'

'You mean Peregrine Baverstock?'

'Yes.' Annabelle was almost smug.

'When have you met that young man and discussed such matters?' her mother demanded, her attention now away from Lydia and firmly fixed on her younger daughter.

'At Caroline's. Twice. And at the lecture I went to with Lydia. He presented me to his parents and they were most gracious to me. Perry says they liked me.'

'And when did he say that?'

'He told me when I met him in the village when I took Hector for a walk. He was riding his horse and I opened a gate for him. We had some conversation—'

'Unchaperoned! Annabelle, how could you!'

'Hector was with me.'

'Hector is a dog.'

'Well, that is by the way. He told me his parents approved of me and that we need not have a long engagement.'

'Annabelle!' their mother exclaimed. 'I cannot believe you have let things go so far without saying a word to me. I hardly know the young man, he might not be at all suitable.'

'Oh, I think he is,' Lydia murmured. 'He will come into a title one day; even if it is only a minor one, it is a title. And I believe there is money…'

'You knew about this?' her mother asked her.

'Not until the night of the lecture.'

'I should have been told. This is not the way a properly raised young lady goes about making a match, Annabelle. Goodness knows what Lord and Lady Baverstock must think of you.'

'Perry will present you to them at the ball,' Annabelle said. 'Then you will be able to judge for yourself, arrange everything as it should be done. Now that Lydia has agreed to marry Sir Arthur, there will be no trouble over a dowry, will there?'

Lydia, who had been dreaming of the handsome

stranger with the laughing eyes, heard her sister's voice, almost strident in its eagerness, and her heart sank. Instead of looking forward to the ball, she began to dread it.

The day before the big occasion, Sir Arthur paid his promised visit to Mrs Fostyn, arriving in his spanking new carriage, dressed in an immaculate coat of dove grey gros-grain and matching breeches tucked into shining calf boots. A froth of lace fell over his hands and cascaded over the top of his green brocade waistcoat. He was wear-ing a new white wig, with rows of sausage-shaped curls on each side, which fitted more securely than the old one. His bulging stomach had been pulled in by a corset which creaked as he bent over Anne's hand.

'Your obedient, ma'am. I hope I find you well?'

'Very well, Sir Arthur. May I offer you refreshment?'

'Thank you.'

She rang the bell for Janet. 'Then please be seated.'

They sat, Anne, Sir Arthur and Lydia, facing each other, not speaking until Lydia, unable to endure the si-lence, asked him if he were going to the ball the following evening.

'Indeed, I am and hope for a happy outcome.'

'Oh.' Lydia paused and then added in a rush, 'Where has that girl got to? Shall I go and find her, Mama?'

'Yes, tell her to bring tea and cakes and then perhaps you should wait in your room until Sir Arthur and I have had our discussion. Or go and help Annabelle finish put-ting the ribbons on her gown. You know what her stitch-ing is like.' She smiled at their guest. 'Lydia is a fine seamstress, Sir Arthur.'

Lydia almost ran from the room in her anxiety to es-cape. She delivered the message to Janet whom she met hurrying along the hall, but instead of going to her room or finding her sister, she grabbed her cloak and left the house. The further away she was when they decided her future, the better. She could not trust herself not to reject the whole idea.

She would visit Mistress Grey, her old teacher. She had been retired a long time but Lydia and her mother visited her from time to time to make sure there was nothing she needed. She was very old now and plagued by rheumatics, but her mind was still sharp and she was full of down-to-earth wisdom and might have some good advice.

Her isolated cottage could be reached using a path through the wood and out across a meadow to a track which had once been an old road, but which the encroaching marshes had made unsafe for vehicles. Lydia set out along the path at the back of the dower house, skirted the park of the Hall, being careful not to look at its mellow stone and mullioned windows in case *he* was there, and plunged into the wood.

It was gloomy among the trees, whose burgeoning leaves dripped rain on to her head and shoulders. The old leaves beneath her feet were sodden and the air smelled musty. It was depressing, which suited her mood, but even in the gloom she could hear the birds beginning to sing after the rain and a frog was croaking in a puddle nearby. Life always returned after the long sleep of winter, she mused. Why then did she feel no joy, why did her winter continue unrelenting?

She had not been this way for some time, not since last summer, and she did not notice that the path she usually took had become overgrown and a new one had been made through the undergrowth until she found herself in a clearing, facing a tumble-down hovel. A shaft of sunlight came out from a cloud at the same moment as she emerged from the trees and shone on the tiny windows, reflecting the trees and the sky. Her face lit up with a delighted smile and she darted forward. She remembered that place! They used to play in it as children, chasing in and out of the broken door, Freddie and Ralph doing their best to throw her off and never quite succeeding.

Six feet from the building, she stopped suddenly. It had a new door which was securely bolted; the welcome was no longer there. She was a trespasser on *his* land, and the friendly games were all in the past and should never, never be recalled. She turned to leave and then gasped in shock. He was standing not ten feet away, his feet wide apart, his long riding coat thrown carelessly from his shoulders, his head bare, not even covered by a wig. And for once, he was not smiling. He looked like thunder.

'I believe you are trespassing,' he said coldly, walking towards her.

'If I am trespassing, then so are you.'

'That is beside the point. This is a dangerous place to be.'

'Dangerous—why?'

He jerked his head towards the cottage. 'This place has been used by smugglers.'

'Smugglers?' She was intrigued. 'Really?'

'Yes. The evidence is plain to see.'

'And why should that make it dangerous? A handful of free-traders would have no interest in me.'

'If it is only a handful. Some of these gangs are vicious and will stop at nothing to carry on their nefarious trade. You would be well advised to avoid these woods.'

'In daylight? O, come, sir, you jest, surely.'

'No, it is not a matter for jest. If you know anything, you would be wise to tell me of it. Who they are, when they might come again…?'

Why was he so angry? Every time they had met before,

it had been a light-hearted exchange, smiles and talk of water nymphs and riding into the sunset, stars and umbrellas, not this lowering look of pure venom. She forced herself to laugh. 'Do I look like a smuggler?'

'They come in all guises.' He didn't know why he had said it, except that some of the free-traders would almost certainly be local men with local knowledge, for few people knew of the tumbledown cottage in his wood. His gamekeeper, Freddie and Lydia sprang readily to mind. His gamekeeper would equate smuggling with poaching and in any case would not do anything to jeopardise his position; Freddie was in exile and that left Lydia. As a child she had been up to all the mischief he and Freddie could devise, a real tomboy, but did that mean she had grown up still behaving in the same way?

'And so, I suppose, do revenue men,' she retorted promptly. 'If you are a revenue man, you will be sadly disappointed in me, for I know nothing of smuggling or smugglers.'

She did not know who he was! But he knew her. Realisation had dawned when he had seen her run towards that hovel, her head flung back and a smile on her lips. Why had he not recognised her before? In the wrong place, he supposed, and time had changed her from a child to a woman. Chelmsford was far enough away for him to be forgiven for not knowing who she was then and even at the lecture in Malden it had not occurred to him that they had met before. But Colston? His own village. Should he not have begun to wonder then?

He had done so for one fleeting moment, but then dismissed the idea on the grounds that he would know an enemy when he saw one, that some inner voice would warn him to beware. But the inner voice had remained silent and here, in this clearing, before this door, time

stood still. He was a boy again, with all the guilt and
sorrow and hate still to come. And she was a child, whom
he tolerated because she was the sister of his friend and
it amused them to tease her. He could hardly look at her
without flinching.

But he did look and the image of the child faded to be
replaced by the woman, the woman who had captivated
him in the rain. She was breathing heavily and her beautiful oval face was flushed, her bronze hair falling about
her shoulders in a cloud. An angel or a witch?

'Then why come here?' he demanded, his voice so
husky it was almost a croak.

'I have said I know nothing,' she said, defiantly, still
bemused by the change in him. 'My presence here is pure
chance.'

'Chance.' He laughed harshly. 'Chance is it, to come
upon a place so well hidden and which leads nowhere
except to the marshes where smugglers might find it easy
to land their contraband?'

'I was making for a track on the other side of the woods
but then, as a stranger, I suppose you would not know it
was there.' She should walk away from him, she realised,
should excuse herself and leave, but she could not. It was
as if he had put a spell on her, depriving her of her will
to move. 'But I think it only fair to warn you that if the
Earl of Blackwater were to find you here, it would be the
worse for you he is not a forgiving man.'

'Is he not?'

'No.'

'You know him well, do you?'

'Well enough.'

'Do you think he knows that smugglers use his woods?'

She shrugged. 'Perhaps. Perhaps he would not care; it
is well known that the gentry shut their eyes to such things

in return for a barrel or two of French brandy, a case of wine, or a few pounds of tea. And I know he is not averse to breaking the law.'

He was so angry he felt like shaking her, shouting that it was because of her he had spent ten years in exile. Yes, her, Miss Lydia Fostyn. She had alerted her father to the duel, that much he had discovered in the confusion afterwards; if she had not, his shot would have found nothing but the empty air and no harm would have been done. He and Freddie would have made up their quarrel, deciding no woman was worth the destruction of a friendship and that would have been the end of it. Instead…

Almost without realising what he was doing, he had reached out and taken her shoulders in his hands, intending to tell her so. He just had time to register the astonishment on her face, before he bent his head to find her mouth with his.

It was a harsh and cruel kiss, meant to hurt. And it did. Bewildered and not a little frightened, she struggled in his arms, kicking out with her feet. He held her fast, determined to punish her in the only way he knew how. At last, too breathless to continue, he flung her from him.

She sank to the wet ground, sobbing. Nothing had prepared her for that, not after their previous encounters, which had been sweet and gently amusing. He had flattered her and touched her lips with his very, very gently. He had lent her his umbrella and said they would meet again because it was written in the stars. How could a man say such things and then behave so cruelly? He was as bad as that fiend up at the Hall.

And then she gasped. He was that fiend! He was the Earl of Blackwater! Why, oh, why had she not recognised him? Why had she allowed herself to dream pleasant dreams about a man she hated?

She struggled to stand and he reached down to help her up, more sorry than he could ever have believed possible for what he had just done. It was unforgivable. 'Lydia…'

'Oh, so you do know me,' she raged, shrugging him off and scrambling to her feet. 'Not content with killing my father and ruining my family, you must add salt to the wound and try to humiliate me. What did you intend? That I should fall in love with you and then you could spurn me, laughing as you did so? I hate you, Ralph Latimer, hate you with every sinew of my body and if I could find a way of punishing you, I would. May you rot in hell.'

'No doubt I will,' he said softly, but she did not hear him, for she had fled, blundering into the thick undergrowth, trying to find the path by which she had come, blinded by tears.

Afraid she would injure herself, he strode after her. 'Not that way, you little fool, the path is this way.'

Desperate to get away from him, she tore at the branches of an alder tree, scratching her hands and face, her feet sinking into the wet earth and dead leaves. He grabbed her arm. She fought him, she fought him for all she was worth, until they both slipped on the mud and fell to the ground in a tangle of arms and legs. She lay still, like a terrified rabbit, holding her breath, her eyes closed, waiting for him to make a move, to complete the ravishment he had started. She had no strength left to continue the fight.

He sat up and looked down at her. She was covered in mud and scratches, her cloak was spread about her and her green taffeta gown was almost in tatters, revealing a pure white shoulder and the rounded top of one breast. He felt an almost irresistible urge to reach out and touch it, to pull away the rest of her bodice and cup that silky flesh in the palm of his hand, to roll the nipple between finger and thumb and feel it harden. To make her want him. It would be a way of punishing her, wouldn't it? Of taking away the pain that was always there, the pain he had never been quite able to subdue, the pain of guilt and exile, of not being there when his mother needed him, of being too late to see either her or his father before they both died. Violent deaths, just as the Reverend Fostyn's had been a violent death.

He reached out, his hand poised above her breast, which rose and fell with her ragged breathing. His glance moved to her face. She had one arm over her eyes as if to shut out the sight of him and what he might do to her and the tension in her slight, but lovely, body was almost tangible. He could not do it. He could not despoil such beauty simply for revenge. He took the torn edge of her dress and pulled it up to cover her breast, feeling her flinch, even from that. 'Lydia, I am sorry,' he said.

Her hand came away from her face and her eyes flew open and the golden lights in them flashed with pure hatred. It was enough to unnerve him.

'Sorry, sir?' she queried, sitting up and drawing her muddied cloak about her, trying to regain her dignity and with it the upper hand. 'Sorry is not enough. You will pay for this, you will pay for all you have done to our family—'

'I have already paid, Lydia, over and over again.'

She did not want to hear his gentle voice, so full of sadness that it was almost enough to soften her anger. She did not want to soften. She scrambled to her feet, hopping on one foot because she had lost a shoe in the mud. 'Oh, no, my lord, your punishment has only just begun.'

He picked her shoe up, intending to return it to her, but

it was full of mud and he took a handful of leaves and attempted to clean it.

'Give me that,' she demanded, holding out her hand for it.

Silently he handed it to her and watched as she crammed her foot into it before setting off again. He should have stayed where he was and let her go, but he could not. He rose and went after her. 'At least, let me see you safely home.'

'I do not need an escort, sir, I know my way.'

'Do you? You are not going in the direction of the dower house.'

'I am going to see Mistress Grey.'

He remembered the old lady with affection. She had been a nursery maid at the Hall when he was in leading strings. When he became too old to need a nursery maid, she had gone to live in the village and taught the Fostyn children until they were old enough to go to school. All except Freddie, who had shared his lessons at the Hall. 'Mistress Grey? Is she still about?'

'Yes. Now, if you do not mind, I find your presence distasteful. In fact, nothing would please me more than never to see you again. Go back to India.'

She had found the path now and marched purposefully forward, head held high, though she looked like nothing so much as a gypsy, mud-spattered and ragged, hobbling because her shoe had split and would not stay on her foot. No doubt she would tell the world he had attacked her and the world would have no difficulty in believing her, the state she was in. It would be one more accusation he would have to live down, unable to vindicate himself. He stopped and watched her back with that lovely hair cascading over her shoulders until she disappeared, then he turned and walked in the opposite direction. Perhaps he should go back to India after all...

Chapter Four

Lydia limped on, wondering if he would come after her again. Was there no end to his perfidy? How had she allowed herself to be taken in by him, believing him to be the stuff of dreams? Because he was handsome and smiled a great deal? Had she assumed that his guilt, carried for ten long years, would have etched deep lines in his face, turned his hair white? Had she expected the returning Ralph Latimer, the new Earl of Blackwater, to look haggard and drawn, years and years older than he was?

He did not look a day over his twenty-nine years, tall and straight and firmly muscular. His eyes were clear and had, until today, been full of gentle humour when he looked at her, his mouth clean cut and... Oh, she had been kissed by those lips, had felt them on her mouth, fierce and burning. And passionate. Even in his cruelty she had recognised that, had felt an answering fire. Love and hate had become so inextricably part of the same passion, she could not separate them.

She found the old Roman track and, a few minutes later, stumbled up to the door of Mistress Grey's cottage and banged on it with her fists, not knowing what she was going to say, how she was going to explain her appearance.

'Lydia!' The old lady who answered the door was almost as round as she was tall; her head barely reached Lydia's shoulders. She wore a black taffeta gown whose voluminous skirts added to the impression. Her plump, rosy-cheeked face owed nothing to paint and her white hair was the colour nature had intended it to be. Her welcoming smile turned to consternation at the sight of the girl. 'What in the name of heaven has happened to you?'

Lydia almost fell into her arms, sobbing and unable to speak for the tumult in her breast. Mistress Grey led her to a sofa and sat down, pulling the distraught girl down beside her and putting her arms round her. 'My poor darling, you are safe now. I won't let anyone hurt you.'

'It was awful,' she mumbled, her head in the comforting warmth of the old lady's ample bosom. 'I thought he—'

'He? A man did this to you? Come, child, tell your old Harriet all about it and he will be punished.'

Punished! Hadn't she told him he would be punished? Was this her chance for revenge? Oh, how sweet it would be! How satisfying! But could she? Could she accuse him of attempting to rape her? It would destroy him. That was what she wanted, wasn't it? She had only to say his name, conjecture would do the rest.

But she knew she could not. Her mother was right, vengeance should be left to God, but she hoped, oh, how she hoped He would not be long in bringing it down. She lifted her head and smiled wanly. 'It is a long story…'

'Then I will make a herbal tea to soothe you while you tell it. And, Lydia,' she added, lifting an admonishing finger, 'it must be the whole story, nothing left out.'

And so Lydia sat by the fireside in her petticoat, gazing

into its flames, sipping herbal tea, and unburdened her heart while the old lady did her best to clean and mend her clothes while she listened. She did not comment until the tale was told and then she did not presume to offer advice, except to say, 'Lydia, dearest, you know right from wrong. Do what is right—you do not need me to tell you that.'

'No.' She rose, took the mended gown and slipped it on. Though it was cleaner and no longer torn, nothing could disguise the fact that she had met with a mishap. 'What shall I tell Mama?'

'A fall in a puddle, perhaps. It is not an untruth, is it? I think it would distress her to know the whole story and she has worries enough, don't you think?'

Lydia bade her goodbye and set off home, half wondering if she might encounter his lordship again, but she arrived back at the dower house without meeting anyone and slipped up the back stairs to her room unseen. The damaged dress she bundled into the back of a closet, before washing and changing into a blue muslin with long sleeves and a high neck which hid the worst of her scratches.

She was calm as she went down to the drawing room, her insides frozen into acceptance of a fate she could not change. Sir Arthur had left and her mother, with a pair of spectacles perched on the end of her nose, was sewing pink ribbon bows on the skirt of Annabelle's ball gown. She set it aside when her daughter came into the room.

'Lydia, where have you been? Sir Arthur wanted to take his leave of you, but you were nowhere to be found. I had to tell him you had the headache.' She paused, noticing the scratches on Lydia's face. 'What has happened to you?'

Lydia sat in a chair near the fire and held her cold hands

towards the blaze. 'I went for a walk through the woods to call on Mistress Grey. The ground was muddy after the rain and I slipped in a puddle…'

'But your face is scratched and there is a bruise above your eye.'

'I fell into a bush.'

'Really, Lydia, I cannot think why you should take it into your head to go visiting today of all days. I asked you to wait in your room, not disappear altogether. Now what are we to say to everyone? I doubt patches will cover those scratches. And that eye! What are we to do about it? Thank goodness the ball is to be masked.'

'I need not go. You can say I am unwell and that is the truth, for I feel considerably shaken.'

'But I believe Sir Arthur is wishful to make his offer.'

'You have reached an agreement, then?' Lydia spoke flatly, as if she were discussing a new gown with the mantilla maker. It was the only way she could hold her emotions in check.

'Yes. It will be as I said. All you have to do is listen to his proposal and give your consent. The wedding can be in June—so much nicer in the summer, don't you think?'

'But that is less than three months away! Oh, Mama, must it be so soon?'

'Why delay? Sir Arthur is a widower; his home is already set up and waiting for you. And I believe he has business in foreign parts which must be transacted before the year is out. He wants to combine it with a wedding tour.'

'Oh, Mama, it is such a big step to take and I am not at all ready for it.'

'Nonsense. Once you have become used to the idea, you will begin to look forward to it, as every young bride does, making plans, buying clothes and fripperies, being showered with gifts from your husband-to-be, arranging your new home...'

With the right man, she might have agreed with her mother, but she was only too aware that Sir Arthur was not the right man. She was almost repulsed by him and if she said yes when he proposed, she had to spend the rest of her life with him! She shuddered, imagining him kissing her, taking her to bed, his naked body against hers. It was abhorrent! She would rather be kissed by the Earl, and heaven knew how much she hated him! Suddenly she found herself reliving the feel of that powerful mouth on hers, the strength of his arms, the hint of laughter in his eyes, and was overwhelmed by such a feeling of desolation that she could hardly breathe and was in danger of bursting into tears again.

Anne was shocked by her daughter's pallor, the bleakness in her eyes and the shaking of her limbs. 'Dear child, you truly are not well, are you?' She reached out for the small bell on the table at her side and gave it a shake. 'Janet shall put you to bed with a tisane and a hot brick to your feet and we will see how you do tomorrow. If you are unable to go to the ball, I am sure Sir Arthur will understand.'

'Thank you, Mama.'

'There is something else I have to ask you. When Sir Arthur was leaving, I tried to return the umbrella, but he denied it was his.' She searched her daughter's face. 'If it is not his umbrella, Lydia, whose is it? You told me you had called at Sir Arthur's house and I naturally assumed it was he who lent it to you. That is what you meant me to think, is it not?'

'No, Mama, I had no intention of deceiving you. It belongs to the Earl. His coach overtook me as I was walking home in the rain and he took me up and brought me to the village. He offered me the umbrella to walk up the drive.'

'Why did you not say at the time that you had met him?'

Lydia shrugged. 'The less said about him the better. You know what I think of him.'

'Do I? I only know what you tell me. But as you consented to ride in his carriage, perhaps you are beginning to realise you misjudged him. He is not a bad man, you know. He was caught up in circumstances which he could not control, just as we all were. You should understand that.'

'Oh, I understand,' she said bitterly. She understood what it was like to lose control, to feel like a leaf on the wind buffeted here and there, to feel there was no hard ground beneath her, no safe haven. She rose and made her way towards the door, as Janet arrived in answer to the summons.

Half an hour later she was in bed and alone, but she knew it was only a temporary reprieve and sooner or later she would have to face up to reality. And the reality was that she must marry Sir Arthur. And Ralph Latimer, Earl of Blackwater, was not the stuff of her dreams. The man of her dreams, the man she had met in Chelmsford, was a figment of her imagination. The tisane must have been liberally dosed with laudanum because she fell asleep in the middle of this thought and did not wake until the next morning.

When Janet drew back the curtains of her room and let in the sunshine, Lydia got up and went to the window. The mist had gone and the sun was glinting on the wet grass of the meadow. She looked towards the wood which she could just glimpse over the outbuildings to her right. The trees seemed to have burst into leaf overnight and it no longer seemed the sinister place of smugglers and ghosts of the past. But Ralph Latimer was no ghost and he held sway over their lives, just as his father had before him, unless she did something about it.

She must put him from her mind, right away, banish him from every thought. But how could she, when he refused to be banished? If she thought of Sir Arthur, Ralph Latimer intruded with his whispered criticism; if she thought about the smugglers, he was there with his accusations; if she thought about her mother, she was reminded of those dreadful rumours and there she was, back where she started, blaming him for what had happened ten years before. There was no escaping him; he was omnipresent, ubiquitous, all-seeing, powerful.

She turned as Annabelle burst into her room. 'Mama says you are not well and we may not go to the ball. Oh, Lydia, how could you? I declare you are only saying it to be perverse; you were perfectly well yesterday.'

Lydia gave a huge sigh; it was no good postponing the inevitable. If she made difficulties for Sir Arthur, he might withdraw his offer, and then what? She sat down on the edge of her bed and looked up at her sister's petulant face. Poor Annabelle! She had set her heart on going to the ball, how could she gainsay her? 'I am quite recovered,' she said. 'Do not concern yourself. We shall go.'

'Oh, you angel!' Annabelle flung herself on her sister with such exuberance they both fell back on the bed.

'Now, be off with you and let me dress,' Lydia said, extricating herself. 'And you had better calm yourself or there will be no dealing with you tonight and Lord and

Lady Baverstock with think you are too excitable to make
a good wife for their son.'

Once Annabelle had left her, smiling broadly at having
her own way, Lydia washed and dressed slowly and made
her way downstairs. It was going to be a long, long day
and an even longer night and she dare not think further
forward than that.

They began preparing for the evening hours before the
time for them to leave. Water had to be heated for them
to take baths before bedroom fires, and then, once in their
undergarments, they had to sit to have their hair dressed
and make-up applied; with only Janet to help all three, it
took a long time. And finally their gowns were slipped
over their heads and the fastenings done up, head-dresses
arranged and feet slipped into shoes. By the time the
coach was brought round at eight o'clock they were ready.

Unable to buy matching braid, the stomacher of Lydia's
yellow brocade had been embroidered with gold and
cream thread and the straight neckline decorated with
cream lace and more cream lace tumbled from the tight
elbow-length sleeves. The skirt was full and unadorned.
Its simplicity and the way it enhanced her neat waist and
uplifted her bosom pleased her. Needing to disguise her
cuts and bruises, she had allowed Janet to use rather more
maquillage than she would have liked, but it enhanced the
green of her eyes; the black patches over the worst of the
marks added to her allure. Her wig was piled high and
decorated with gold-dyed feathers. A velvet cloak fastened with a large brooch from her mother's rapidly dwindling collection of jewels, white stockings, satin slippers
and a brocade mask to match her dress completed her
ensemble.

'I say, Lydia, you look like a princess,' her brother said,

coming from his room to watch his mother and sisters depart.

She smiled. 'Then where is the prince?'

'Never mind about a prince,' their mother put in with a smile. 'Sir Arthur cannot fail to be impressed.' She turned to her youngest daughter. 'And you look very fine too, Annabelle dear. I am so glad I kept those old gowns.'

'You are not to say they are old,' Annabelle said, looking down at the pink silk with its dozens of large pink bows sewn all over the skirt and the white and aquamarine gauze ruching over the bodice. Pink silk rosebuds filled the décolletage and, instead of feathers in her hair, she wore more rosebuds in a coronet. 'Nor that we made them up ourselves. They came from the best mantua maker in London and are the latest mode.'

Anne smiled. 'Of course. Now let us be off.' Picking up her fan, she sailed out of the front door, followed by her two daughters, watched by John and Janet.

The Assembly Rooms were already filling up as they arrived. A long line of carriages stretched from the door, right down the street, and from them emerged the upper crust of the local society and the town's dignitaries. Others arrived by chair or on foot, accompanied by link boys carrying lanterns. Light spilled from the door and they could hear the musicians tuning their instruments as their own carriage finally reached the entrance and they were able to alight, ducking their heads low so as not to disturb their head-dresses.

The noise of laughter and conversation hit them as they entered the ballroom which was a-glitter with jewellery and silks and satins, besides the crystal candelabra which hung above their heads. 'Brought from the Hall,' Anne whispered to Lydia. 'I heard the Earl had promised to lend them for the occasion.'

The Earl. It was the first time his name had been mentioned all day, but he had, Lydia realised with a start, never been far from her thoughts. She didn't know why she kept thinking of him, when it made her so angry. And now as they made their way into the room, she realised his name was on everyone's lips. How generous he had been, how handsome he was, and still unattached, or so it was thought. Matrons with eligible daughters looked smug.

'Where has he been all these years?' everyone wanted to know, but Lydia, who could have told them, remained silent. She could not bear to speak his name, let alone enter into conversation about him.

'I believe he will come,' Lady Baverstock was saying as they approached her. She turned when she saw the newcomers. 'Mrs Fostyn, do come and join us.' She smiled at Lydia, inclining her feather-decked head in greeting, and then turned to appraise Annabelle. 'Annabelle, how charming you look.'

Annabelle blushed and curtsied. 'Good evening, my lady.'

'I was just saying we thought his lordship will attend tonight, though Bertie…' she indicated her portly husband with her fan '…thinks he will not on account of being in mourning. What do you think?'

'I am sure I do not know,' Anne said, while Lydia looked round for a way of escape and Annabelle stood searching the room for Peregrine, who was to be seen talking to a group of young men in a corner. He came over when he spotted Annabelle.

'He was hardly close to his parents, was he?' her ladyship went on. 'The late Earl sent him away and he made no attempt to return…'

'There was a reason for that,' Anne said.

'Oh, as to that, I cannot believe that to have been sufficient reason for staying away all these years.'

Lydia could feel her mother's discomfort and felt like slapping the insensitive woman. She longed to shout that the man she found so agreeable had tried to rape her but, knowing the furore that would cause, she could not do it. Even in her anger, she knew it would be an unjust accusation.

'Prudence, I think such talk is upsetting to Mrs Fostyn,' her husband said. 'Pray change the subject.'

Lydia gave him a look of gratitude and he smiled benignly at her as his wife began profuse apologies. 'I did not think. Oh, my dear Mrs Fostyn, please forgive me. It has been so long, one is inclined to forget there were others involved. Do you ever hear from your son?'

'Occasionally,' Anne lied bravely. 'He is serving in the army…'

'Ah, yes, but now we are at peace, he will come home?'

'Perhaps.'

Lydia wandered off to speak to other acquaintances, but there was no escaping the subject of conversation. Even Robert Dent, who was dressed in puce satin decorated with pounds of silver lace, was talking about the new occupant of the Hall.

'I believe his lordship has plans to refurbish the Hall,' he said, after sweeping her a bow and asking her for the first dance which was then beginning. 'And not before time. It has been sadly neglected.'

'I know nothing of it.' Her answer implied she did not want to know.

'There is rumour that he is preparing it for a wife.' His

grip on her hand tightened as she stumbled. 'Oh, did I tread on your toe? How clumsy of me. I beg your pardon.' And then he continued with the conversation as if there had been no interruption. 'It is surprising if he has not married, but if he has, why did he not bring her back with him?'

'Why is everyone talking about that man?' she demanded, as they promenaded down the line of dancers, to meet the couple from the opposite end.

'Because, my dear Miss Fostyn, this is a small town where very little happens and the arrival of the prodigal is a source of much curiosity.'

'Prodigal! He is a murderer.'

'Oh, my dear, such vehemence! Surely you are not still harbouring that view of the matter. I was there and I assure you it was an accident—'

'It need never have happened.'

'Oh, I agree wholeheartedly, but I do not blame Ralph Latimer.'

'Why not? I do.'

'I can understand you feeling like that ten years ago, you were only a child then and to children everything is black and white...' He paused to look down at her and added softly, 'Now you are a very beautiful woman, and I should have thought able to view things more objectively.'

'How could you? You were Freddie's second; you should be loyal to him.'

'I am, but that does not blind me to the fact that Freddie asked for it.'

'What was the fight about?'

'You do not know?'

'I would not ask if I did.'

'A young lady Freddie had fallen in love with. Unfortunately she did not feel the same way about him and, well, you know Ralph was, even then, a deuced fine fellow…'

'Oh.' She had not known about the young lady. Had Ralph taken the unknown girl, kissed her, made love to her, just as he had tried to do with her only the day before, knowing how Freddie felt about her?

'That makes it worse and I do not wish to speak of it again,' she said primly.

He was prevented from saying any more as they circled the opposing couple, which was just as well, and they finished the dance in silence. He escorted her back to her mother, bowing before her and asking how she did. Anne was gracious towards him, which only added to Lydia's torment.

She hoped fervently that his lordship's mourning for his parents meant he would not come. So why was she continually looking towards the door, her heart beating madly as if she were waiting for a lover to arrive? But the only other person to come through the door was Sir Arthur. He was dressed in a suit of pale lilac satin. The lapels of the coat, the huge turn-back cuffs and the flaps of the pockets were intricately embroidered with red silk and trimmed with silver braid. His breeches were fastened with ribbon bows just beneath the knee. She could not help noting that his calves were spindly and his white hose a little wrinkled. Seeing Anne and her daughters, he walked over to them, his red heels clicking at every step.

'My dear Mrs Fostyn.' He swept Anne a magnificent bow, so that the top of his new white wig was presented to her gaze. And then he repeated the process towards Lydia. 'Miss Fostyn, I hope you are fully recovered from your megrim?'

'Indeed, I am, Sir Arthur.' She smiled at him. She really

must be pleasant towards him, she really must, however much it cost her.

He turned and greeted Annabelle who had just returned from dancing with Peregrine, and then bowed to Lord and Lady Baverstock, remarking on the good attendance and the weather, which was more clement than it had been of late. As soon as the orchestra struck up the next dance he took Lydia's hand and led her into the set. He danced correctly, but stiffly, as if it was a chore to be got over but not enjoyed and, because he had to concentrate on the steps, he hardly spoke. Lydia's smile became stuck, as she moved like an automaton beside him, moving in and out, round and under his raised arm, her feet obeying the music while her mind wandered.

This was going to be her life, stiff, correct, no real enjoyment and no fire. She could not imagine him raising his voice or quarrelling with her, nor could she imagine his face lit by the sheer pleasure of being alive. When the dance came to an end, he did not return her to her party, but tucked her hand into his arm and led her to a quiet corner beside a pillar which had been decorated with greenery. My goodness, she thought, looking about her in dismay, he is surely not going to attempt to kiss me? And then, looking past his shoulder, she saw a slight movement by the door, people giving way, small curtsies from the ladies and then *he* was there.

Tall, arrogant and magnificent in black velvet with white ruffles, he stood in the doorway, surveying the scene, utterly composed. His dark wig was so like his own hair that, for a moment, she thought he had come without one. Diamonds glittered in the folds of his cravat and on his fingers. Sir Arthur felt her tension and turned to follow her gaze. 'Ah, the Earl,' he said. 'I was not sure he would grace us with his presence, but he has hit just the right

note with that black suit. No doubt he is only putting in
a token appearance and will soon leave again.'

'Yes,' she said flatly.

'We will go and greet him. Perhaps I can persuade him
to stay for our announcement. Shall we ask him if he
would be so kind as to make it for us? It will be quite
fitting, don't you think?'

'Announcement?' she echoed as he almost dragged her
unwillingly across the room. Now the time had come she
was almost in a panic and racking her brains to find a
way of stopping him.

'Why, yes. Surely your mama told you I hoped it would
be made tonight?'

'Sir Arthur.' She stopped so suddenly he was obliged
to come to a halt himself. 'Sir Arthur, you are in too much
haste. We have not discussed this properly. Mama said
you would be speaking to me tonight, not that you would
take it as *fait accompli.*'

'Oh…but Mrs Fostyn led me to believe you would
agree, that you would put up no resistance.'

'Sir, you have given me no opportunity to agree or
resist.'

'No, 'tis true, but I did not know when, or even if, the
Earl of Blackwater would appear, but as he has come, his
approval would set the seal—'

'I care not one fig for the Earl of Blackwater's partic-
ipation in what should be a private affair,' she said tartly.
'And if you think it so important, pray, let us postpone
the whole matter to another time.'

'But do you not wish to be presented to his lordship
and receive his congratulations?'

She became aware that Ralph had noticed them
crossing the room towards him and then had seen them
stop; a slight smile crossed his face, almost as if he knew

what the altercation was about. She lifted her chin defiantly and laid her hand on Sir Arthur's sleeve. 'Very well, sir. Let us greet the Earl of Blackwater.'

They continued their stately way, until they stood before the Earl who was surrounded by sycophants, young men who wanted to be like him and eager mamas, anxious to present their daughters.

'My lord,' Sir Arthur began. 'May I present—?'

'No need, old fellow,' Ralph said, grinning wickedly at Lydia. 'Miss Fostyn and I are already well acquainted. You do not mind if I take her off to dance with her, do you? I have been promising myself that pleasure all evening.' And without waiting for the astonished Sir Arthur to frame a reply, he had taken Lydia by the hand and drawn her away on to the middle of the dance floor where a minuet was just beginning.

'How dare you!' she exclaimed in a strangled whisper.

'Now, I would have expected you to be thanking me…'

'What for?'

'For saving you from making a terrible mistake.'

'I don't know what you mean.'

'Oh, I think you do. Sir Arthur is not your father, that much we established long ago, but he is conducting you about with a proprietorial air which, added to the rumour that he is thinking of marrying again, I find very disturbing.'

'Why should you be disturbed? It is none of your business.'

'Do you mean to tell me you want to be married to that…that… Words fail me.'

She laughed, in spite of herself. 'Then it must be the very first time.'

'Do you?' he asked quietly.

She made the mistake of looking up into his face and

saw those deep, dark eyes, looking down at her with a softness that completely unnerved her. Her heart began to beat uncomfortably in her throat and it was difficult to get any words out. 'Do I what?' she managed, at last.

'Do you want to marry Sir Arthur?'

'He has yet to ask me.'

'Good. I arrived in the nick of time.'

'But I believe he will do so before the evening is out.'

'That is not an answer to my question. Do you want to marry him?'

'Yes,' she said defiantly.

He leaned forward to put his mouth close to her ear, so that his warm breath sent shivers tingling through her abdomen and down her legs almost to her toes and, for the second time that evening, she stumbled over her own feet. 'Liar!' he whispered.

She hated him, she told herself, hated him with every fibre of her and the tingling sensation coursing through her body was fury. But she could not forget what he was like before she found out who he was. Which was his real self? The devil or the handsome nabob? But this devil did not have horns and a tail, this devil had a smooth tongue and searching eyes and it could see right into her heart and make it beat faster or slower at will. What had gone through his mind when he discovered who she was? When had he made that discovery? Had he known her identity all along? Had he been playing with her, as he was playing with her now?

But each of their meetings had been by chance. He could not have known she would be at that lecture or have foreseen her coming out of Sir Arthur's house, or expected her to be walking through the woods on a wet day. He had not engineered the encounters; they had all been the hand of a cruel fate. Cruel because she could not get him out of her head; her brain simmered with angry thoughts of him, mixed inexplicably with a kind of longing she could not understand and would not allow her to settle.

He could see her uncertainty in her hazel eyes. What was she thinking? He was prepared to swear it was not of Sir Arthur. Was she reliving that encounter in the wood? It was one he would dearly like to forget. But he could not. He had only to shut his eyes and he could see again her creamy breasts rising and falling, and what he had so nearly done choked him and filled him with shame. He must have been mad. If only he could put the clock back ten years, ten days even. But ten days would make no difference. She was still who she was and you did not fall in love with your mortal enemy. But who had made her his enemy? She had. He did not want her for an enemy. Was she really going to marry Sir Arthur?

He found himself, against his will, feeling sorry for her. Her father's death and her brother's banishment must have hit her very hard at a time when she was not old enough to understand what had happened. And now she was being promised to a man of middle years with a gaggle of daughters. Why was Mrs Fostyn allowing it? That shot, that single shot from a duelling pistol had ruined so many lives. How could he maintain the feelings of hate and resentment he had harboured for so long?

His punishment had been nothing compared with what she and her mother had suffered. He did not know what it was like to be poor and to lose the one who provided. His father had been able to send him money and he had been in a position to make it grow. But for that one thing, his life had been tolerable, if not happy. She was not happy. But what could he do about it? How could he right the wrongs perpetrated so many years ago? How could he extend her suffering by his awful behaviour?

'Don't do it,' he said, surprising himself. 'Don't marry Sir Arthur Thomas-Smith.'

She looked at him in astonishment. 'Why not?'

'He is not the man for you.'

'Oh? I should have thought you would be the last person to advise me against it. After all, the sooner I am wed, the sooner you will be rid of the Fostyns from your land and will no longer be plagued by guilt every time you see one of us—'

'I? Plagued by guilt?'

'No, of course not,' she amended swiftly. 'I cannot imagine you allowing anything like guilt to creep into your heart.'

'Nor compassion in yours,' he retorted.

The dance came to an end before she could think of a fitting reply. He bowed to her with a flourish and she sank into the deepest of curtsies, her golden gown billowing around her, and then, as he held out his hand to raise her, he realised everyone was moving into the supper room and surprised himself a second time by saying, 'Will you do me the honour of allowing me to escort you into supper, Miss Fostyn?'

She was taken aback and tilted her head to look at him. His face and voice were so gentle, she could almost imagine he was her umbrella man again. But he wasn't. He was 'that man', her enemy. She was about to refuse when he added, 'Please, Lydia, I must speak to you.'

'What about?' She pulled herself together sufficiently to regain her dignity, at least on the surface. 'And I do not remember giving you permission to address me by my given name.'

'Do I need permission?' he asked softly.

'If you think that what you did entitles you to famil-
iarity, then I suggest you think again, my lord,' she said.
It was easier to be angry with him than answer his softly
spoken words with politeness.

'What I did?'

'You know very well what I mean.'

'A kiss?'

'That is what you call it, is it? I call it an assault.'

'It is about that I wish to speak to you. In private.'

'Oh, no, you will not catch me out like that.'

'Catch you out?'

'Yes, if you are thinking of repeating your effrontery…'

'No.' His smile was almost a grimace. 'I would not
dream of doing so.'

'Then you are worried about what I told Mama when
I arrived home and whether you have to face another scandal.'

'Oh.' Now she had mentioned it, he did begin to wonder. Had she cried rape? 'What did you tell her?'

'Wouldn't you like to know?'

'If it makes any difference, I am very sorry for what
happened.'

'It doesn't. Now, I think I shall let you simmer in your
own evil, for a while. If you will excuse me…' She looked
round her for a way of escape because what he was doing
to her peace of mind must never be allowed. She was
melting, slowly dissolving under the power of those
searching eyes, which were asking, almost pleading with
her, for understanding, for that compassion he had said
she lacked. No, that was all a sham. He did not have a
sorry bone in his body or he would not have come tonight
and forced her into dancing with him when it was the last
thing she wanted, nor would he have made her mother
humiliate herself before him in order to have a few weeks'

grace in the house they had lived in unmolested for ten years.

Sir Arthur was bearing down on them to reclaim her. She turned to Ralph and smiled at him, a watery smile which did not reach her eyes. 'I am sorry, my lord, but my mother and sister and I are engaged to join Sir Arthur and his sister for supper.' She smiled at Sir Arthur and refused to look at Ralph as she was borne away.

It was a lively crowd that gathered for a supper of capon and ham and meat pies, bread and salad, junket and fruit tarts, washed down with punch. Annabelle was as happy as a lark because Anne and the Baverstocks had agreed that Peregrine might call on her and, properly chaperoned, she might attend one or two social functions with him, although they were both too young to put it on a formal footing. Even her mother was looking brighter than she had been for weeks, chatting away to Sir Arthur, for all the world as if they were already related. If her mother liked him so much, why didn't she marry him herself? She was only a few years older than he was and she had many more years of life ahead of her.

Oh, Lydia knew the reason well enough; Sir Arthur wanted someone young, someone who might give him the son he craved. Daughters were not enough. She, Lydia Fostyn, eighteen years old, was to be the sacrificial lamb or, more crudely, the breeding cow. She shuddered at the thought. She could not marry him, she really could not. She looked at her mother, wondering how she could tell her, and then at Annabelle, happy with her love, and knew she was going to have to go through with it.

Sir Arthur, sitting beside her, helping her to food, was as complacent as ever. 'My dear, tonight has not gone quite to plan,' he said. 'On such an occasion as this it is not possible to control events. At first I thought Lord

Blackwater's arrival was fortuitous, but now I realise it
was ill-timed from our point of view; it quite threw me
off my stride.'

'You will regain it, I am sure,' she murmured.

'I had some further conversation with your dear mama
while you were dancing with his lordship,' he went on.
'You are still very young and perhaps I have been a little
impatient.'

She turned to face him, her spirits suddenly lifting; was
he offering a reprieve? 'Oh, if Mama said that I am sure
she did not mean that as a criticism.'

'Mrs Fostyn offered no censure at all—the opposite, in
fact. She said you were a little overawed by the honour I
wish to bestow on you and that you needed a little more
time to accustom yourself to the idea of becoming Lady
Thomas-Smith.'

Lydia was so annoyed that she felt like slapping him
and telling him in tones that would leave him in no doubt
that she did not view it as an honour at all, but a dire
necessity, but good sense prevailed; it would hurt her
mother and Annabelle if she made a scene and there
would be yet another scandal to live down. 'You are too
kind,' she murmured.

He reached out and patted the back of her hand. 'In
view of that, I will not press you tonight. It is not a suit-
ably romantic occasion, after all. We are here to celebrate
the end of a war.' He waved a be-ringed hand in the
general direction of the company who seemed to be trying
to outdo each other in jollity. 'It is too crowded and noisy
and there is nowhere where we might be private.'

She could find no answer which would not give away
her immense feeling of relief and confined herself to,
'Thank you, sir.'

He laughed as if it were a load off his mind, making

her wonder if he had had second thoughts about her. Half of her rejoiced at the idea, the other half was dismayed because it could only mean he had found out something against her, or her family. Had he heard the story of what had happened ten years before, enhanced by repetition as it was bound to be? Or worse, gossip about her mother and the late Earl of Blackwater?

'Now, my dear, do not look so melancholy,' he said to her. 'We may have started off on the wrong foot, but it is nothing we cannot put right. Young ladies like romantic proposals and declarations of undying love, I understand that…'

'Is that what my mother said?' Now she was fighting laughter and it was all she could do to hide it behind her fan, pretending the room was excessively hot.

'Did you think I could not work that out for myself?' he said, sounding hurt.

'No, of course not, Sir Arthur. You are, I am sure, a very sensitive man.' Her efforts to remain serious received a jolt as she looked up over her fan and saw the Earl of Blackwater regarding her with amused brown eyes from across the other side of the table where he was tackling a chicken leg. Had he heard?

'We will devise another occasion,' Sir Arthur bumbled on. 'I will hold a musical evening and supper at my house for a select gathering of the people of Colston and Malden who have been so kind to me since my arrival in a strange town and that will be a more appropriate occasion to make an announcement.'

'Sir Arthur,' she said, with a light laugh, afraid he might detect her relief and deciding to tease him. 'You have not yet asked for my hand…'

'No, because I have been given no opportunity,' he said

solemnly. 'But it will be done on a suitable occasion before the evening in question.'

'Then I will look forward to it,' she said, wondering if he had any sense of humour at all. 'You shall have my answer then.'

Supper over, he escorted her back to the ballroom for the next dance, and after that relinquished her to others. Knowing there would be no announcement that evening, she was suddenly light-hearted and she danced with several young men, including the Comte de Carlemont, the young Frenchman that Annabelle had mentioned as an alternative to Sir Arthur as a suitor.

He was certainly handsome in his yellow coat and lace ruffles, and very charming, but she detected a certain falseness and wondered aloud what he was doing in Malden, a sleepy little town with no pretensions at all. She would have expected him to have gone to court to celebrate the end of the war.

'Court gives me the *ennui,*' he said airily. 'So much ceremony and so much intrigue…'

'Is there? Intrigue, I mean.'

'*Naturellement.* So many stabbings in the back, so many assignations. It is more dangerous than war.'

'In France, perhaps, but not in England, surely?'

'France, England, it makes no difference.'

'Have you met King George?'

'*Oui.*'

'And yet you prefer to live here?'

'I 'ave what you call the connections,' he said airily. 'English cousins who gave me 'ospitality when I was exiled from my 'omeland on account of the war. I was staying with them and could not return.'

'Will you go back now?'

'Soon, perhaps. I must look after my estates.'

'Where are they? Are they very extensive?'

'They are in the south, where it is warm and the vines grow excellent grapes for the wines. But you will see them for yourself before the year is out. Sir Arthur 'as promised to bring you on a visit during your wedding tour.'

'Has he?' she asked in surprise. 'I did not know you knew him well.'

'Oh, we have been acquainted for some time. Business, you understand.'

The dance came to an end and she was claimed by her next partner, but she was puzzled and intrigued. There was so much she did not know about Sir Arthur, so much she needed to know. Had he told her mother all about himself or had he held some things back, secrets he would rather keep hidden?

'You know you are wasted on Sir Arthur,' her partner said. 'And I will happily step into the breach should you have second thoughts.'

She laughed, knowing he didn't mean it, but she allowed him to flirt a little and cheer her up. She was laughing at some joke he had made when she saw Ralph watching her from the doorway. His eyes seemed to bore into her, to be asking what she thought she was about. She deliberately turned her head away and whispered something to the young man, making him throw back his head and laugh aloud. Sickened, Ralph turned away, but he did not go far because the dance had come to an end and the Master of Ceremonies called for a drum roll.

'My lords, ladies and gentleman,' he said as the sound died away and everyone fell silent and turned towards him. 'This is indeed a happy occasion. Not only are we celebrating the end of the war which has taken so many of our young men, both on land and at sea, but we give thanks for the safe return of the Squire of Colston, the

Earl of Blackwater.' He paused while everyone applauded and Ralph squirmed, wondering what the man was going to say next.

'We offer our condolences in his sad bereavement,' he went on. 'The late Earl was dearly loved and respected by everyone who had the privilege to know him, but we also give thanks that his son is back among us and has condescended to grace us with his presence tonight. My lords, ladies and gentlemen, I give you the Earl of Blackwater.' He raised his glass while the company raised theirs and echoed his toast.

Ralph, who had only intended to put in a token appearance and had changed his mind when he saw Lydia, felt obliged to answer. He stepped up on the dais on which the orchestra played so that he could look round the company and make himself heard. A sea of faces was turned up to him, all smiling, even Lydia's, though he sensed hers was a little forced. If only he could make her smile at him in genuine pleasure… He pulled himself together to address them.

'My lords, ladies and gentlemen, I thank you for your expressions of loyalty to my late parents and for your kindness to me, though to many of you I am a stranger. I am very glad to be home again and I am ready to take on the mantle of my late lamented father. I shall do my best to execute those tasks expected of me and I hope that if anyone has any problems which I can solve, he or she will not hesitate to come to me.'

He waited for the applause to die down, then went on. 'Finally, let me thank everyone who had a hand in making tonight such a successful occasion. I do not intend to bore you with any more speech, except to ask you to raise your glasses in a toast to peace and prosperity, the end of conflict and the beginning of forgiveness and understanding,

and continuing friendship.' He raised his glass and looked directly at Lydia as he spoke. She felt her face beneath its mask flame with such heat that she thought she would faint. Was he trying to humiliate her again? Was he telling everyone she hadn't a forgiving bone in her body?

'Why did you not tell me your gentleman was the Earl?' Annabelle whispered beside her. 'I nearly fainted away when he arrived and Perry told me who he was.'

'He is not my gentleman.'

'You gave me your fan to stop me telling Mama about him and that makes me wonder what you are trying to hide. I do believe you are only pretending to hate him.'

'There is no pretence about it, I promise you. I loathe him.'

'Then why—'

'I did not know who he was then, did I?'

'Then you were as surprised as me to discover his identity?'

'Yes, now do be quiet, everyone is looking at us.'

They were not, they were looking towards the Earl and raising their glasses. The toast drunk, he turned and spoke to the leader of the orchestra and they began to play another minuet. Everyone, except the old dowagers, paired off to dance: Annabelle with Peregrine, Lord Baverstock with Lady Brotherton, the Marquis of Brotherton with Lady Baverstock, Robert Dent with Caroline Brotherton, the Comte with an overdressed young lady Lydia did not know. Even Sir Arthur had taken her mother on to the floor, no doubt to appraise her of the conversation he had had with her daughter and tell her how well it had gone.

Lydia stood uncertainly and then found a seat behind a pillar where she hoped she would not be noticed. Ralph had gone and she should have been feeling relieved that his gaze was no longer on her, but she felt nothing but a kind of numbness, as if her mind and body did not belong together; the one in conflict with the other.

She became aware of the dowagers, nodding their feathered head-dresses as they gossiped. 'They say he has come back very rich, which is strange seeing the old Earl hardly had a penny piece except his lands,' one said.

'If he has, then perhaps things that have been neglected too long might be done.'

'Is he married?'

'I haven't heard tell of a wife.'

'Do you think he knows his mother was mad? Anyone who married him would have to look out if there was madness in the family. You could say it was part of the price he had to pay for what he did.'

'You mean that duel? Did that have anything to do with the Earl's affair with Mrs Fostyn?'

'Affair?'

'I've heard it said it was not the Countess Mrs Fostyn went to visit when she went up to the Hall, but the Earl. They say his lordship kept his wife locked up because she was mad with grief and jealousy and it left him free for dalliance with the widow.'

Lydia, unable to listen to any more, got up and hurried from the room, though where she was going she had no idea, just anywhere away from those malicious tongues.

Ralph had been saying goodbye to the civic dignitaries, who had congregated to congratulate him and to say good-night, and had not yet left the premises. A footman was just handing him his overcoat and hat. He ignored the man and seized her shoulders, making her stop in front of him.

'Miss Fostyn, what is the matter?'

'Nothing.' She forced herself to stop and face him. 'There is nothing wrong with me that your absence would not cure. Now, please release me.'

He dropped his hands from her as if he had been stung, took the coat from the servant and flung it across his shoulder, and then the hat, which he clamped on his head. 'Then I will accommodate you. Goodnight, Miss Fostyn.'

The door was opened for him and he went out into the night, leaving her staring after him in such a rage she hardly knew how to contain herself.

Chapter Five

Without waiting for Partridge to open the door and let down the step, Annabelle jumped from the carriage, rushed into the house past her startled sister and up the stairs to her room where she flung herself across her bed in a flood of tears. Lydia ran to comfort her. 'Annabelle, Annabelle, whatever is the matter?' She took her sobbing sister into her arms. 'Come, tell me what has happened?'

'It's Perry…'

'Peregrine Baverstock? What about him? Surely he has not acted improperly?'

'No, of course he has not,' Annabelle snapped. 'He says his parents have forbidden him to see me on account of— Oh, it's all a lie, isn't it? Tell me there's no truth in it.'

'How can I when I don't know what you are talking about?' But she did know. The gossip must have reached the ears of Lord and Lady Baverstock.

The whole village seemed to have taken sides, just as they had ten years before, but now there was an additional element, the story that Anne and the late Earl had been lovers and Freddie Fostyn had found out about it and leapt to the defence of his mother. It was why, so they said, the Reverend was at the scene of the duel. He thought

Freddie was going to fight the old Earl and, considering the quarrel was his, had been determined to take his son's place and put an end to the man who had cuckolded him. Ralph had only stepped in to save his father. It was, Lydia realised, a very plausible tale and until now her concern had been for her mother, for how could she fail to hear of it?

'They are saying the most dreadful things about the old Earl and Mama.'

'They?'

'Everyone. Caroline Brotherton told me. She's the one spreading the rumours, she thinks if she spoils it for me, then Perry will marry her instead. And her family have bags more money too... Oh, Lydia what am I to do?' And she burst into fresh tears.

Annabelle had met and spoken to Caroline after church on the Sunday before and had been invited to take tea with her and a few of her friends, an invitation which had Annabelle in a froth of excitement because invitations had been few and far between since the night of the ball and the promised social occasions with Peregrine Baverstock had not materialised and he had been invited too. And this was the result.

'If Perry believes tittle-tattle, then he is not worthy of you, dearest,' Lydia said firmly.

'It isn't Perry's fault,' Annabelle sniffed. 'He'd marry me anyway, he told me so, but he dare not oppose his parents. They would cut him off without a shilling.'

'I am dreadfully sorry, Annabelle,' Lydia said. 'It will blow over. I sincerely hope so, for if it reached Mama's ears it would make her dreadfully unhappy.'

'The rumours would stop if you married Sir Arthur,' Annabelle said. 'You must do it quickly before he hears—' She stopped suddenly. 'Lydia, you don't suppose that was why he did not make the announcement at the ball?'

'No, he only wished to give me more time to consider.'

'Consider! What is there to consider? It was all arranged between him and Mama but you insisted on keeping him in suspense and this is the result. If he hears the gossip, it will be he who has more time, time to change his mind and withdraw his offer.'

Lydia half wished he would. It would be a great weight off her mind, but the other half of her, the half that was sensible and practical, knew that would be a disaster.

'Lydia, you do want to marry him, don't you?' Annabelle persisted. 'You said you would. And when Lord and Lady Baverstock see what a good match you have made, they will allow Perry to marry me.'

'You seem very sure of that.'

'I am.' She paused. 'Perry said so.'

'If Ralph Latimer had not come home, this would not have happened,' Lydia said angrily. 'And even now, he could scotch the rumours if he had a mind to. He could refute the lies and tell the truth. He could publicly admit it was all his fault and had nothing to do with Mama or the old Earl, but he remains silent.'

He had not only remained silent, he had remained out of sight. She had not seen him since she ran from the ballroom a whole week before when she had shouted at him, told him all she wished for was his absence and he had taken her at her word. It had been a week of misery for her, made worse because it was so silent. She could not tell anyone of her unhappiness, mainly because she did not want to upset her mother, but also because she could not put it into words. She did not want to marry Sir Arthur, but she had known that before the ball and accepted that she must, so why had the prospect since then become not only disagreeable, but abhorrent?

And why, whenever she thought about Sir Arthur, did she hear again Ralph Latimer's insidious voice whispering in her ear, 'Do not do it. He is not the man for you'? Why should those words, uttered by that abominable man, upset her so? Did he know how much they would torment her? Did he know that she would go over and over them in her mind, trying to find a motive for uttering them, to hear the hidden meaning, to deny their truth. Was he truly trying to persuade her against such a step? But why?

Lydia could not bear to think about it any more and scrambled off the bed. 'I think we had better dress or we shall be late for supper.'

Annabelle mopped up her tears and stood up. 'But you have not told me. Are you going to tell Sir Arthur you have made up your mind to say yes?'

'When he comes calling.'

'And suppose he does not? You must find some way of communicating with him.'

'Mama will do that.'

'And you will tell her tonight?'

Lydia heaved a sigh. 'Yes. But not a word to her about those rumours, do you hear? Now, go and dress.'

Annabelle smiled and kissed her sister before leaving the room. Lydia sat in a chair before her dressing mirror and, picking up a comb, began to rake it through her bronze curls. They were to have the evening *en famille,* so there was no need to have her hair dressed. 'I look too pale,' she told herself. 'And there are dark rings beneath my eyes.'

She touched the spot where the scratches had been. They had healed over nicely and there was no scarring, but she could still imagine the feel of the twiggy branches scraping along her face. But that was not so bad as the remembrance of strong lips bruising hers, the sensations they produced in every part of her body, which she could not shake off. Day after day she relived the encounter and day after day her hatred of the man who had done this to her grew. It would not let her be still. The sooner she was married the better.

Sir Arthur called two days later in answer to Anne's invitation, arriving in his magnificent carriage drawn by two spanking horses which were put into Partridge's care. This time Lydia remained with her mother to receive him. He was, as usual, immaculately dressed, today in shades of blue, dark for his coat and breeches, light aquamarine for his shirt and waistcoat. His new wig sat firmly on his sparse hair as he made his bow to them both in turn and was offered refreshment.

They sat and asked each other how they did, remarked on the springlike weather, spoke of the success of the ball and commented on the news from London where the Earl of Bute's ministry had fallen and Henry Fox, on his elevation to the Lords, was resolutely refusing to give up his lucrative post of Paymaster-General, and generally skirted around the subject which had brought him to the dower house.

'Mrs Fostyn,' he said at last, sipping the claret and nibbling the little cakes from the plate Janet had brought him. 'I believe I know the reason for your invitation. Miss Fostyn has decided—'

'Yes, I have,' Lydia said, wishing he would direct his remarks to her.

He turned to look at her in her plain pink muslin gown, chosen for its simplicity. Anne had said she wanted the demure look and Lydia had done her best to achieve it. 'I, on the other hand, have grave misgivings.'

'Sir Arthur, surely you have not changed your mind?' Anne asked.

'I have heard rumours, very unsettling rumours and, to be honest, I am undecided.'

Lydia opened her mouth to speak, but a look from her mother made her close it again. 'Tell us about these rumours, Sir Arthur.'

'I am not sure they are repeatable, madam.'

'If they are about me, as I think they are, then you must repeat them, so that I may refute them. That is only justice.'

'Very well, madam. It is said that you and the Earl of Blackwater, the late Earl, I mean, were—' He stopped, apparently too embarrassed to continue.

Lydia looked at her mother, wondering how much of the story she had heard and how she could protect her, but her mother simply smiled. 'Lovers, Sir Arthur? Do not be afraid to say the word.'

'So be it.' He inclined his head. 'Lovers, and that your husband found out and set out to revenge himself, but in the fracas he was the one who died.'

'Yes, he died,' Anne said, so calmly Lydia was astonished. 'But not for the reasons the tattlers would have you believe. I shall tell you the whole story and you may judge for yourself. I have nothing of which I need be ashamed and most certainly my daughter has not.'

'Mama, you need not…' Lydia put in. Even though it had been ten years ago, that duel was still fresh in her memory and still as painful.

'I need not, but Sir Arthur has a right to know.'

He listened attentively while she outlined the events of

ten years before, ending, 'It was a tragic accident, Sir Arthur, nothing more sinister than that.'

'And since then?'

'Since then?' she repeated.

'Your visits to the Earl?'

'My visits to the Countess, you mean. We had both lost a son, Sir Arthur, we had a great deal in common and we gave each other comfort. She, poor lady, was more delicate than I and she sent for me whenever she was unwell. Can you not understand that? We bore no grudge towards each other.'

'And the present Earl? Do you bear him a grudge?'

'No,' Anne said firmly, though Lydia sucked in her breath and bit her lip to stop herself speaking.

He saw it and smiled. 'I think Miss Fostyn is not so magnanimous.'

Lydia forced herself to sound calm. 'The past is past, Sir Arthur, we cannot change it and must go forward.'

'Yes.' His smile was oily. 'Forward together, eh?'

She bowed, clutching her closed fan in her lap, wishing it were all over. But it would never be all over and this was only the beginning. 'If that is your wish, Sir Arthur.'

'Is it your wish?'

She took a deep breath. 'Yes, sir, it is.'

He smiled again and reached forward to take her hand. His touch was clammy and she shivered slightly. 'Then we will overlook the past and I ask you formally if you will become my wife.'

Now was the time to stop, now was the time to look him in the eye and say 'No, no, no, a thousand times no!' It was the last chance she would have. The prevaricating was done, the arguments for and against were all made and answered, the teasing and the hiding behind doubt were all in the past. And that quiet voice, telling her she was making a mistake, must be silenced.

'Yes, Sir Arthur, I will become your wife.' She looked up at him then, straight into his pale eyes, and added, 'Subject to the arrangements my mother made with you being put in place: a home for her, schooling for my brother and a dowry for my sister.'

He sat back, his satisfaction evident on his face. It was not a smile so much as a smirk. 'You come very dear, Miss Fostyn, but I am persuaded you will be worth it.'

'She will be a dutiful wife,' Anne said.

'Then the sooner the better,' he said. 'Three weeks from now, shall we say?'

Lydia glanced at her mother, her expression giving away her dismay.

'I think three months might be more easily managed, Sir Arthur,' Anne said. 'There is much to do, bridal clothes to buy, a feast to arrange. Word to be got to my brother-in-law, Lord Fostyn. I do not think Lydia needs his permission, but he is the head of the family and courtesy demands I ask it.'

'Let us compromise,' he said. 'Let us say the second week in May. A pleasant time for a wedding, don't you think?'

'Very well, Sir Arthur,' Lydia said. What was the point of putting it off? She had agreed to marry him and that was almost as binding as a marriage, so why delay the inevitable? But oh, how much she longed for someone like her umbrella man. Why did he have to turn out to be Ralph Latimer? Why did her dreams have to be shattered so cruelly? Had she done something very wicked, that she must be punished for the rest of her life?

She looked at her mother and smiled weakly. And her

mother, seeing it, found tears welling in her own eyes and had to turn away.

'We will announce the coming nuptials at the soirée I am having at my home next week,' Sir Arthur said, addressing Mrs Fostyn. 'Is there anyone you would particularly like me to invite? I will, of course, be sending invitations to all the local dignitaries and what passes for the *haute monde* in this part of the country.' There was a slight tone of disparagement in his voice which was not lost on Lydia.

'I cannot think of anyone at such short notice,' Anne said. 'There is no time for my two other daughters or Lord Fostyn and his wife to make arrangements to travel, though no doubt they will come for the wedding.'

'Very well. What about the Earl of Blackwater?'

'No,' Lydia said.

Sir Arthur turned to her with a smile of satisfaction. 'You have no love for the Squire of Colston, my dear? I can hardly blame you for that, I am not over-fond of him myself, but I think to exclude him will only add to the gossip when it were better we buried it. After all, this is a small community and we have to put the past behind us and learn to live together in harmony.'

'Yes, of course,' said her mother. 'I have no objection to his lordship and Lydia will overcome her enmity of him when she realises how lucky she is to have you to protect her from malicious tongues.'

'Then I will take my leave and look forward to seeing you Friday se'ennight.' They all rose, he bowed to Anne and kissed the back of Lydia's hand and was escorted to the door by Janet. They heard the door close and the sound of his carriage leaving. Mother and daughter sank back on to their seats with huge sighs of relief, Anne because she had managed to overcome the gentleman's reservations, Lydia because he had gone and she did not have to endure his presence any longer. The effort to be civil had taken all her self-control.

But what of the future? Day after day, living with him. How would she manage it? She must try to see the good in him, she told herself, the pleasant side of his character, which had accepted her mother's version of events without question and was prepared to help them face down their critics, to enjoy her new-found wealth, which in some ways would give her a certain freedom to do as she liked. As long as she never fell in love. She must guard against that, whatever happened.

She had a week more of freedom and she must make the most of it, doing all the things she liked doing, so she would spend it going into Chelmsford shopping, visiting old friends, reading and walking, usually with Hector at her side.

The day before Sir Arthur's soirée, she walked through the village and on to an old track that led through the marshes to the sea. There were many such tracks and Lydia, who had lived in Colston all her life, knew most of them. So did Hector, who scampered ahead of her sniffing the ground and chasing the gulls who dared to land near him.

When she reached the beach she stood with the wind blowing her skirt against her legs, threw back her head and breathed deeply, filling her lungs with fresh, salty air. As a child she had done exactly the same, laughing and carefree. Sometimes her father had been with her, or one of her older sisters, and they would chase each other down to the beach and stop to watch the ships sailing down the coast to London, or up to the east coast ports, speculating on the merchandise they carried. With the parlous state of

the roads, taking goods by water was still the best way.
There had been warships too, and Lydia would wonder
what great sea battles they had fought and would read the
newspapers for news of them.

And sometimes ships came inshore by stealth on dark
nights and sent out boats to land contraband. Freddie had
often told her of seeing lights flickering out to sea and
answering ones from the shore. He had, he told her, crept
out after he was supposed to be in bed, to see what was
going on. He made it sound exciting and dangerous and
she had marvelled at his courage.

She didn't think there had been so many smugglers
during the war, certainly not any involving local men,
who were all patriots, but if what she had heard was true,
there had been some illegal activity and more than tea and
brandy involved. Spies had been brought ashore, who disappeared into the darkness to do their nefarious work.
Today she could see sails on the distant horizon but they
were too far away to identify.

She sighed and turned towards Hector who was splash-
ing about it the shallows, tugging at a piece of cloth he
had found submerged. She took it from him. 'No, Hector,
drop it. It is time we went home.'

She tugged the cloth from him and realised it was a
man's coat, a brown leather jacket such as the oyster fishermen wore. She looked about her, half afraid there might
be a body, but there was nothing and no one to be seen
except half a dozen men, bending over the mud flats with
their oyster baskets. Donkeys harnessed to carts with huge
wheels stood patiently waiting to be loaded.

She was about to fling the garment into a patch of mar-
ram grass when she realised it was heavy, and not just
with the weight of water it had absorbed. Feeling in the
pockets, she pulled out an oilskin-wrapped package. Hec-

tor had rushed off to find new treasures, but she stood with the package in her hand wondering what to do with it. She supposed she ought to hand it over to the coastguard or the revenue men. But supposing it implicated one of the villagers in smuggling? Could she bear to be the one to betray him?

Thinking about smugglers set her mind whirling towards the subject she had been able, just for an hour or so, to banish from her mind. She tried not to allow it to happen, tried calling Hector and throwing a stick into the sea for him to retrieve, laughing when he emerged, dripping water, his soft coat flattened to his skin, anything rather than permit her unbridled thoughts to flow.

That encounter in the woods still played on her mind. She could not forget that kiss which had been so brutal and demanding and yet she had felt herself respond, passion with passion. She was ashamed of that, ashamed that he might have deduced she enjoyed being treated so roughly, that given the opportunity she might welcome his advances. It was one more reason to hate him. She thrust the package into the inner pocket of her cloak and turned her back on the sea.

'Come, Hector, time to go home.'

The dog followed her over the wet sand and across the dunes, swept into hills and hollows by the wind, then onto the path which led back through the marsh. It was easy ground for smugglers if you knew the difference between solid land and weed-covered bog, where stepping off the path might mean sinking without trace. It took local men to know that, men who had lived on the marshes all their lives, men she had known since she was old enough to walk the lanes of the village. She could not betray them.

When she reached the firmer ground alongside Colston woods, Hector disappeared, sniffing among the trees for rabbits, and he would not return when she called him. She had promised herself she would never go into those woods again and would take a two-mile detour rather than do so, but she could hardly leave the dog. She stood undecided, listening to the scuffling sound of his progress through the undergrowth and the sighing of the wind and the hairs began to stand up on the back of her neck and her mouth felt dry.

'Hector!' she shouted, and her voice sounded unnaturally loud. 'Come here, boy!'

She had to call several times but at last the dog emerged, wagging his tail. Behind him strode the tall figure of the Earl of Blackwater. He was dressed in a rough tweed coat and thick leather breeches and boots; he wore no wig or hat and was carrying a pistol in his belt. If she had not known who he was, she would have taken him for one of his own labourers. She bent to grab the dog by his collar and save herself having to speak to him, but he had stopped and was standing, feet apart, not three paces from her. 'Good day, Miss Fostyn.'

She straightened up to face him. 'Good day, my lord.' Her voice was cold and precise.

'Not a bad day.'

'No, my lord.'

'But the wind is sharp, especially down by the shore, do you not think?'

'Yes, it is,' she answered, wondering if he had been watching her. Had he seen her take the package from that old coat? Would he demand she hand it over? 'But it is very invigorating.'

'Oh, to be sure, but more sheltered in the trees.'

'I have not been in your wood, I was exercising my dog and he ran in.'

He looked down at the animal. 'I heard you call him Hector. Is he the original Hector?'

'Freddie's puppy, yes. Twelve years old now, but still as ungovernable.' For a tiny fraction of time, their memories united them, pleasant memories of two boys, a little girl and a dog.

'That I surmised. Does the beast ever come when called?'

'Sometimes.' The moment had gone; the hint of criticism was enough to send it flying into the past where it belonged. 'But if he finds something that interests him...' She stopped. Now was the time he would ask what she had found on the beach and she was determined to deny finding anything but a ragged coat which she had thrown away.

'In my woods?' He smiled, wondering why she looked so guilty. Her face was scarlet and she seemed unable to look him in the eyes which, in his experience, was not at all like her.

'Perhaps a rabbit, my lord, but, as you see, he failed.'

'I do not begrudge a rabbit for your pot, Miss Fostyn.' He laughed suddenly. 'But do not tell the rest of the villagers or I shall be hunting poachers as well as smugglers.'

She looked up then. 'Are you still hunting smugglers?'

'I am looking for the men who have had the effrontery to use my land and buildings for their activities, as I have every right to do.'

'Indeed, sir.' She stopped, unwilling to continue the conversation; it was too unsettling. In fact, any interchange with him was unsettling and especially so, if you imagined you were carrying evidence of some kind. 'But surely they have gone now? They would not stay once they have landed the contraband?'

'True. But that cottage has been used regularly, I will swear to it. They will be back.'

'Then I shall take great care to avoid this path while I am still living in Colston, which you will be pleased to hear will not be for much longer.'

'Ah, I see. I have received an invitation from Sir Arthur to attend a soirée at his home tomorrow evening. Am I to assume that is to celebrate your betrothal?'

'Yes, my lord.' She forced a smile from her stiff lips. 'The wedding will be in early summer. Will that be time enough for you?'

'Me?' He was genuinely surprised. 'Why should I have an opinion on the matter?'

'The sooner I am married, the sooner you will be rid of me and my family from the dower house. That was the arrangement you made with Mama, is it not?'

'Yes, but I still say you are making a mistake. What do you know of the man?'

'I know all I need to know. He is an honourable man who knows how to treat a lady. Good day to you, my lord.' And with that parting shot, she left him.

He stood, watching her departing back, held so rigidly upright, and smiled. Proud she was, but was pride enough? What did she really know about Sir Arthur? Why did he think he had met the man before? Not recently, he was sure of that, but in another place, another time. Where? He had travelled the length and breadth of Europe and half of Asia in the last ten years and it could have been anywhere. India, perhaps. But he had never come across anyone called Thomas-Smith while he was there, he was sure of it. Had the man changed his name?

Ought he to find out? But why? So that he might inform Miss Fostyn, who would rage at him for interfering and tell him to look to his own business? He shrugged. It was nothing to do with him what the Fostyns got up to; the sooner they were off his land and he need never think about them again, the better. He had enough to occupy him with the work being done on the estate, the decorating and refurbishing of the Hall.

He smiled to himself as he strode home; there was talk in the village that he was preparing it for a wife and curiosity as to who she might be. Having no one in mind, he was curious himself. It was time he married and settled down, but there had never been a woman in his life, not one he would have considered marrying, that is. Mistresses in plenty, pretty ones too and satisfying in many ways, but not wifely material. But then who was? What kind of woman would she be? Young, beautiful, passionate and compassionate, he told himself, attributes not often found all together in one woman.

Lydia. Her name sprang to his mind completely unbidden and shocked him. They were sworn enemies. She hated him and the feeling was mutual. Then why did he keep thinking of her, why when she suddenly appeared as she just had, looking windblown and vulnerable, did he want to detain her, to taste her lips again, to experience again that feeling of tenderness which was so alien to him and had been for ten long years?

If she were not Freddie's sister, he would almost say he was falling in love with her. But he had no love for any of the Fostyn family. They were to blame for his mother's madness and the early demise of his father as well as his own exile. If he had not been sent away, both parents would be alive now. If there was something murky in Sir Arthur's background, so be it, he would do nothing to disillusion them.

As soon as she arrived home, Lydia went to her room and took the package from her pocket. She laid it on the table by the window, took off her cloak and hung it away before returning to look down at the flotsam. Or was it jetsam? Had someone deliberately thrown it overboard from a ship? Had the jacket clothed a dead body? If so, where was the body? She picked it up and weighed it in her hand. How long had it been in the water?

She sat on her bed and carefully unwrapped it. It contained documents, a map and a velvet bag containing several glittering stones which could have been diamonds. The documents were so badly stained with sea water they were illegible except for an odd word here and there and a large red seal. The sea had stained the edges of the map as well, but it was drawn on linen and some of it was still clear. Lydia spread it out, realising it was a plan of the marshes between Malden Water in the north and the Crooksea Water in the south. Mersea Island with its defending fort on the south-east corner was marked, so was Malden, Southminster and Burnham in the mouth of the river Crouch. Colston and its Hall, the dower house, the church and woods were clearly marked, including the empty hovel and Mistress Grey's cottage. And there was a cross on the Southminster road where it branched off to Chelmsford.

Her first thought was that it was a smuggler's map, but why would smugglers need a map when most of them were almost certainly local men? And were the stones really diamonds? Who did they belong to? What were they worth? And what, in the name of heaven, should she do with them? What had she stumbled on? She felt a frisson of fear run down her spine as if the package portended evil and she wished fervently she had not picked it up.

'Lydia, is that you?' She heard her mother's voice and then her footsteps climbing the stairs. Quickly rewrapping the bundle, she put it at the bottom of her clothes chest beneath the yellow ball gown, shut the lid and called, 'Yes, Mama. I was taking off my cloak.' Then she left the room to carry on as if it were a normal day.

But it was hardly that. She was possessed of something that frightened her; she had met and spoken to the Earl of Blackwater and if she had hoped that after an absence of a week, the effect he had on her would be any less disturbing, she had been wrong. And tomorrow would be her betrothal day and she must prepare herself, not only by trying on her gown and the new white wig, but mentally. And that was hardest of all.

Sir Arthur had sent money and required her to buy herself a gown suitable for the occasion and all the accessories that went with it and though she would have liked to refuse it, Anne had persuaded her that to do so would be foolish. 'He will look after you from now on,' her mother had said. 'And you should not hesitate to take advantage of his generosity. Look on it as your due.' And viewed in that light, she conceded her mother was right. If she had to marry him, she would make sure he paid. She ignored the little voice in her head which told her she was being unfair.

The gown she had gone to Chelmsford to order from the best mantua maker there was of white grosgrain, heavily embossed with silver embroidery of flowers and vine leaves. The stomacher was stiff and forced her breasts so high the rounded tops of them appeared above the low square-cut neck. The sleeves were narrow to the elbow and then fell in a cascade of lace over her wrists. The skirt was wide and heavy and supported by several petticoats, one of them padded. White stockings, white slippers embroidered to match her gown, a white wig topped with three Prince of Wales feathers and long white gloves, completed an ensemble which had her mother in tears and her sister green with envy.

'No jewels,' her mother said, 'for undoubtedly Sir Arthur will present you with something special as a betrothal gift.'

Sir Arthur sent his coach to fetch them and so they were saved having to arrive in the old carriage which would surely have looked incongruous. Anne, in a dark blue taffeta, was quietly satisfied, Annabelle in white silk, was quivering with excitement and Lydia shaking with nerves as they rode the two miles to Sir Arthur's mansion, every window of which was ablaze with light.

He greeted them in the vast hall, whose marble floor echoed the footsteps of everyone crossing it, took both Lydia's hands and held her at arm's length to appraise her. 'Beautiful,' he said. 'You have good taste, my dear.'

'Thank you.' She found herself looking wildly round her, as if searching for a way of escape, but there wasn't one. The door to the large reception room was open and most of the guests were already there, taking their seats while the musicians tuned their instruments. Behind her the door to the street had been closed.

'Miss Fostyn, may I present my sister, Mrs Sutton, who is housekeeping for me.' He turned to the tiny thin-faced woman who stood beside him clothed in purple. 'Martha, this is the lady who has done me the honour of consenting to marry me, Miss Lydia Fostyn.'

Lydia curtsied, wondering as she did so how the older woman viewed her arrival on the scene.

'You are welcome,' Mrs Sutton said. 'And will be doubly so when you make this house your home. I will then be able to hand over my nieces to your care and return to my own family.'

'The little girls,' Lydia murmured. 'I look forward to meeting them.'

'It is late now and they are asleep.' Sir Arthur put in. 'But come tomorrow afternoon and take tea with us. I shall allow them to join us and you shall make their acquaintance.'

'Do they know...?' She paused.

'Of course. I told them a week ago and they are all agog to meet their new mama.'

'Constance is the oldest,' Mrs Sutton put in. 'She is thirteen and Faith is eleven. They are dark like their father, but little Gracie, who is four, is fair and blue-eyed. She never knew her own mother, who died when she was born, and the idea of having one fills her with pleasure.'

Lydia wondered how the older two had reacted to the news, but decided not to ask. If they resented her, she would find out soon enough.

'Before we make our entrance, I have something for you,' Sir Arthur said. 'Come with me. Your mama will excuse us, I know.'

Anne nodded and he took Lydia's hand and led the way into the library whose shelves were stocked with brand new books, all of the same size, and unlocked a drawer in a desk. From it he withdrew an enamelled box which he brought over to her. She watched as he opened it and took out a diamond and emerald ring, which he slipped on to her finger. It was huge and ostentatious and she hated it.

'The betrothal ring,' he said. 'Do you like it?'

'It is beautiful,' she croaked, hoping he would mistake her husky voice for awe. Even though she had known what was going to happen she felt stifled, unable to breathe. Until now she had almost managed to convince herself it would never happen, that some thunderbolt would come down and prevent it. But it had happened and it was so very, very final.

'Only the best will do,' he said, his strange falsetto voice filled with self-satisfaction as he returned to the drawer for another, larger box from which he lifted a matching necklace of diamonds and emeralds set in filigree silver. 'And now my betrothal gift to you, my dear.'

She stood, frozen into immobility as he fastened it about her neck and then bent to kiss her bare shoulder. She must not flinch, she told herself, she must not.

'Magnificent,' he said, though she was sure he was speaking of the jewels and not her. 'Now let us make our entrance.' He offered her his arm and they walked slowly to join the company, who stood and applauded.

She heard the applause at the end as if from a long way off, was only half aware of movement about her as servants circulated with champagne for everyone. Then Sir Arthur's hand took hers and his high-pitched voice announced their engagement and invited everyone to drink to his future bride, but Lydia hardly heard a word of his flowery speech.

'Smile,' Anne, who stood a little to one side, commanded her in an undertone. Lydia obeyed like an automaton as Sir Arthur led her to the front row of the chairs which had been arranged facing the musicians, and the entertainment began. She could not afterwards have said what they played, nor what the enormous soprano had sung. She was numb from head to toe.

As the applause died away, Sir Arthur announced that supper was served in the next room and afterwards there would be dancing or cards for those who did not care for the exercise.

'Come, my dear,' Sir Arthur said, lifting her hand and

putting it on his sleeve so that the ring was prominently displayed. 'Let us go into supper.'

She did not eat a thing, could not swallow it, though she did drink two glasses of champagne which only served to make her light-headed. Her jewels were admired by everyone and the young ladies present admitted their envy of her. If they only knew!

After supper Sir Arthur led her in the first dance and then she was claimed by almost every young man in turn, except the Earl of Blackwater. He stood on one side of the large room, leaning against an imitation Greek pillar. He was wearing the same black suit he had worn to the ball; she supposed because he was still in mourning, but he looked magnificent. A head taller than anyone else in the room, he seemed to dominate it without doing anything to bring that about. His tanned features were set in an expression of disinterest, but she knew that was far from the case. Even from across the room, she could see that his dark eyes were watchful, scanning the company.

Determined not to let him upset her, which was evidently his intention, she danced with great verve and laughed at her partner, putting on a very convincing act of being happy. 'La, sir,' she said, hardly aware of who that partner was, though Sir Arthur had introduced them. 'All this exercise has made me thirsty.'

'Then allow me to fetch you a drink. A cordial or more champagne?'

'Oh, definitely champagne,' she said as he took her to a seat and disappeared.

When he brought it she drank it far too swiftly and, on an empty stomach, it had the inevitable effect. The room began to revolve around her and she felt decidedly queasy. 'Oh, dear, please excuse me,' she said and, getting up, made her way to the door, trying not to stumble.

She just managed to reach the room set aside for the ladies to refresh their toilettes and grab a chamber pot before she was sick. 'Drunk,' she said, wiping her mouth on a towel and looking at herself in the mirror. Her wig was awry, her eyes unnaturally bright; her cheeks, which had seen no rouge, held twin spots of bright red. But underneath her skin was a translucent greeny-grey. 'Whatever will he think of me?' But it was not of Sir Arthur she was thinking.

There was a carafe of water and glasses on a table in the room. She poured herself a glass and drank it greedily. And then another. 'Got to go back,' she told her reflection. 'Got to show myself beside my betrothed, got to be pleasant to him. More than pleasant. *Loving*.' Setting her wig straight and making liberal use of the bottle of perfume which had been provided, she pulled a face at herself in the mirror and then, straightening her shoulders, went back into the hall.

At the foot of the grand staircase, she hesitated. She needed to draw a few big gulps of air to steady herself before returning to the heat and noise of the drawing room.

'Miss Fostyn.'

She whirled round to face the speaker, her heightened colour betraying her discomfort. 'My lord, you startled me.'

'So I see. Who or what are you hiding from?'

'Hiding?' she repeated, wishing she felt more in command of herself. Being sick had sobered her, but not enough. 'I am not hiding. I was merely getting my breath back after the exertions of the dance…'

'Oh, I see.' His brown eyes were gleaming with amusement.

'No, you do not see,' she said, trying to look past him

to the drawing-room door, afraid someone might see them together and draw quite the wrong conclusion, but he was too tall and too bulky. All she was aware of was the breadth of his chest and the way his own hair curled round his ear beneath his wig. She found herself wanting to reach out and touch it.

'Oh, but I do. I see a bosom heaving gently and bright eyes and hands always on the move.' He was referring to her swift use of her fan and she shut it with a snap that threatened to break it. 'I see agitation.'

'Stuff and nonsense! Being a peer, and the Squire of Colston *and* our landlord, does not give you the right to make insulting remarks.'

'I was not making insulting remarks, quite the contrary. You look every inch a duchess.'

'Don't be silly.'

'A countess, then.' His voice was soft, appealing, and she realised he was doing it again, creeping in beneath her guard with gentle words and tender looks, like a purring cat waiting to pounce. She did not feel well enough for another battle of words with him. In any case, she always lost.

'Please stand aside.'

'After you have explained to me why you did not take my advice.'

'What advice was that?'

'Not to marry Sir Arthur.'

'I have not married him.'

'Not yet, but you have agreed you will and that is not something you can retract without a scandal.'

'Why should I retract?'

He smiled. 'Second thoughts, my dear.'

'And why should I have second thoughts?'

He shrugged. 'Regrets. We are all entitled to those. The

difficulty is to admit to them, to undo what has been done.'

'And you should know,' she snapped. 'But the dead cannot be brought back to life.'

'No.' He paused. 'Does Sir Arthur know the grisly details?'

'Of what?'

'Come, my dear, I never took you for obtuse. I was referring to the accident. Ten years and two months ago. I could give you days and hours too, if you wish.'

'I do not wish and it was no accident.' She heard her voice rising and paused to add in a lower tone, 'I do not want to talk of it, particularly to you.'

'I think perhaps I am just the one you should be talking to about it.'

'No. Out of my way.' She pushed against his chest with both hands and he caught them in his own and held them against him, virtually imprisoning her.

'Would your haste to be tied to Sir Arthur have anything to do with the latest *on-dit*?' he asked. 'A way of scotching it, perhaps.'

'Latest *on-dit*?' she echoed.

'About my father and your mama. You have heard it, I suppose?'

'I should think the whole world has heard. And if you thought Sir Arthur would turn against me when it reached his ears, you would be wrong, for he says it makes no difference.'

'I wonder why not?' he murmured, more to himself than to her.

'Because Sir Arthur is a gentleman and believes the word of a lady,' she said. 'And I wonder you can be so sanguine about it. It is your father they are talking about—'

'And your mama…' He paused, watching her face. 'Do you believe it?'

'No, of course not. Do you?'

'I revered my father and know he could not have done anything to hurt my mother; it was not in his nature, any more than it would be in your mother's nature to bring shame on her family. I have the greatest respect for her.'

'You could put an end to the rumours, if you chose, you could refute them publicly.'

'I think, perhaps, that might make matters worse. There is nothing like denying a rumour to confirm it. It is human nature.'

'Then why mention it?'

'I was merely questioning Sir Arthur's altruism.'

'You do not like him, do you?'

'I am entirely indifferent.' That was untrue, he admitted to himself. If only he could remember where he had seen the man before he might be able to understand his unease. 'And just to show there are no ill feelings, allow me to escort you back to the dance floor.' He released her hands and offered her his arm.

She laid her fingers upon his sleeve and even through the shiny material she felt a shiver pass through her body. Hate him, she commanded herself, hate him. It is the only way.

They made a handsome couple as they took to the floor, the one in black, the other in white and silver, and if anyone thought they were better matched than Sir Arthur Thomas-Smith and Miss Lydia Fostyn, they were not so indiscreet as to say so, but the looks they gave each other, the heightened colour in her cheeks and the smile he could not quite hide were noted.

After the dance ended, he took his leave, although it was still not yet midnight. He sent his carriage home and set out to walk, musing on his latest encounter with Miss Lydia Fostyn. His hate for her had been dissipated, blown away on the wind which came in off the sea. But hers for him? He could not tell. She appeared friendly one minute, full of venom the next, and when she was like that, he found himself answering fire with fire. He was curt, brusque, hurtful, when he did not want to be any of those things. What did he want? Did he even know that? And what difference did it make now? She was betrothed to Sir Arthur Thomas-Smith and nothing short of death or at least a huge catastrophe could put an end to it.

Chapter Six

After Ralph had left, Lydia turned to go back to the company, but the bubbly effect of the champagne had worn off and she felt sick and tired. The music was too loud, the conversation nothing more than a babble of voices, the smell of hothouse lilies, overheated bodies and congealing food all crowded in on her until her senses reeled. She wanted her bed. She wanted to lie down and lose herself in sleep.

She found her mother vigorously fanning herself by an open window and listening to the Marchioness of Brotherton talking about a performance of *The Beggar's Opera* which had recently been put on in Chelmsford by a minor theatre company. Seeing her daughter approaching, she excused herself and left the lady in mid-sentence.

'Lydia, is something wrong?' she asked in an undertone. 'You do not look at all the thing.'

'I feel a little unwell, Mama. Do you think we could go home?'

Anne had seen her daughter's too-obvious efforts to appear happy and guessed what had made her run from the room, but she made no comment on that. 'Perhaps it would be best. I will go and speak to Sir Arthur, but you must pull yourself together, dear, and say goodnight to everyone or they will think you ill-mannered. And, Lydia,' she admonished, 'do smile.'

They circulated round the company, saying goodnight, explaining that it had been such a wonderful exciting day, she was quite overcome with fatigue. Sir Arthur, all consideration, said of course she must not overtax herself and kissed her cheek, before relinquishing her to her mama. Then they collected a protesting Annabelle and went out into the night where she gulped in huge breaths of cold air and willed her rubbery legs to support her.

Someone had been sent to alert Sir Arthur's coachman and the carriage rolled up a few minutes later. They climbed in and were driven away with Annabelle still grumbling that they had dragged her away just when Lady Baverstock was softening towards her. They overtook the Earl of Blackwater, walking home alone, but no one in the coach saw him.

Once back at the dower house, Anne helped Lydia to bed because Janet had been told not to wait up for them. 'Go to sleep, my dear child,' she whispered, pulling the covers about her daughter's shivering shoulders. 'You will feel better tomorrow.'

Long after her mama had left, she lay staring at the ceiling. Would she feel better tomorrow? And what of all the other tomorrows? Soon she would be in another bed in another house and she would be mistress of it. She ought to be elated. There was no natural law that said you had to be in love with your husband. According to some of her mother's friends being in love with one's husband was exceptional, and was more likely to lead to misery than happiness. A husband's role was to provide a home, clothes for his wife's back, and any trinkets or luxuries he could afford in return for someone to run his household and have his children, to provide him with an heir, more than one if possible.

His wife should quietly attend to her duties and not question his decisions, or even ask what he did when he was not with her. If she suspected he had a mistress, the very last thing she should do was accuse him of it. She must turn a blind eye and never complain. Would Sir Arthur take a mistress? Did he have one already? She would not mind, she told herself, if it meant he did not expect too much from her. What a way to begin a marriage!

It could have been so different. If only her umbrella man had been real and not that hated man. She had met him three times before she found out who he was and in that time had woven all manner of fantasies around him. She shut her eyes, trying to bring him back into focus, trying to regain that joyful, slightly breathless feeling she had experienced on those three occasions. She was in the swaying coach, smiling and offering her lips to him and he was smiling back with those soft brown eyes and kissing her…

Musing on the conversation he had just had with her, the man in her thoughts strode home along the narrow roads, passing the familiar landmarks of his childhood, the ancient church where generations of his family had worshipped and been buried, the village green, the two taverns. He remembered the carefree child she had been, the lovely woman she was now, lovely but embittered. He supposed she had cause to be bitter, especially when his return had set the tongues wagging all over again as those who had lived in the village for years enlightened those who had not. And it did not matter to the tongue waggers if what they said were accurate or not.

Could there possibly any truth in the story about his

father and Mrs Fostyn which, until Robert Dent had told him of it earlier in the day, was new to him? His father had been a healthy and virile man; it would not surprise him to learn he had a mistress, many men kept paramours and their wives accepted it. Some even said it made the marriage all the sweeter, though he could not subscribe to that view. When he married—if he married—it would be because he was in love and he would want no one else. But he was the exception, he realised that. His parents' marriage had been negotiated by their parents, so perhaps his father could be forgiven for letting his attention stray.

But so close to home! To the wife of the Rector, whose living he had in his gift! Had it happened before or after the Fostyns came to live in the village? Had the living been part of the arrangement? He found the idea so abhorrent, he could not believe it. His father would never have done anything so base. But if there was no truth in it at all, how had the rumour started? Did Miss Fostyn believe it, even though she had denied it as vehemently as he had?

Had Freddie heard it? Was that why he had been so angry that day ten years before, not over the girl who had simply been the catalyst, but because he wanted to hit out at someone and, unable to confront the Earl himself, had chosen to vent his spleen on his son? Did the Reverend Fostyn believe it too? The Rector had not spoken a word on that fateful morning, had not been given an opportunity to do so. Poor Lydia! No wonder she hated him. But she was no longer a child, she was a woman and it was time she faced up to reality. Until she did, she would never have any peace. And neither would he.

Walking home in the dark, he went over and over it, trying to dredge up from his memory anything that had happened in his childhood to give credence to the story or, better still, disprove it. He needed to know the truth. He could hardly confront Mrs Fostyn, the only person alive who knew it. Perhaps his father had kept a diary or documents which had not turned up in his admittedly casual search of the house since his return. Tomorrow he would look again.

Having made that decision, he hastened his steps. Arriving home, he dismissed his valet who had waited up for him and undressed himself. Pulling his nightrail over his head, he went to the window to draw back the curtains and gaze out on the dark landscape. This was his home, the people out there were his responsibility and he must mete out succour and justice impartially. If they would let him! But to do that meant he had to overcome prejudice and gossip and that was not easy with Lydia Fostyn living not a quarter of a mile away. Damn all the Fostyns and Miss Lydia Fostyn in particular!

What was it the military pundits were always saying? The best method of defence was attack. If he wanted to silence the rumours and live in peace with his neighbours, including the Fostyns, he had to do something positive about it. He sat in the window alcove and leaned his head back on the cold stone, trying to think of something to fit the bill, but his mind kept drifting to Lydia Fostyn engaging herself to Sir Arthur Thomas-Smith.

The man was twice her age and not even handsome. He was too fat, his eyes were too colourless and that high-pitched voice grated on the ear. He could not imagine why she had allowed herself to be coerced into marrying him. True, he was rich—the house and its furnishings proved that—but was wealth enough for a young and beautiful girl who could surely find others more pleasing to look at who were eligible? He chuckled suddenly; if wealth was the criterion, then the Earl of Blackwater could match it, even surpass it, and Colston Hall was every bit as elegant as that new pretentious mansion on the road to South-minster.

The alterations to his home were nearly finished and it would once more be the elegant home it had been when his father had brought his bride there, and though there was no bride now, he could throw it open. He would have a party, a huge *bal masque*, with sumptuous food, elegant decorations, a full orchestra for dancing, and fireworks to finish it all off. He would invite everyone who was any-one, including the Fostyns, and they would all see that he did not believe the rumours and held no grudges. He might even ask Mrs Fostyn to be his hostess—that should put an end to the rumour that the Latimers and Fostyns were in conflict. Oh, it was a capital idea!

Smiling to himself, he left his perch in the window and climbed into bed, refusing to acknowledge he would be doing it to spite Miss Fostyn, to prove to her that she had made a terrible mistake in choosing that mushroom for a husband when he had so much more to offer. Not that he would have offered for her; there was a limit to forgive-ness and forbearance.

In less than five minutes he was asleep, but his dreams were full of the colour and noise and the smell of an Indian bazaar. A very fat bearded man whom he half rec-ognised was talking to one of the stallholders, muttering in a low voice while the other listened, nodding his tur-banned head every now and again, but not speaking. Then the stallholder picked up a bag of spices from his stall and the European paid for them and left.

Five minutes later the Bengali packed up his stall and hurried away. He was soon lost in the crowd. The col-ourful bazaar faded from the dream and was replaced by an English ballroom crowded with dancers. And among them was Lydia Fostyn. She was throwing back her lovely head and laughing. Even in his dream, his body ached with the need to hold her in his arms, to feel that soft flesh against his, but as he reached out for her, the vision faded and he woke to find the sunshine of a new day streaming in the window.

A quarter of a mile away, Lydia opened her eyes to find Janet in the room, drawing back the curtains. There was a steaming dish of chocolate on the table by the bed and a jug of hot water on the washstand. She tried to sit up and moaned because the movement sent a little man with a hammer to work inside her head. That was what too much champagne did for you, she scolded herself. She had been foxed, there was no doubt about it. She still felt uneasy in her stomach and her head was as fluffy as a pillowful of feathers, and heavy as lead at the same time.

'What time is it?' she murmured, shutting her eyes against the strong light.

'Half past ten, Miss Lydia. What will you wear?'

'Oh, an undress robe will do, I think.' Reluctantly she opened her eyes again. 'Later, you may put my pink muslin out for this afternoon. We are to visit Sir Arthur.'

The maid picked up the white dress from a chair where Lydia had discarded it. 'Shall I put this in the chest?'

'Yes,' she murmured and then, remembering the hidden package, added. 'No. No, leave it. It needs airing first. I am sure it smells of smoke and drink...' And sick, she added to herself as she left the bed to wash in the warm water the maid had poured for her.

Janet draped the gown over a chair, smoothing the rich material of its skirt, sighing as she did so. 'It is so beautiful. Did you enjoy the evening, Miss Lydia?'

'Yes, thank you.' Her flat reply did not deceive the

maid, who knew her too well, but she made no comment. Instead she went to the dressing table and picked up the betrothal ring.

'Is this it? Oh, my, it's something, that is. Is that a real diamond?'

'Yes.' Lydia had neither the heart nor the energy to scold the maid for her impertinence. 'And the green one is an emerald.'

'And this?' The maid held up the shining, heavy necklace. 'Did 'e give you this too?'

'Of course.'

'Ooh, you are lucky to have someone like Sir Arthur to marry. It's like a fairy story.'

Lydia could not bear any more of this nonsense. 'Janet, are you going to fetch me my robe or not?'

'Yes, Miss Lydia.' The maid put the jewellery back where she found it with a deep sigh and went to obey.

Ten minutes later Lydia joined her mother in the little parlour where she was presiding over the breakfast table and reading a letter with a small frown on her brow. Lydia went to kiss her cheek; as she did so, she could not help noticing the Blackwater crest at the top of the page. 'What have you got there, Mama? Not more demands, I hope.'

Her mother looked up and smiled. 'Demands, no, but it is an invitation to take tea with his lordship tomorrow afternoon.'

'Good heavens, whatever for?'

'It does not say. Perhaps he simply wishes to be neighbourly.'

'After telling us to move out! I don't think so, Mama. No doubt he wishes to make sure we are truly going.'

'He did not need to ask us to take tea to do that.'

'Us?'

'Yes, the invitation is addressed to you too.'

'Me? I cannot think why he wants to give me tea unless it be to gloat.'

'Gloat, my dear?'

'Over my downfall.'

'Downfall?' Anne repeated in dismay. 'Lydia, what have you done?'

'Engaged myself to be married.'

'But, dearest, in no way can that be described as a downfall, quite the contrary. It is a triumph.'

'Yes.' Lydia sighed. 'But his lordship is not pleased about it, or so he says.'

'When did he say that?' her mother asked sharply.

'Last night.'

'Then he is jealous that you have been snapped up from under his nose.'

The idea was so ludicrous, Lydia laughed until she cried. 'Oh, Mama, you say the strangest things. He hates me as much as I hate him and I will not give him the satisfaction of thinking he can order me to come and go on his whim.'

'Lydia, it is a politely couched invitation, not an order.'

'You mean you want to go?'

'Why not?' She smiled suddenly. 'I must admit to being curious. Aren't you?'

'Perhaps, just a little.'

'Then you will come too?'

Lydia smiled again and reached out to put her hand over her mother's. 'How could I let you beard the lion in his den all alone?'

'Good,' her mother said with satisfaction. 'Now, do not forget we are engaged to call on Sir Arthur this afternoon to meet his daughters.'

'I had not forgot.'

They ate a frugal dinner with John and Annabelle, who

was still grumbling that they had forced her to leave the party just when she thought Lord and Lady Baverstock were coming round. She had not even had time to say goodbye to Peregrine and she had no idea when she would see him again, and it was all so unfair. But both her mother and her sister were too engrossed in their own problems to pay any attention to her.

Lydia dressed slowly that afternoon, trying to delay the inevitable, until her mother called out to her to make haste, that Partridge had had the coach at the front of the house for the past ten minutes. Sighing, she put a wool cape over her pink muslin dress and went to join her mother, taking with her gifts for the children.

Sir Arthur was stiff and formal, the little girls too shy by half and only answered Lydia's questions in mumbled monosyllables. She sensed the older two resented her and the youngest clung closely to the apron of her nurse, sucking her thumb, though she accepted the doll Lydia gave her with a shy smile. Constance and Faith, given games, bobbed a curtsy each and said, 'Thank you, Miss Fostyn,' in tones which told her they had been rehearsed.

'I wonder if I will ever be accepted as their new mama,' she remarked to her mother when they were once again in the coach and going home.

'Of course you will, given time. You must be patient.'

'You know, Mama, I often wonder why Sir Arthur chose me. We are as unlike as two people can be. He is so serious, almost pompous, he rarely smiles and I do not think I have ever heard him laugh. And he is so correct, I am sure I shall never be able to live up to his high standards. Why do you think he picked me out?'

'You underestimate yourself, my dearest. You are beautiful and lively, how can anyone fail to fall in love with you?'

'You are biased, Mama,' she said. And even then thoughts of Ralph Latimer intruded which was silly because he was immune from falling in love, certainly with her.

'Perhaps.'

They rode on in silence for several minutes while Lydia found herself wondering what it would be like to have several handsome young gentlemen all vying for her hand. They would shower her with gifts, extravagant compliments and protestations of undying love and she would play along with them, favouring one and then the other before someone came along to sweep her into a love affair, whose passion nothing could extinguish.

He would be bigger in every way, not only in stature but in presence. He would be more handsome, more powerful and richer and every whim she had would be satisfied because he loved her to distraction and she loved him. And she would honour him and try to please him and they would be happy together for the rest of their lives. She sighed heavily. That only happened in stories of romance, and dreaming impossible dreams was a waste of time and only brought heartache. Better to face reality: marriage to Sir Arthur Thomas-Smith. And the coming visit to the Earl which must be endured.

They walked up to the Hall at four o'clock the following afternoon. It was the first time Lydia had been there since Ralph's return home. Even before that she had rarely ventured there and, in spite of her avowed animosity, she really was curious.

The drive had been cleared of weeds and the garden tidied. The house itself was massive, built of stone and

crenellated like a castle. Lydia, looking up, was reminded
of the Countess and that dreadful leap from the roof.
Whatever she thought of the Earl, it must have been very
sad for him to come home to that and she found herself
feeling sorry for him. Telling herself not to be such a fool,
she took her mother's arm and they proceeded along the
drive, their taffeta skirts rustling as they walked.

The newly varnished front door was opened as they
reached it and a footman stood aside to allow them to
pass into the entrance hall with its marble tiled floor, massive fireplace and grand staircase which went up from the
centre and divided to left and right. There was a very long
window on the half-landing and at the top was a gallery
which had doors all round it evenly spaced.

Lydia tilted her head. The walls above the doors were
covered in an enormous mural: a peaceful pastoral scene
on one side and a battle scene on the other. 'You didn't
tell me it was like this,' she murmured to her mother in
wonder. 'It's like a fairy castle.'

'Mrs Fostyn. Miss Fostyn.'

Lydia had been so immersed in looking about her that
she had not heard Ralph's footsteps.

Startled she swung round to face him. He was dressed
in a plain grey kerseymere coat with biscuit-coloured
breeches and stockings and wore a small brown wig. He
was smiling pleasantly. Almost her umbrella man. But not
quite. Her mother was curtsying and bowing her head to
him. 'My lord,' she said.

Lydia, against her inclination, found herself doing the
same and chided herself for her weakness when she
should have been haughty and merely given him a nod.

'Your obedient servant.' He acknowledged the obei-
sance with an inclination of the head and a smile. 'May

I offer my congratulations on your betrothal, Miss Fostyn. I did not have a proper opportunity to do so on the night.'

Only because you were quizzing me and telling me how much you disapproved, her errant mind told her. 'Thank you, my lord,' she said aloud.

He threw his arm out to encompass the room. 'Do you like it?'

'Very baronial,' she said.

'Exactly,' he said. 'Meant for show. There are other rooms which are more comfortable. Would you like a short tour?' He smiled suddenly. 'Oh, I forgot, Mrs Fostyn, you are already familiar with the house.'

'Yes, my lord, but you have changed it beyond recognition. I remember this hall as being rather gloomy.'

'I thought so too, which is why I enlarged the window. Come up and see.'

He led the way up to the half-landing and they stood looking out of the window, which gave a magnificent view from the rear of the house. Below them was a cobbled courtyard, enclosed on two sides by other buildings. Ahead was a wide archway, which led to the gardens and from there to the park and beyond that the marshes and sea. They could just make out the glimmer of it in the distance.

'I like to stand here and watch,' he said.

'What do you watch for?' Lydia asked, thinking of smugglers.

'Oh, the changing seasons, the different shades and patterns of the greenery, the animals and seabirds, the fishermen. I think I might set up a telescope and watch the stars and the ships going about their business.'

'You can see the ships out to sea?'

'On a clear night with a good glass I could.'

'But we cannot see the beach from here.'

'True.' He smiled, guessing she was thinking about his determination to catch the smugglers, and that thought led inexorably to their first encounter by the hovel, the day he had realised who she was. It made him squirm with shame to think of the way he had chased her and kissed her. But she deserved it. And she had responded. Oh, she had not wanted to, he knew that, but the answering passion had been there and, in any other circumstances, the outcome could have been so different.

That kiss was something he would never be able to forget; it would come back to haunt him over and over again, a reminder of what could never be. He found himself looking down at her, wishing he could explain why he had done it, but what was there to say? He had been angry, or weak, or had given in to temptation, that if he could roll the clock back it would never have happened— how could he say that? She would not listen and it was not the truth. What was the truth? He did not know.

She was looking at him with a puzzled frown, as if trying to read his thoughts. He shook himself and addressed himself to Anne. 'There is something else I must show you, Mrs Fostyn. Follow me, if you please.'

With both ladies behind him he led the way up the remainder of the stairs and through a double door opposite the long window. They found themselves in a huge room which took up almost the whole width of the front of the house, along which long windows, elegantly draped with ruby velvet, were spaced at regular intervals. The plastered ceiling was intricately carved and gilded and supported six huge candelabra. The walls were papered in red and gold and the floor was polished to a mirror brightness. 'The ballroom,' he said. 'It has not been used since my parents were young and was in a parlous state of disrepair.'

'It's very grand,' Lydia said. 'Don't you think so, Mama?'

Anne was standing in a kind of dream, her eyes misted over and her mouth slightly open, and there was an expression on her face which was half-joyous, half-sad.

'Mama, is something the matter?'

Suddenly aware that her daughter had spoken to her, Anne pulled herself together and smiled. 'No, my dear. It is magnificent.' She turned to Ralph. 'But how did you know what it looked like in the old days? Recently I believe it was used as a repository for old furniture and anything no longer in use.'

'I know, and you would be surprised at the strange things I found when I cleared it out: stuffed animals and birds, broken statuary brought home by my father from his Grand Tour, gruesome pickled things in jars, ancient chests and sideboards, thrown out when Mama decided to refurnish in the French style, bed hangings eaten by mice, documents and letters—'

'Letters?' Anne queried.

'Yes.' He smiled, knowing why she had reacted in that way. He had found a bundle of letters from her which his father had kept. But there was nothing she need be ashamed of and one day, when the time was right, he would return them to her. 'That is how I knew what to do to restore it. I found my great-grandfather's instructions to the architect.'

'Oh, I see.' She sounded relieved. 'It is done so exactly right.'

'I thought you might remember it.'

'You were here?' Lydia asked her mother in surprise.

'Yes, when I was young. The first Earl and his wife held a great many balls and I was lucky enough to be invited to some of them.'

'The first Earl was my grandfather,' Ralph explained to Lydia. 'I believe your mama is speaking of a time before my father married.'

'Oh, yes, indeed. I never came after that.'

Lydia looked sharply at her mother whose face was flushed with colour, but she was still looking at Ralph, almost as if she were trying to convey something to him, something more than the words she spoke. She felt a great wave of tenderness for her mother; to have to deny rumours, without actually mentioning them, must be very difficult. Was that why Ralph had brought them here, to try and catch her mama out? Oh, it was hateful of him!

'Let us go down and I will have tea brought in,' he said. 'Then I will tell you why I asked you here.'

They followed him down to the hall again and he ushered them into a small comfortably furnished room, where a fire burned in the grate and teacups with handles were already set upon the table.

'Mrs Fostyn, will you preside?' he asked, pulling out a chair for her.

The next few minutes were occupied with the ritual of pouring and drinking tea and the offering and nibbling of little cakes, while Lydia seethed with impatience and irritation. Just what was he playing at?

'Dear lady, do you think it would be a good idea for me to hold a ball here at Colston Hall?' he asked Anne.

'Why, if that is what you wish to do, then I can see no reason why you should not.'

'You do not think it is too soon to be entertaining?'

'I think your people might be pleased to know that you are going to stay and live among them again.'

'That is exactly what I thought,' he said. 'Thank you for confirming it.'

'I cannot think why you have asked Mama's opinion

on the matter,' Lydia said, unable to resist the opportunity to score a point. 'We shall soon be gone from Colston.'

He smiled, refusing to be drawn. 'Because it is important your mama and her daughters are present.'

'So that you may crow over us,' Lydia put in. 'I told you so, Mama, didn't I?'

'Lydia!' Anne was appalled.

'No,' he said. 'That is not what I had in mind. You said I could do something to put an end to the rumours if I had a mind to and you were right. I want to show everyone that the Latimers and the Fostyns bear no enmity towards each other, that they can live in peace together and then those factions who have been taking sides will also live in harmony.'

'Very commendable,' Lydia said tartly. 'But to do that, we must both want it.'

'I agree. I, for one, want nothing so much as to put the past where it belongs, in the past—'

'You may do that, my lord, you are home and comfortable,' she retorted. 'Freddie is not home. We have no idea where he is and certainly cannot vouchsafe he is comfortable. And as for the rest of the family, under notice to quit—'

'I said you may stay until you are married,' he snapped. 'I did not mean you should accept the first man to ask you. You could have taken all the time you wanted.'

'Sir Arthur was not the first man to ask me, do not think that for a moment. You have hardly been back in Colston a month and you think you know everything about me—'

'Then I beg your pardon.' He bowed to her, determined not to allow her to disturb him, but it was an uphill struggle and, if her mother had not been present, he would have put her over his knee and spanked her. And after-wards kissed her soundly.

'I have no wish to be under an obligation to you, my lord,' she went on. 'Nothing would please me more than to be out from under your jurisdiction.'

'Then that is something we are able to agree on,' he said, with a sardonic smile.

'Lydia, there is nothing to be gained by going over old ground,' Anne said, desperate to take the heat out of the exchange.

'My point precisely,' he said. 'I wish to hold a ball but as I have no wife to be my hostess, I would be honoured if you, Mrs Fostyn, would take that role for the evening and also help me to plan it. I am sure if it were left to me I should forget something important.'

'Oh, no, I won't let you do it,' Lydia said. 'Mama, he means to humiliate you, to humiliate us.'

'Nothing was further from my mind,' he said, wondering how he was ever going to pierce that armour. Once he almost had, once he had seen her eyes soft and dreamy with desire, had tasted lips that answered passion with passion before she shut him out again. Was it difficult for her to maintain that searing hatred or did she have to cultivate it, nurture it to keep it alive? 'I am perfectly sincere. There was a time when I hated as passionately as you appear to do, but I have learned it is as likely to destroy the hater as the hated.'

'Well said, my lord,' Anne put in. 'I shall be delighted to do as you ask. Tell me, when do you want to hold the ball?'

'May Day,' he said promptly.

'May Day,' Lydia echoed in dismay. 'Why, that's only two weeks before my wedding. In a little over four weeks I am to be married.'

'Four weeks?' he echoed, making no attempt to disguise his surprise. 'So soon?'

'There is no reason to delay, my lord.'

He could think of a dozen reasons, none of which he could utter. 'No, but I always thought ladies took an unconscionable time preparing for their weddings.'

'It depends, my lord, on what has to be done. And Sir Arthur is impatient to make me his bride.'

He smiled suddenly, his eyes full of humour, and for a tiny moment she saw her umbrella man again. 'I can easily understand that, Miss Fostyn. May I wish you happy?'

'You may, my lord.' But do you mean it, she wondered, or do you wish me in purgatory because that is undoubtedly where I shall be?

'But I cannot see that it makes any difference. I want the ball to be as soon as possible or the reason for it will be lost.' He smiled mischievously. 'After all, May Day is a traditional time for celebration, is it not? A joyous time, looking forward to the summer and the bounty of summer. And it will not be the same if you have to come from Southminster instead of the dower house.'

Walking home with her mother afterwards, Lydia was seething. 'He's doing it to upstage me, to ruin my wedding day,' she said. 'Why? What have I ever done to him? And why did you agree? It is too mortifying.'

'Only if you allow it to be so,' her mother said placidly. 'If we enter into the spirit of it, everyone will come and I do believe it will put an end to those terrible rumours. When the time comes for your wedding, it will be the happy occasion it should be.'

No, it wouldn't, Lydia thought—she would be miserable. She would be miserable twice over, because the ball at the Hall would only serve to emphasise the emptiness

of the wedding ceremony. And he knew it! He was doing
it on purpose!

He had anticipated Anne's acceptance and had given
her a list of all the things he wanted done and the people
he thought should be invited and asked her to go over it
and then they would meet again at her convenience to
discuss it further. To Lydia it seemed that her mother was
betraying her father's memory and a dreadful worm of
suspicion wriggled itself into her mind and would not go
away.

Were the rumours true? Did Ralph Latimer know they
were true? Had her father known? Had Freddie? 'The Earl
knew how occupied you were going to be,' she said, stub-
bornly. 'It was unkind of him to add to your burdens.'

'Lydia, dearest, they are not burdens. How can dressing
your daughter for her wedding be a burden? And as for
the ball, I am only acting as an adviser, which is no trouble at all. We have not had an occasion like it for years
and years and I am quite looking forward to it.'

Lydia wished that she was.

The next two weeks were unbelievably busy. The or-
ganisation of the ball meant Anne having frequent meetings with the Earl and trips to Chelmsford to book musicians and arrange for food to be cooked and delivered,
for flowers and decorations to arrive at the proper time.
Often she took Lydia with her, not only to ask her opinion
on anything she might buy on his lordship's behalf, but
because they could combine it with a visit to the mantua
maker who was making Lydia's wedding gown and those
of her sisters who were to be her attendants.

Sir Arthur had insisted that the wedding feast would be
held at his house; the dower house was not large enough
for the number of guests he had in mind and consequently

his sister would be in charge of everything. Lydia and her
mother were not consulted at all. Anne was a little put
out, but Lydia said she did not mind and her mama ought
to be relieved the burden of it was being taken from her
shoulders, otherwise she would never have managed.

As the day of the ball approached Lydia began to dread
it more and more and could not be enthusiastic, unlike
Annabelle who could think and talk of nothing else, convinced that was the night Peregrine Baverstock would
make his offer. Lydia would like it to be all over, but that
meant her wedding day would be only two weeks away.
Two weeks! But first they had to go to that ball.

Naturally Sir Arthur was to be their escort and he arrived in his coach at eight o'clock on the evening of the
first of May dressed in a plum-coloured satin suit with
pink- and yellow-striped waistcoat straining across his
corseted front. He wore a cream shirt with acres of cream
lace at the throat and wrists. A huge emerald pin nestled
in his cravat and his fingers winked with more precious
stones as he flung out his hands.

'Ladies, I am honoured,' he said in his affected voice,
sweeping off his hat and executing an exaggerated leg to
each in turn, which had Annabelle giggling and Lydia
hard put to keep a straight face. But the smile was soon
wiped from it when he took both her hands in his and
held her at arm's length before planting a damp kiss on
each of her cheeks. Then he kissed her mother's hand and
said, 'Ladies, your carriage awaits.'

It was quite a squeeze because the three ladies in their
ball gowns took up a great deal of room. In the interests
of economy, Lydia had chosen to wear her white gown
again, but she had changed it by adding a diaphanous
overskirt, graded from deep green at the hem to almost

white at the waist. It floated about her like moving water.
The bodice under the bust she had trimmed with rows of
green velvet ribbon. Matching ribbon had been used to
decorate her wig and naturally she was wearing Sir Arthur's jewels. Anne had made over a deep blue velvet
which was among the clothes in the attic and Annabelle
was in white silk trimmed with spring flowers.

They settled themselves in the coach and spread their
skirts as far as possible to minimise creasing, which meant
Lydia's gown was spread across Sir Arthur's knees. It was
kind of intimacy which he obviously savoured for his
hand strayed to stroke the shiny material as if he could
not wait until they were married and he could take such
moments for granted, could undress her and…

She refused to allow her thoughts to roam along that
track and took refuge in thinking about the evening to
come. There was no doubt it was going to be a very grand
affair. The whole county had been invited and it seemed
every single one of them had accepted. Whether they were
coming out of curiosity or out of genuine friendship towards the Earl, or simply for a free meal with plenty to
drink, she did not know. What she did know was that her
mother had surpassed herself and in doing so she and the
Earl had become very good friends.

In the face of that it was impossible for Lydia to keep
up her enmity without quarrelling with her mother and as
the loathing she felt for his lordship was on her mother's
behalf, it seemed rather inconsistent to maintain it. But it
was so difficult to let go! To do so would mean being
disloyal to her brother and to the memory of her father
and besides, Ralph Latimer had said and done so many
things to annoy and upset her since he came home that
she did not feel disposed to weaken.

The coach turned in at the gates of Colston Park and

proceeded up the drive at a brisk trot. There were lanterns strung across the terrace before the front door which swayed and winked in the slight breeze coming off the sea and almost every window was ablaze with light. As Anne was to act as hostess, they were of necessity the first to arrive and servants were still scurrying to and fro with flowers and garlands and huge trays of glasses and the members of the orchestra were tuning their instruments.

They stood in the vast hall and had their cloaks taken from them by waiting maids. Sir Arthur handed his hat to a footman and adjusted the frills at his cuffs, before putting up his quizzing glass and gazing round him. What he thought about it he did not say and it was impossible to tell from his expression. Lydia wondered if it might be envy and a determination to outdo the Earl for munificence two weeks later.

His lordship appeared on the gallery and hurried down to greet them. Lydia caught her breath when she saw him. He was dressed in black from head to toe: a black velvet coat; long black brocade waistcoat heavily embroidered with silver thread and pearls; black breeches, stocking and shoes. His shirt was white silk, his cravat black lace in which a huge diamond pin glittered. He made Sir Arthur look very ordinary.

'My dear Mrs Fostyn,' he said, raising Anne from her curtsy before she had time to execute it fully, 'please do not stand on ceremony. I need you to come and help sort out a little contretemps in the kitchen over how to serve the quails. I am sure Sir Arthur and your daughters will excuse us.' He called to a footmen to conduct Sir Arthur and the Misses Fostyn to the ballroom and bore Anne away.

Lydia began to wish she had allowed her mother to take

their own coach and arrive early by herself. She and Annabelle could easily have come later. Now they were left
standing in the vast ballroom, feeling conspicuous and out
of place and the rest of the company would not begin
arriving for another half an hour.

'Ostentatious,' Sir Arthur, said looking about him. 'The
man has more money than taste.'

'Oh, do you think so?' Lydia said. 'Now I always
thought my mama had exquisite taste.'

'Oh, I did not mean the decorations,' he blustered.
'They are indeed very fine and to be admired. I was referring to the Earl's dress. All that black and white makes
him look like a checkerboard.'

'He is still in mourning.'

'Why do you defend him, ma'am, when he was responsible for the ruination of your family?'

'I am not defending him, Sir Arthur, simply stating a
fact.' She paused, looking about her almost wildly for
something to say to change the subject. 'Oh, we can see
right down the drive from this window and there are some
more arrivals. Who do you think they are?'

He came and stood beside her as the first of several
carriages drew up below them. 'I do believe that's the
Comte's carriage,' he said.

The Comte de Carlemont, in bright yellow and cerise,
was followed by Lord and Lady Brotherton with Caroline
and then the Baverstocks, much to Annabelle's delight.
More arrived as they watched and soon the ballroom was
no longer empty but filled with men and women sump-
tuously dressed, all talking at once, looking about them,
commenting on the changes made to the house, reminisc-
ing about what it had been like in the old days, remarking
on the other guests, often maliciously.

A long line of liveried footmen walked into the room

carrying trays of champagne and cordial which they offered to everyone. A few minutes later Anne entered on the arm of the Earl, a master of ceremonies announced the first country dance and his lordship led his hostess into the first set. Sir Arthur seized Lydia by the hand and joined them and the evening had begun.

Lydia had made up her mind she would not enjoy it, was determined she would not, but the music and gaiety wore her down and she began to relax. By the time Ralph claimed her for a polka, she had drunk two glasses of champagne and her feet were tapping. He bowed before her and held out his hand without speaking. She took it silently and then they were in the middle of the floor, careering up and down in breathless abandonment.

By the time they finished she was flushed and laughing. He knew he loved her then. There would never be anyone else for him. The enormity of the discovery hit him like a physical blow and took his breath away. He had been fooling himself if he thought his motives were simply to end the long running enmity of two families and end the rumours which he knew to be untrue. He wanted more, much more. But it was too late, much, much too late. He could not have her.

He raised her from the deep curtsy she had made at the end of the dance and forced himself to smile as he offered her his arm. She laid her fingers on it and walked sedately with him back to her mama and Sir Arthur where he bowed and raised her hand to his lips. His expression as he did so puzzled her. It was sardonically humorous, quizzical and yet slightly melancholy. 'Miss Fostyn,' he murmured softly, leaving her bemused.

'Come, my dear,' said Sir Arthur brusquely. 'I believe they are serving supper in the dining room.'

She trailed after him, her feet dragging when only

minutes before they had been flying round the ballroom
as if they had wings. She did not want to eat but, remembering how the champagne had affected her at Sir Arthur's
soirée and not wishing to disgrace herself a second time,
she forced a little food down her throat. He tried coaxing
her with more titbits which only made her angry and she
excused herself and fled before she gave herself away.

Down the passageways of that huge house she went,
not knowing where she was going. She needed somewhere cool and private to think. But what was there to
think about? She had burned her boats. She could not
escape from the hateful engagement and nothing had really changed; they were still under notice to quit the
dower house and there was still the question of John's
schooling and Annabelle's dowry. Nothing had changed.

'*The Mermaid* is lying out to sea.' She stopped in her
tracks, frozen by a man's voice coming from an open door
ahead of her. She stood, afraid to go on, unwilling to go
back. There was a dank smell of soil and warmth ema-
nating from the room and she remembered the Earl showing her and her mother the conservatory he had recently
had erected on a south-facing wall and stocked with exotic
plants. Beyond it was the garden. 'If the moon and tides
are right, I expect it to come in close soon after midnight,'
the voice went on. 'The boat will be lowered when the
signal is given. Have the men and the cart ready. I'll send
word.'

'Where will you be?' The voice was gruff and had a
local twang, though Lydia did not recognise it.

'Combing the dunes.'

'What for?'

'You know what for.' It was said angrily. 'Now go.'

Lydia felt a cool draught flow around her ankles, as the
outer door was opened and then shut. She guessed the

roughly spoken man had gone, but at any moment the other would come through the door behind which she was hiding. Afraid of being discovered, she hurried away to the other side of the staircase where she might see anyone coming out of the conservatory from between its banisters. She had not recognised the voices and it was important to know who the men were. 'Combing the dunes,' one had said. That implied looking for something that was lost. But he would not find it, because it was in the chest in her bed chamber.

She crept away, all thought of flight forgotten, and for a moment her concern for the dilemma she was in over Sir Arthur was superseded by another, more mystifying and in many ways more terrifying. Did the Earl know men were plotting under his roof? Who were they? Should she tell someone? The Earl?

'There you are, my dear. I have been looking for you everywhere.' She was startled by her mother's voice behind her.

'I was just coming, Mama. I needed some fresh air.'

'We are all going into the garden for the fireworks. You will find fresh air enough there.'

It was then that she realised everyone was crowding down the corridor to the conservatory from which they could enter the garden where the fireworks were to be let off. She and her mother went with them, but there was no sign of anyone furtively hiding among the plants; whoever had been there had blended with the guests and was gone.

Sir Arthur joined them in the garden, arriving silently at Lydia's side as they were ushered onto the terrace behind the ropes which had been strung across it for safety's sake, and the men Ralph had hired from London set off a spectacular display.

Rockets fizzed and flared into the sky and burst into myriad dancing lights in red, yellow and green before falling to earth leaving a pall of smoke and an acrid smell. The display ended with a set piece, a mock-up of a castle with imitation guns sticking out from every embrasure, which were detonated in a single flash, and the guns popped and sent cascades of starry brilliance upwards, illuminating the castle in an eerie glow.

The spectators let out a combined sigh as the lights died and everywhere was once again in darkness. And then they applauded and shouted huzzah as footmen went round with mulled wine and cakes. It was almost an anticlimax after that as everyone went back indoors, cloaks and hats were found and carriages called to the door.

'Where is Annabelle?' Anne asked Lydia, as Ralph stood at the door to bid each of his guests goodnight.

'I don't know. She was standing beside me in the garden, but then she disappeared.'

They turned to search her out among the departing guests. Lord and Lady Baverstock were approaching and beside them a red-faced, scowling Peregrine. They passed Lydia and her mother without speaking, said goodnight to the Earl and went out to their carriage.

Two minutes later, Annabelle appeared. She had little to say as they stood and waited for the remainder of the guests to depart. Lydia wanted to be gone but she knew she would have to go through the ritual of saying goodnight to their host and she did not know how she was going to go through with it. He spoke to her mother, lavished her with praise for her part in making the evening the success it had been, teased Annabelle a little and nodded curtly to Sir Arthur, who was smiling broadly, almost triumphantly.

'We shall expect you for the nuptials in two weeks' time, my lord,' Sir Arthur said.

'Wild horses wouldn't keep me away.' He turned to Lydia, took her hand in his and put it to his lips. 'Miss Fostyn, goodnight.' That was all. Nothing more.

She almost choked as she hurried down the steps and clambered unaided into the carriage. By the time the others had joined her, she had composed herself. As they bowled away down the drive she risked a look behind her through the rear window. Ralph Latimer was standing outlined by the light behind him, watching them go.

Chapter Seven

Lydia dreamed of the duel that night. It was a strange and disturbing dream because not only was she present, but so was her mother and the old Earl and Sir Arthur clothed in gold. Everyone was arguing and shouting, waving their arms about. Duels were supposed to be silent affairs, weren't they? They should be sombre, as befitted an occasion when one person was intent on killing another, not a noisy debate. The real protagonists stood slightly apart, watching those they loved arguing the rights and wrongs of it, as if it had been taken out of their hands.

She wanted to join in, but found she had no voice; she was simply an onlooker forced to watch by the man at her side, the man in gold who held her wrist in a grip so tight that she could not move. Her brother looked old, almost as old as her father, when she knew perfectly well he was only seventeen, and Ralph, whom she had, until this dreadful night, always thought of as a friend, was a giant, towering over everyone else, his face so dark that she could see nothing of it but the eyes, glowing like twin fires. The arguing suddenly stopped, the two young men paced out the ground and turned and raised their pistols.

In her dream Lydia watched as Ralph slowly lifted the hand that held the gun and pointed it at Freddie, who did nothing, made no move to raise his own weapon. Then that hateful man slowly turned away from her brother towards her father. She tried to shout 'No!' but no words came. Then he turned again, facing her, pointing the gun at her. She could not breathe, could not free herself from the man who held her. Mesmerised by the gun, she could not take her eyes off it. Ralph laughed; he was going to shoot her dead. There was a loud bang and at the same instant she felt Sir Arthur's grip on her slacken as he crumpled to the ground.

The shock of it woke her and she sat up in bed, shaking uncontrollably. It had been so real, like a scene from a macabre play. She dare not lie down again and, wrapping herself in a robe, went to the window to gaze out on the cloudy night. What had it meant? Why was Sir Arthur there, dressed in gold when everyone else was in black? Why was her mother there? And the old Earl? Why had Ralph Latimer shot Sir Arthur? By doing so, he had released her.

It was wishful thinking, she told herself firmly, because only the death of one or the other of them would free her from Sir Arthur now. And because there had been so much talk about the duel recently, coupled with the return of Ralph and the rumours about her mother, her sleeping brain had conjured up the dream, allowed her father to live and made Ralph Latimer her saviour, a situation which could not possibly come to pass.

Something else had happened last night. She had heard men plotting, whispering in the dark, whispering of boats and searching the shore. Or had that been part of her nightmare too? But she had not dreamed that coat and the bundle in its pocket, a bundle the man she had overheard was determined to find. Who was he?

How long had she slept? She did not know. The nightmare had woken her so thoroughly there was no question of going back to sleep. She rose and went to the window, drew back the curtains and stood looking out on the quiet countryside. There were a few ragged clouds scudding across the sky, hiding the moon, which every now and then peeped out and bathed the garden in its silvery light. To her left were the dark woods, while in front and to the right, the marshes gave way to the shore. She could not see the beach which was down below the dunes, but she could just glimpse the sea on the horizon. She smiled to herself, remembering Freddie's talk of lights at night, Freddie her beloved brother who had crept out of the house to see what was going on.

Without stopping to consider what she was doing or its consequences, she rose and lit a candle, then went to her bedroom door, opening it a chink and listening. There was no sound; nothing and nobody stirred. She crept along to the room which her mother always kept ready for her son's return. In the closet she found breeches and a shirt and coat in a warm brown fustian which Freddie had worn when out on the marshes shooting ducks. She took them back to her own room and put them on.

She was a little smaller than her brother had been, but that was a good thing; the looseness of the coat concealed her curves. The breeches she pulled on over her own stockings and tightened a belt about her waist, pushed her feet into her walking boots and went to the mirror to comb her hair back from her face as tightly as she could, before cramming it under her brother's old tricorne hat. She had no idea if she looked like a boy or not, but the clothes would certainly help her to move about more easily.

In the kitchen she picked up a knife and put it in her belt before letting herself quietly out of the door. It made her feel more masculine and in command of events, which was silly considering she would never have the courage to use it. She slipped out of the outer kitchen door, closing it softly behind her, and in a matter of minutes was skirting the Earl of Blackwater's woods. They were dark and eerie, silent as the grave except for the soughing of the wind in the tops of the trees and her own ragged breathing. She had not consciously been heading for the hovel, but she found herself approaching it furtively. It was in complete darkness.

She shivered and turned away. Leaving the woods to the ghosts who inhabited it, she made for the shore, but the familiar paths were not visible in the dark and several times she found herself up to her knees in water. She must be mad, she told herself. What was she doing here? What was she hoping to achieve? How could wandering about in the dark cure her ills? She could drown, her body could disappear without trace and her mother would have one more sorrow to bear. She should go home.

She had been looking at the ground, carefully picking her way, but now she lifted her head to return and it was then she saw the light out to sea. There was one flash, followed after an interval by two more and though she waited, there was no answering signal from the shore, though it might have been hidden round the headland.

She felt a prickling sensation in the back of her neck as if she were being watched. Her feet were squelching in her shoes and her heart was thumping so loudly she thought the men on that vessel out to sea must be able to hear it. She was torn between an inclination to run and find safety at home and curiosity about who the smugglers were and what it was they were smuggling. Curiosity won and she moved forward, trying to be as silent as possible for surely there were others on the shore waiting, as she waited.

Having safely negotiated the marshes, she made for the nearest dune which would provide cover. The next minute she was thrown to the ground and someone big and heavy was sitting on her, holding her arms down each side of her head. A shriek of surprise and fear was forced from her as she struggled to free herself. Her hat fell off and her hair spread itself over her shoulders in a dark cloud.

'Who the devil are you?' her attacker demanded, removing the knife from her belt.

'There's no law says you can't take a walk on the beach, is there?' she retorted breathlessly, relieved to have recognised the voice; it belonged to Robert Dent. 'But there is a law against smuggling.'

'Who are you?' he demanded. 'Some young jackanapes thinking to join in?'

'If you like. Now let me get up.'

'And have you give the game away? Oh, no, my lad. You'll stay where I can keep an eye on you…' The moon came out from a cloud and he saw her clearly for the first time. 'Lydia Fostyn, by all that's holy!' He scrambled off her. 'What are you doing here?'

'I'm out for a walk.' She sat up and tried to brush the sand from her clothes.

'In the middle of the night? And why are you dressed like that?'

'I needed to clear my head, too much champagne, you know, and I am not used to it. You, on the other hand, are accustomed to drink deep, so you have no such excuse for wandering abroad at dead of night.'

He did not see fit to explain his presence, but stood up and reached out his hand to help her to her feet. 'I believe

you are still a little disguised,' he said and she laughed at
his unintentional pun which only served to confirm his
diagnosis. He reached down and picked up her hat, knocking it against his leg to remove some of the sand before
handing it to her, together with the kitchen knife. 'You
know, you could hurt someone with that.'

'It was only for self-defence.'

'Then I am mightily glad I took you by surprise.'

'I'm sorry. I don't think I could have used it.'

'Not in cold blood, perhaps, but in a struggle to save
your life I think you might. Go home, Miss Fostyn, stay
out of harm's way.'

'So there is danger.'

'The only danger on this beach is you,' he said, with a
low chuckle. 'Now, let me take you home.'

'Don't you have to answer that signal?'

'What signal?'

'I am not a fool, Mr Dent. I have seen the light out to
sea and the hovel in the woods...' She decided not to
mention the packet she had found.

'Miss Fostyn, I strongly advise you not to meddle.'

'And miss the fun?'

'There is no fun and you could be hurt. These are desperate men.'

'Oh, surely not? They are only a handful of villagers
bringing in a little contraband. Where's the harm in that?'

'None, so long as that is all they are doing. Now, be
off home with you. And take care to stay on the path.'

They were standing close together, almost touching, sil-
houetted against the lighter sky above the horizon. Ralph
saw them quite plainly from his position on the track
above the dunes, though he could not identify them. He
saw the smaller of the two bid the other goodbye and walk

towards him. He ducked out of sight behind a windblown bush and watched.

The figure passed within two feet of his hiding place and he almost gasped aloud.

She was dressed as a boy, but there was no mistaking the russet tresses and rounded curves of Miss Lydia Fostyn. In spite of her protestations she really was in league with the smugglers. He was tempted to confront her, to demand that she tell him what she knew. Did she, for instance, know there was more to what was going on than a few cases of wine and brandy? But she appeared to be leaving the scene, sent home by the man she had met. Did that mean she was a courier, a taker of messages?

He half wished he had not come out, but he had been unable to sleep for the thoughts that whirled round in his head. The ball had probably been a success if all he meant to do was put an end to the rumours and establish himself where he belonged in the community, but as for the feud between the Latimers and the Fostyns, he was not so sure.

Mrs Fostyn had never blamed him, he knew that now, and she had been grateful when he had given her back those letters, admitting to her he had read some of them and wished he had not. They were too private and he had felt like an intruder in sorrows which had happened so long ago. But Lydia was different. He had been no nearer reaching an understanding with her at the end of the evening than at the beginning. Why was he even trying? She still loathed him.

He had turned back indoors after seeing everyone off the premises and gone back to the ballroom. There were empty glasses everywhere, fading flowers and drooping greenery. There was even mud on the floor, walked into the room on the shoes of those returning from the garden. Servants had been extinguishing the lights and piling up the debris. 'Leave it until tomorrow,' he said and they had scuttled thankfully away.

He had stood in the darkened room for a moment, looking out on the drive. Sir Arthur's carriage had long since disappeared. He could not see the dower house because it was screened by trees, but he could imagine Lydia at home there, saying goodnight to her mother and sister and preparing for bed, taking off that lovely gown, having her beautiful hair brushed, climbing between the sheets and he wished he were there with her, part of her life. Would she sleep well? Would he? He sighed and left the room shutting the door behind him.

Reluctant to go to bed himself, he stood on the half-landing, looking out on the marshes, home of seabirds, eels, oysters and crabs, a grand place for scavenging schoolboys. And smugglers. Almost as if he had conjured them up, he spotted the light out to sea. It had winked once, then twice, and then gone out.

He had run to his room, stripped off his black suit and dressed in the nondescript clothes he had worn on another such occasion and set out for the hovel in the woods, intending to wait until the smugglers arrived with their booty and he could catch them on his land. There had been no sign of them, but he had seen the boy making his way furtively along the path towards the shore and he had followed.

Only it was not a boy, but the girl who was constantly in his thoughts. He had believed her assertion that she knew nothing about the smugglers because he had wanted to believe it, but how could he deny the evidence of his own eyes? He let her pass, waiting for bigger fish. But the man she had been talking to had disappeared among the dunes and though he watched another hour, becoming increasingly colder, there were no more signals.

He supposed she had warned them off and there would be no landing tonight. But he was not beaten; the smugglers would not give up, they still had to deliver their cargo if they wanted their money and he would be ready for them.

He stirred his cramped limbs and went home, furious with Lydia for frustrating him. Lydia Fostyn, young, beautiful, contrary, defiant, a thorn in his flesh, so deeply embedded he did not know how to rid himself of it. Having her arrested with all the others might serve. He knew, even as the thought entered his head, he could not do it. Somehow he must make sure she was safe before he made a move.

Lydia did not wake until noon and then she did not feel as though she had slept at all, though Janet assured her she had been so deeply slumberous she had been unable to rouse her at her usual hour and Mrs Fostyn had said to leave her be. Watching Janet busying herself about the room, tidying scattered clothing, Lydia hoped all the evidence of her night's excursion had been safely stowed away in Freddie's room.

'My, Miss Lydia, how did your boots come to be so wet and muddy?' the maid exclaimed, picking them up from the corner where Lydia had kicked them off.

'I went walking yesterday afternoon,' Lydia said quickly.

'Did you? And why didn't you leave the boots in the kitchen to be cleaned as you usually do?'

'I forgot.'

'Seems to me you haven't got your mind on anything these days, Miss Lydia. Excitement, I suppose, for that is what your mama told Sir Arthur when he arrived not half an hour since.'

Lydia sat up with a jerk. 'Sir Arthur is here?'

'No, he left when your mama said she would not disturb you.'

'Oh.' She sank back on the pillows. 'I think I will go back to sleep.'

'Mr Dent has called too. I heard him tell the mistress he was afraid you were unwell last night and he came to see how you did. I think he is waiting for you to appear for he has settled himself in the best armchair and is drinking all the claret. I think your mama needs rescuing from him. And the Earl of Blackwater left his card and said he would come back later.'

'The Earl! What does he want?'

'I am sure I do not know,' Janet said huffily. She was usually privy to everything that went on in the Fostyn household and the huffiness was due to the fact that this time she had been kept in the dark.

'I had better dress and put in an appearance,' Lydia said, swinging her legs out of bed. 'Fetch me the yellow stripe, will you? And see what you can do with my hair.'

'It looks as though a bird has been nesting in it,' Janet said bluntly as she took the brush to the girl's dark tresses. 'You must have tossed and turned all night. No wonder you look so pale.'

'Do I? Then I shall put a little of Mama's rouge on my cheeks.'

Twenty minutes later she was dropping a curtsy to Robert Dent, resplendent in a red coat with an enormous collar and huge pocket flaps, who had risen to greet her.

'Miss Fostyn, your obedient,' he said, studying her face under cover of a sweeping bow. 'Are you well?'

'Perfectly, sir. A little fatigued, that is all.'

'Is it to be wondered at?' he said. 'So much going on,

so much to think about and do. I wonder you are not prostrate with exhaustion.'

'I am young and healthy Mr Dent,' she said, glancing towards her mother, who looked slightly startled by the undercurrents beneath the seemingly banal conversation. 'I can take a great deal more activity that I have had so far, I do assure you.'

'Oh, I am sure you can, but let me caution you, my dear Miss Fostyn, against over-exertion. It could lead to all manner of ills. Night air, I believe, is particularly harmful.'

'Whatever are you talking about?' Anne put in. 'Lydia has not been out in the night air, unless you mean when we were in the garden watching the fireworks—'

'Quite, ma'am,' he said, bowing towards her.

'Mr Dent, I cannot think why you should mention it. I am perfectly able to look after the health of my daughter until she marries and then, of course, her husband will take care of her.'

'I beg your pardon, ma'am. I only spoke because when I saw Miss Fostyn last night, I thought she was not feeling quite the thing and it is only common civility to call and ask if she has recovered.'

'I was never ill, sir,' Lydia said. 'But I will take note of your concern about the night air.'

He took his leave soon after that and she wondered if he took her assurances as an indication that she would not pursue her interest in the smugglers. It was what she wanted him to think, but she had no intention of doing anything of the sort.

'I do declare that man is a little touched in the head,' her mother said, when he had gone. 'Whatever was he talking about?'

Lydia shrugged. 'I have no more idea than you, Mama. Perhaps he was drunk.'

'In the middle of the day?'

Lydia picked up the claret bottle; there was hardly a thimbleful left. 'How much was in this when he arrived?'

Anne smiled. 'It was more than half full. I tried to tell him you were sleeping, but he seemed determined to stay. What is going on? He knows you have accepted Sir Arthur's offer, so it is too late to put in one of his own.'

'I doubt that was his intention, Mama.'

'Then what? I do hope he is not going to spread more rumours…'

'What could he say?'

'That you have a tendency to over-indulgence when it comes to champagne. You drank too much at your own betrothal party and had to be taken home early. And last night too, judging by his hints.'

'Mama! You make me sound like a soak.'

'Not at all, but you did leave the supper table very suddenly last night. What Sir Arthur thought of that, I do not know. He went looking for you, but fortunately I found you first.'

'I did nothing wrong.'

'No, but that is not how other people perceive it. Sir Arthur has called, you know. I had to tell him you were still abed. I said it was over-excitement, what with the ball and the wedding coming so soon on top of one another.'

'And did he accept that?'

'He seemed to. But, Lydia, if you do anything else to embarrass him, he will begin to think he made a mistake in offering for you.'

Lydia would have loved to retort that nothing would please her more than for Sir Arthur to have second thoughts, but she knew that would upset her mother and that was the last thing she wanted. 'I am sorry, Mama. It won't happen again, I promise you.'

'Good,' her mother said, picking up the bell from the table at her side and giving it a few shakes. 'I'll tell Janet to serve dinner.'

But when Janet came it was not in answer to the summons but to tell them the Earl of Blackwater was in the hall.

'For goodness sake, girl, do not keep him standing outside,' Anne told her. 'Show him in.'

Before Lydia could gather her scattered wits he was standing before them in a riding coat of deep forest green, nankeen breeches and highly polished boots. He wore no wig and his dark hair was drawn back and tied with black ribbon. 'Mrs Fostyn, Miss Fostyn, your obedient,' he said, bowing to each in turn.

'My lord.' Anne rose and curtsied. 'You are very welcome.'

No, you are not, Lydia said to herself, as she executed her own curtsy. Aloud she said, 'My lord, what brings you here?'

'A courtesy visit, Miss Fostyn.' Looking at her was doing all manner of strange things to his insides, stirring him with a desire which he knew he must suppress at all costs. He deliberately turned from her to her mother. 'Ma'am, I came to tell you how magnificently you managed everything for me last night. Everyone tells me it was a great success.'

'Thank you, my lord.' Anne smiled. 'But you thanked me sufficiently when we left.'

'Did I? Oh, but it does no harm to say it again.' He paused. 'Ma'am, if you should find living at Sir Arthur's not to your taste, you are welcome to stay here.'

'What did you say?' Lydia demanded, unable to believe her ears.

'I said I find I do not need the dower house after all, and if your mama wishes to make it her home after you have married, then she is welcome to stay.'

'How could you? How could you be so cruel?' Lydia cried, so full of anger and frustration she could not keep silent. 'You knew perfectly well what that notice to quit would mean for us all and yet you were determined to see us go. Oh, but I do see. You baited the hook, Mama was caught like a poor fish and is reeled in by your apparent magnanimity so that she forgets how you wronged her and now you are trying to make fun of me—'

'Not at all,' he said coldly. 'I was thinking of your mama. And there is nothing the least amusing about that outburst. I begin to think you are not well.'

'I am perfectly well, my lord,' she said.

'Lydia, his lordship is right, you are beside yourself and I am ashamed of you.'

'I am sorry, Mama. It is just… Oh, why does he have to come offering an olive branch now? It is all too late. Much too late.' She was so vexed she was on the point of bursting into tears and she must not do that.

Anne turned to Ralph, her face creased with concern. 'My daughter has had too much excitement of late, my lord,' she said, giving what had now become her stock answer. 'What with her engagement and arrangements to be made for the wedding and last night's ball… I am not complaining about that, you understand, it was a great occasion.'

'Indeed, it was splendid, thanks to you. And I cannot believe Miss Fostyn was overcome by it. She looked radiant.' That was not the right word, he decided, it was not radiance but a kind of haunting beauty which made him sad.

He turned from Anne to Lydia as he spoke, with a gaze so deep and compelling, she fancied he could see right into her soul, to understand things about her she did not understand herself. She could hear her own heartbeat, thumping in her chest like a blacksmith's hammer, and her hands were shaking so much she was forced to hide them in the folds of her skirt.

'Thank you, my lord,' she murmured, wishing he would take his leave.

'Will you take refreshment, my lord?' Anne asked, glancing at the empty claret bottle. 'Coffee or tea perhaps?'

'No, I thank you, I am expected back at the Hall. There is much to be done clearing up from last night and estate work to supervise…'

Before he finished speaking Janet came into the room and said Cook wanted to speak to Mrs Fostyn in the kitchen. Anne looked surprised and unsure whether she ought to leave his lordship and Lydia alone together, but evidently decided there was no danger of them doing anything but be coldly polite to each other. She asked to be excused for a moment; he bowed in acquiescence and she followed Janet from the room.

As soon as she had gone, Ralph, who had given Janet half a guinea to find some way of taking Mrs Fostyn from the room, took a step closer to Lydia. 'Miss Fostyn, I must take the opportunity while we are alone to ask you if you know what you are doing?'

'Marrying Sir Arthur? Yes, I do, and do not tell me again that you think it is a mistake, for I will not listen.'

'No, I know that would be a waste of breath. I was

referring to other matters. It is a dangerous game you are playing, you know.'

'Game, my lord? What can you mean?'

'Don't play the innocent, Miss Fostyn. I was referring to the smuggling.'

'La, sir, a lady smuggler, how droll.' Her laughter was meant to show how amusing she found him, to demonstrate she had nothing to hide, but it was too forced to deceive him and she knew it. She stopped laughing and effected anger. 'My lord, I find your accusations insulting, but then I should have expected no less from you, who would blacken my name if you could, just as you blackened my brother's.'

He refused to be distracted and stood his ground. 'Lydia, if you have got in too deep to extricate yourself, I beg you to confide in me. I can help. In spite of your enmity, I would aid you if I could.'

It was strange, she thought, that whenever she raised her voice in anger, he lowered his and spoke gently, taking all the heat from her fury. It took a monumental effort to maintain her animosity. But she had to stay on that path, because to step off it was to drown, just as she would drown if she lost her way on the marshes. 'My lord, I do not know what you mean. I have no need of help, none at all, and even if I had then I should apply to Sir Arthur Thomas-Smith.'

'Of course. I bid you good day, Miss Fostyn.'

A curt bow, which she answered with no more than a tiny inclination of the head, and he was gone, leaving her fuming. Every word he had uttered had been calculated to upset her, to accuse, to admonish, as if it were any of his business what she did. How much did he know? Did he know anything about that package which, even now, reposed in the bottom of her clothes chest? If he had seen her pick it up, surely he would have said so when he had accosted her on the day, not left it until now?

She was reminded of that long window at the Hall. Had he been watching from there last night? But the beach was not visible from there and he certainly would not have been able to recognise her from that distance. And why was he offering to help her? She would never turn to him for assistance, for what price would he extract for it? It would be like turning to the devil himself and the cost would be humiliation at the very least.

She turned as Anne came back into the room, surprised to see only her daughter there. 'Where is his lordship?'

'Gone, Mama. He had said all he came to say and there seemed no reason to detain him.'

'Oh, and I did not bid him goodbye. I really do not know what Cook wanted that was so urgent. She knew she could not serve dinner until he had gone and we could not have asked him to stay, not at such short notice. It is only mutton chops.'

'I am sure he understood, Mama.'

'Did you give him back his umbrella?'

'No, I forgot.'

'Lydia, you are really become quite empty-headed, but I suppose there is some excuse for it. We shall no doubt see his lordship again, unless you would like to walk up to the Hall and return it yourself.'

'No, I would not,' she said, so quickly her mother looked at her in surprise. 'I mean, you are right, we are bound to see him again.'

The chops had been kept hot and gone leathery; Lydia, whose stomach was already in turmoil, could not eat. It was all Ralph Latimer's fault, she told herself, stoking up her anger. If he had not chosen to call when anyone with a grain of sense would know it was the dinner hour, the meal would at least have been palatable. And if he had not spent three-quarters of the time finding fault and making accusations, she would not have lost her appetite.

She was not the only one to lose her appetite. Annabelle pushed her plate away with a grimace of disgust. 'Mama, it is time you let Cook go. She becomes worse and worse.'

'I don't like to,' her mother said. 'She has been with us so long and it was not her fault today. The Earl arrived just at the wrong moment.'

'Well, she will have to go when Lydia marries, I cannot imagine Sir Arthur employing her. He has a French chef.' She laughed suddenly. 'Just think, Lydia, when you are married you will never have to cook another thing yourself.'

'I like cooking.'

'Then it is a pity you did not cook these chops instead of playing society hostess to his lordship.'

'I did not do so from choice,' her sister said. 'But I could not let him bully Mama, could I?'

'Bully me?' Anne queried. 'How can you say that? He was a perfect gentleman. Do you know, Annabelle, he has said we do not need to leave here after all, if we do not wish it.'

Annabelle looked at Lydia in alarm. 'Does that mean you are going to break off your engagement? Oh, that would be the last straw. There will be more talk and our names will be even more decried. Peregrine will never be allowed to marry me. It was bad enough last night…' The diatribe ended in a wail.

'What do you mean last night?' Anne demanded. 'What happened last night?'

'Nothing.'

'Come along. I want to know. What happened?'

'Perry kissed me.'

Anne allowed herself the ghost of a smile. 'Oh, Annabelle, it was very wrong of you to allow it, you should know that, but I cannot see what that has to do with Lydia.'

'Lady Baverstock saw it. We were coming from the garden and it was dark and he…he kissed me, just as her ladyship came up behind us. She was very angry.'

'I do not doubt it. Peregrine should have known better.'

'She was not angry with Perry. She was angry with me for luring him on. She said…' The girl hesitated and then went on, talking through sobs. 'She said she wasn't at all surprised, it was no more than you would expect from a Fostyn.'

'The devil she did!' Lydia exclaimed. 'Mama, we cannot let that rest. We cannot.'

'I don't know what we can do about it,' Anne said. 'Making a fuss would only make matters worse.' She paused and turned back to Annabelle. 'Dearest, I really do think it would be wiser if you did not see that young man again. He has little backbone if he is prepared to allow you to take the blame for something he did. He is older than you and should be wiser in these matters.'

'He did try to defend me,' Annabelle cried. 'His mama struck him and grabbed him by the arm and dragged him away. If Lydia breaks off her engagement, I will never be allowed to marry him.'

'Goodness, do you still want to?' Lydia asked.

'Of course, I do. You cannot blame someone for what their parents do.'

'You certainly shouldn't,' Anne murmured. 'But you know what they say about the sins of the fathers…'

'I didn't mean that,' Annabelle said, aghast that she might have hurt her mother. 'Lydia, tell Mama. You know what it is like to love someone so much that it doesn't matter what he does.'

'Do I?' Lydia queried in surprise.

'Yes.' Annabelle looked meaningfully at her. 'You and your umbrella man.'

'Annabelle, what are you talking about?' Anne said.

'Nothing, Mama,' Lydia put in. 'Annabelle is weaving fantasies. I met a stranger at the lecture at the Assembly rooms and spoke a few words to him. She has made a romance out of it.'

'Yes, but he turned out not to be a stranger, but the Earl of Blackwater,' Annabelle said.

'Which just proves it was a fantasy,' Lydia said. 'I cannot abide the man, as you very well know.'

Anne looked from one daughter to the other and sighed. 'Girls, will you stop arguing? Annabelle, I do believe you have some studying to do. Go and do it, please. I wish to speak to your sister.'

Annabelle rose and flounced from the room, leaving Anne facing a very flushed Lydia. 'Now, child, I think you should tell me exactly what has been happening.'

Lydia took a deep breath and told her mother about her meetings with the man with the umbrella, trying desperately to sound light-hearted, making a jest of it, saying what a strange coincidence it was that the young man who had sheltered her with his umbrella should turn out to be the Earl of Blackwater.

'And you were determined to hate him,' Anne said gently.

'With good reason. All those years we've had to live like paupers without Papa and Freddie and look what has happened since he returned. Our lives have been turned upside down.'

'Only if you allow it to be so, Lydia. You would still have had to find a suitable husband sooner or later—'

'Yes, but would it have been Sir Arthur Thomas-Smith?'

'Him or someone like him. You cannot marry an imaginary man. A husband has to be flesh and blood.'

'Yes, but—'

'Lydia, dearest, I know how you feel, truly I do. You are upset and confused, torn between what you think you want and your duty.'

'Why is duty so hard?'

'It will become easier. You know, I was once in your position, when I was about your age. I thought I was in love with someone completely unsuitable.'

'Really?'

'Yes.' Anne smiled at her daughter's surprise. Why did children never think their parents were capable of deep emotion? 'He was an aristocrat, heir to a title and estates, and I was simply a doctor's daughter, not suitable material to make a countess. Neither parents would allow it. His parents contracted his marriage to a duke's daughter and mine arranged for me to marry your papa.'

'But you loved Papa!'

'I certainly grew to love him, but it was not so in the beginning. The match was considered a very advantageous one for me because, as you know, your father came from a titled family and, though he was unlikely to inherit himself, it did mean I had a certain standing. My father pointed out my duty to me and no doubt the young man I loved had his duty pointed out to him and so we parted.'

'Did you never see him again? The young man. Did he inherit?'

'Yes, he became an earl and married his countess and I married your papa.'

'He was the Earl of Blackwater, wasn't he?'

'Yes.'

'So the rumours are true.'

'No, Lydia, they are not. After we both married we did not meet for years until Papa was offered the living in Colston. He was so pleased to have it, how could I argue against accepting it?'

'He did not know the truth?'

'No, I could never have hurt him by telling him. He was a good and devout man, who was a loving husband and an indulgent father, as you well know.'

'But why did the Earl offer him the living? He must have known it would be difficult.'

'The living your father had was a poor one and we already had five children and I was expecting John. The future looked rather bleak. Colston was a richer parish. The Earl did it to help us. We were able to avoid each other, except for the normal intercourse of neighbours, and we did nothing wrong. Ever. And then Freddie was foolish enough to get into that duel and his lordship came here and we decided what had to be done. You know the rest.'

'But you went often to the Hall after that.'

'I went to keep the Countess company, I have already explained that. I felt sorry for her.'

'Did the Countess know about you and the Earl?'

'I don't know. I do not think so.'

'She didn't jump from the roof because of you?'

'No, she was deranged, Lydia, had been for years.'

'But you must have met the Earl at those times.'

'Not often and then we were simply polite to each other. Until the night he had the fall that led to his death, we never spoke of our love. It was nothing more than a memory, which faded with each passing year.' She paused. 'I have not been unhappy, Lydia. I loved your father and took pride and joy in my children. What I am trying to say, dearest, is that happiness comes from following the right path, even if you don't see that at the time.'

'Yes.' But she knew she would never come to love Sir Arthur and could not be convinced it was the right path for her. And her mother's revelation had confused her more than ever.

'You must not continue to bear a grudge against the Earl for what happened,' her mother went on. 'We have to live as neighbours whether we stay here or move to Sir Arthur's house.'

'Who do you think started those rumours?' Lydia asked. It was a question which had been taxing her brain ever since they started. 'Annabelle says it was Caroline Brotherton, but she could not have known anything unless she heard others talking. Who would even have guessed? You don't think it was Mistress Grey? She was in service at the Hall for years.'

'No, she would never say anything to hurt the Earl or the Countess, she loved them both. But there were other servants in the house who had served the family for many years, the old Earl's valet for one. He must have been privy to any number of secrets and Ralph dispensed with his services when he came home. He may have borne a grudge. But you know, it does no good to speculate. The important thing is to live our lives as we know we should and hold our heads up. You are betrothed and in two weeks you will be married and so busy with your new life, this will seem like a dream.'

Or a nightmare, Lydia told herself. Her duty had been clear to her long before her mother's revelation, and longing for another man, especially one who did not even exist, was a futile waste of time, a drain on emotions which were better used dealing with real people. Oh, she hoped and prayed her mama was right and it would become easier.

But she could have some adventure before she settled down to domesticity, she told herself. She could try to solve the riddle of the smugglers and the package and if there really was something nefarious going on, something more than bringing in a little contraband for local use, then she might be instrumental in bringing the criminals to justice. And it would serve the Earl of Blackwater right if she did it before he did. She had evidence; he did not. Oh, it would be great fun and certainly very satisfying to best him.

Had they brought in the contraband last night or had the master of the ship postponed coming in with it when his signal to the shore was not answered promptly? Had it been answered from some cove somewhere, which could not be seen from the land? But if it was all over, why had Robert Dent taken so much trouble to call on her and warn her off? He did not want her anywhere near the beach again tonight. Neither did the Earl of Blackwater and that was reason enough to go.

It was all very well to make plans in the safe atmosphere of the dower-house dining room, a very different matter to put those plans into effect, when it meant leaving a warm bed and venturing out into the night, especially when that night was as black as pitch, made all the more impenetrable by thick fog. When the time came, she almost changed her mind, but the thought that the contraband might be landed and dispersed under cover of that very fog and she would miss the going of it, kept her resolve.

At midnight, dressed in Freddie's clothes, she made her way down to the path beyond the wood, but once on the marshes, the mist was thicker than ever, eerily silent. She stood to get her bearings, wondering if she dared go on, remembering how she had stumbled into the water the previous night when visibility had been a great deal better. Would the boats even be able to find their way in?

She heard a sharp sound like a seagull calling and then another. It broke into the silence like a thunderclap and she realised that was how the men would get their bearings: sound carried for miles on such a night.

Feeling her way step by step, making sure each foot was on solid ground before she put her weight on it, she crept forward. And always ahead of her, she could hear the cry of the seagull, though she was sure it was no bird which made the sound. Someone was out there, on the beach, guiding the boat in. Her breathing was erratic and she was shivering although she was far from cold. Every now and again she stopped to listen, turning to peer behind her in case she was being followed.

And then she felt soft sand beneath her feet and knew she had safely negotiated the marshes and was on the beach. She stopped to catch her breath and decide what to do next. The gull had stopped calling. And then she heard the creaking of an oar, so close it startled her. A slight breeze coming off the sea lifted the mist a little, so she could just make out the dim shape of a rowing boat. There were men on the beach, wading out to pull it in and low voices. They had only to turn round and they would see her.

She made for one of the hollows in the dunes close by and threw herself face down. Her fear of the fog was nothing compared to the terror she felt now. What, in heaven's name, had made her think she could take on a band of smugglers single-handed? Did she imagine they would surrender the minute she challenged them?

Robert Dent had been right to warn her of the dangers and so had the Earl of Blackwater. Ralph Latimer. What wouldn't she give to have him here beside her now? The thought brought a wry smile to her lips as she remembered her refusal to allow him to help her. Slowly she lifted her head. The men were unloading boxes and casks onto the beach, their low voices carrying easily to her hiding place.

'What 'appened last night?' The voice had a slight accent which Lydia thought might have been French.

'We couldn't let you land, too many strangers on the shore.'

'Where's the cart?'

'Joe is bringing it up now. It ain't easy in the dark, you know, specially with this fog. Can't see a hand in front of your face on the marshes.'

'Where's Gaston?'

'He ain't here. Disappeared. Reckon the revenue men got 'im.'

'And the map and stones?'

There was no immediate answer and then an explosion of verbal abuse, which was all the more sinister for being in French in a hissed whisper.

The cart, pulled by one heavy horse and driven by a huge man bundled up in cape and hat, arrived while this was going on and the men began loading it. 'What about our money?' one of them asked.

'You shall have your money, just as soon as this lot's been delivered.' This was said by the man on the cart.

'That means I'll 'ave to stand off another night. Two nights are dangerous enough, but three is suicidal.'

'Can't be helped. You want paying, you come in again tomorrow night.'

Lydia, who hardly dared lift her head to look, heard the boat shoving off and the creak of oars and wondered how many men were still on the beach. Dare she risk a peep? Slowly she lifted her head. The cart was being driven inland. Besides, the driver, there were three other men walking beside it and would pass very close to where she lay. She pressed herself down into the sand and tried not to breathe. The cart wheels creaked as it was pulled over the sand closer and closer to where she lay. Whoever was driving it would need to know the track very well, she decided, a local who knew the marshes.

And then it was past her and rumbling up on to firmer ground. Thinking herself safe, she sat up, just as one of the men, walking beside the horse's head, turned to look back. She froze, but she was clearly outlined against the eastern sky, just beginning to lighten with a rose-hued dawn. He spoke to the man with the cart, evidently telling him to carry on, then made his way over to where she crouched.

She rose and started to run along the beach. He followed, chasing her among the dunes, though he did not shout. He did not need to, for he was gaining on her with every step; when she stumbled he threw himself on top of her. 'Got you, my hearty.'

He was a big man and his weight was pressing her face into the sand so that she could not breathe. Just when she thought she would choke to death, he sat up, pulling her up beside him. 'Now let's take a look at you.' He stopped and chuckled. 'It's a girl. I've caught me a girl. Who are you, girl?'

In the half-light of a new dawn, she stared at him with her mouth open and her eyes wide in surprise, then she grinned at him, a stupid, happy smile. 'Don't you know me?' she asked, looking up into his face. 'Don't you recognise your own sister, Freddie Fostyn?'

Chapter Eight

Freddie stood and stared at her. 'My God, Lydia. What are you doing here? And dressed like that.' He chuckled suddenly. 'Are they my breeches?'

'They are.' She was grinning all over her face. 'I came watching for smugglers. I never dreamed you would be one of them. Oh, Mama is going to be overjoyed to see you.'

'No, Lydia, she is not to know I am home.'

'Not to know? Freddie, how can you say that? She has lived for your homecoming for ten long years...'

'Then a day or two more will make no difference.'

'Don't you want to see her?'

'Of course, I do, but I have unfinished business to do before I can present myself to her. I need to have something to show for my absence—I cannot return with empty pockets.'

'She will not mind that at all, she will be overjoyed to know you are home safe and sound. Forget the free-traders.'

'I can't. I cannot explain it now, little sister, but later I will come home and there will be a reunion such as we have all dreamed of.'

'Where have you been all these years? Oh, there is so much to tell you.' She paused. 'I suppose you must know much of it, for Robert Dent will have told you.'

'Robert? What has he to do with it?'

'Is he not one of the smugglers?'

'If he is, I have not come across him. But then, how could I? I have only just landed. Now I must go, or the others will stop and come back for me. I don't want them to see you. Wait until we have all gone and then go home. And remember, not a word to anyone. Especially to Ralph Latimer.'

'Why would I tell him anything? I hate him for what he did to Papa and you, I always have. Besides, he knows.'

'Knows? Knows what?'

'About the smuggling. He discovered the hideout in the woods and is determined to catch you.'

'The devil he is!'

'Oh, he's that, no doubt of it,' she said. 'I came to warn you. At least, not you particularly, because I did not know you were one of them, but if they were village men, I did not want them to be arrested.'

'Is this the truth?'

'Of course it is. Why should I lie?' But it *was* a lie, because she had had no thought of warning them when she set out. But if it meant Lord Blackwater was frustrated, then no one would be more pleased than she was.

'Then all the more reason to go home. Leave us to deal with him.'

'What will you do?'

'I don't know. It depends what he does. Now, off you go.'

'But, Freddie, where will you be?' Having been re-united with him, she did not want to part from him again.

It was like a miracle, but there were ominous undertones to what he said, which frightened her.

'It doesn't matter. I'll find a way to send word.'

He looked about him, scrambled out of the hollow and darted across the sand. In two minutes he was out of sight. For a moment she sat hugging herself, thinking of the joy there would be in the house when her brother came home. It was wonderful, glorious, the happiest day of her life. Or it would have been if he had not been so mysterious. In a dream, she picked up her hat and began plodding home, so filled with the strange reunion with her brother, she forgot to be vigilant.

A hand grabbed her arm and spun her round and another hand was raised to strike her. She cried out in terror. The raised fist dropped to her assailant's side, though he maintained his hold on her arm. 'Oh, it is you again,' he said. 'I might have known.'

'Ralph Latimer!' The family name, without even the courtesy of a title, was out before she could stop it. But she would not apologise, she would not.

He noted it but did not comment. 'As you see.'

She tried to tug her arm free. 'You are hurting me.'

'I will hurt you a deal more if you do not stop wriggling like an eel.'

'Then release me.'

'No, you are going to come with me and we are going to get to the bottom of this once and for all.'

She struggled every inch of the way. The longer he spent trying to subdue her, she decided, the longer Freddie and his accomplices would have to escape. Now it was not simple curiosity and a notion to best the Earl of Blackwater which motivated her, it had become more important than that. Her brother's freedom, perhaps even his life, was at stake; she was not going to allow *that man* to ruin it a second time.

Still struggling, she was half-dragged, half-carried back to the Hall. He pushed her ahead of him through a side door left unlocked for his return and through a series of corridors to the main hall and into the book-lined library, where he threw her into an armchair and perched himself on the edge of his desk near enough to make a grab for her if she tried to leave.

Silently she struggled to sit up and restore some of her dignity. But how could you be dignified when you are dressed as a young man in coat and breeches, both of which are covered in dirt and sand, and your hair has come untied and is all over your face, and you are shivering with cold and shock?

He smiled slowly; she was in a pickle, there was no mistake about that but, in some way, it served to make her even more attractive. He admired her courage, for how many genteel young ladies would dare to venture forth at dead of night and join a band of smugglers? He had told himself he would not allow her to creep under his guard and throw him off his stride, that he would interrogate her as he would any other lawbreaker, but how could he when it was all he could do to stop himself taking her in his arms and telling her he would make everything right again. His heart had turned traitor to his head.

He turned and poured a glass of brandy from the decanter on the desk beside him and, leaning forward, handed it to her. 'Here, drink this, it will warm you.' Then added, with an ironic smile, 'It is duty paid.'

She hesitated before accepting it, but she needed something to warm her or he would take her shaking for fear. The fiery liquid caught in her throat and made her choke before it spread its glow into her stomach, but it did little to make her feel better. Where had Freddie gone? What was he doing? When would he come home? How could she go back home and spend tomorrow as if nothing had happened, when she was bursting with the news that Freddie was back?

He watched her sipping the drink, trying to fathom what was going on in her head, then he took the empty glass from her and set it down on the desk beside him. 'Now, Miss Fostyn, I will have the truth, if you please.'

'The truth, my lord, is that I like to roam about the shoreline at night,' she said defiantly. 'There is no law against it, is there?'

'No law of the land against it, but it is against every law of respectability and good sense.'

'And of course, you are an authority on those.'

'No, or I would not be sitting here with you now, but I am sure Sir Arthur is.'

'What has he to do with it?'

'You hope to marry him, do you not?' He smiled sardonically. 'I imagine he might have something to say on the matter, if he were to know of this escapade. And others.'

'And no doubt you will ensure he does know.'

'Not at all. I have no wish for your reputation to be ruined by gossip, but it seems to me you are making a good hand at doing that without anyone's help. If you wish your wedding to go ahead as planned, don't you think you would be wiser to stay at home at night?'

'And you, of course, have an interest in seeing that the nuptials take place, for the sooner I am wed, the sooner I shall be gone from here and no longer able to frustrate you.'

He smiled and inclined his head; she certainly frustrated him. 'As you say. But that is not my only interest in your moonlight walks. I take exception to smugglers trespassing on my land and using my property to hide their contraband. I told you so before.'

'What has that to do with me?'

'Oh, I think you know.'

'I do not. In any case, they are doing no harm. They are simply poor men who have wives and families to provide for and, with taxes so high, who can blame them for bringing in a few goods and avoiding the duty?'

'So you do know who they are?'

'I do not.'

'Then how do you know they are poor villagers?'

'Who else would they be?'

'They could have come from anywhere, men of bad character, evil men leading the Colston men astray. Some are undoubtedly French. And they are doing more than bringing in contraband...'

'Spies, you mean?' she queried, remembering the man who spoke French. 'But the war is over.'

'There is trouble in America and nothing would please the French more than we should lose the colony. And India too. And the Jacobite threat is not entirely eradicated; the Young Pretender might even now be planning to come again. People who conspire with such men are traitors.'

'Oh, no!' She was genuinely dismayed. If the man who faced her now had been anyone but who he was and if her brother had not been implicated, she might have been tempted to tell him about the package she had found, to take the weight of it from her shoulders. She was frightened and exhausted and if she did not go home soon, she would be missed and then what could she say to her mother?

She stood up and faced him defiantly, but even standing, the top of her head only reached his chin. 'You have been away from home too long if you think any of the good people of Colston would turn traitor,' she said.

'Maybe I have,' he said softly. 'But whose fault was that?'

'Not mine and certainly not my brother's. You ought never to have challenged him. You knew Freddie very well, you knew he was impulsive and headstrong…'

He smiled. 'I do believe that is a family trait. Impulsive and headstrong describes you exactly.'

'We were not talking about me—'

'No, but I would much rather talk about you than that wayward brother of yours.'

'Wayward,' she repeated sharply. 'How do you know he is wayward?'

'Oh, we are quick to defend him!'

'Why would I not be? He is my brother.'

'Whom you have not seen for ten years, so I have been given to believe.'

Had he seen Freddie? Did he know he was home? Was he implying he knew what Freddie had been doing since he had been away? Spying? Never! She would not believe that. 'Ten years,' she repeated. 'Ten years since your father sent him away and for what? He had done nothing wrong, it was you who broke the law, not him. I did not understand why he had to go. I was only a little girl—'

'And look at you now. A lovely woman.' He took her shoulders in his hands and held her at arm's length to appraise her. She was afraid; it showed in her eyes, in the tense way she held her body. Did she think he would kiss her again? Or did she have something to hide? 'Oh, Lydia, there is nothing to be afraid of. Simply tell me who these men are and I will take you home. You will be quite safe.'

'Safe?' She attempted a laugh of scorn, but it turned

into one of hysteria. The events of the last two nights, coupled with lack of sleep and everything else that had happened, had been too much for her. Freddie was home and yet he was not home. And this man, this hated man, was doing it again, snuffing out her anger with soft words. 'Why should I not be safe? No one in Colston would harm me.'

'No? Why do you think I brought you here if not to protect you?'

'Protect me! Interrogate me would be more accurate, I think. Now, if you have finished quizzing me, I will take my leave.' She tried to shrug his hands from her shoulders but his grip tightened. 'My lord, let me go. I have nothing to say to you.'

In spite of the harsh words they were saying to each other, their determination to maintain the enmity they had nurtured over the years, there was something stronger even than that drawing them to each other, and when she lifted her eyes to his she saw he knew it too.

If he had remained the same man she had met in Chelmsford, the man who had lent her his umbrella; if the episode in the wood had not taken place; if he had not accused her of being hand in glove with the smugglers, she might even have said she was falling in love with him. But how could she love the man who had killed her father and turned her brother into a violent and embittered man?

'Lydia, we are not, and never should be, enemies,' he said.

'Oh, and what else should we be?' She was trying hard to maintain her belligerence but she was so tired, so very, very tired. Her legs felt almost boneless and her head as heavy as lead. If he had not been holding her upright, she would have sunk to the floor in a heap at his feet.

'Friends,' he whispered. 'At least, let us be friends.'

'We cannot.'

'Why not?'

She did not answer. He smiled and put one finger beneath her chin and raised her face so that she was forced to look into his eyes. 'Why not, Lydia? Can you not put the past behind you and accept that I have lived with remorse for ten long years and need to hear that you have forgiven me?'

'Never!'

'But even unforgiving, you cannot look me in the eye and say there is nothing between us, a thread that joins us whatever we do, however we might like to free ourselves of it. We are shackled by the past. Do you not feel it?'

'No, you are being fanciful.' But why had he mentioned a thread when that was how she had thought of them when they first met, when he was her umbrella man? Sometimes she could almost imagine he was that man, gentle, humorous, kind.

'I do not think so. I shall prove it, shall I?' And he took her face in his hands, bent his head and kissed her.

The effect it had was almost the same as when he had kissed her in the wood, but not quite. Before he had wanted to dominate and was harsh and cruel and she had, even when her traitorous body had been responding, wanted it to stop. She had been outraged. Now his lips were soft and yet gently insistent, setting up a quivering sensation in her belly which trickled like water into her thighs. She tried to hold back, but her efforts were futile. Her mouth opened of its own accord and his tongue, gently probing, sent her into delicious transports of desire, so that she clung to him, wanting him to hold her forever. Safe. In his arms she felt safe.

'You see,' he said, drawing back at last but still cupping her face in his hands. 'You cannot deny the undeniable.' He was looking into her eyes, seeing her inner thoughts, her longing, her need of him, and she was ashamed. Hate him, she had commanded herself, hate him and whatever you do don't fall in love. But she had. Hate and love, two sides of the same coin and she had been fool enough to flip it over. Well, she must flip it back again, because otherwise she would never survive.

She wanted to hurt him, wanted to take away the hurt he was inflicting on her. Wresting herself away from him, she grabbed a vase from the mantelshelf and threw it at him with all her strength. He ducked and it shattered against the desk, scattering shards all over the carpet.

'That was worth a small fortune,' he said mildly.

'Good! And I hope this is too.' She picked up a small figurine and hurled it after the vase. Her aim was better this time and it caught him on the forehead, making it bleed. Horrified by what she had done, her hands fell uselessly to her sides and she stared at the blood trickling down his face. But even then she could not bring herself to admit she had been wrong, horribly wrong. 'I hate you!' But by now she was sobbing, her anger completely dissipated.

He was beside her in a single stride and she was in his arms, sobbing against his chest. 'My poor Lydia,' he said gently. 'I should never have put you through that.'

'No, you should not,' she retorted, regaining some of her spirit and pulling away from him, refusing to look up at him for fear he should see the bleakness in her eyes. 'I am engaged to marry Sir Arthur Thomas-Smith, or had you forgot? We are not, and can never be, friends.'

'No, you are right,' he said, realising the truth of that. He wanted her for his wife, nothing less would do and that could not be. Friendship alone would put an impossible strain on them both. 'I can only offer my sincere apologies and beg forgiveness.'

Apologies could not undo what had been done, could not turn back the clock to a time when she did not know how much she loved him, could make no difference to the fact that she was engaged to be married to someone else and there was no way out of that which would not bring calumny down on herself, her mother and sisters. And there was Freddie, skulking about on the marshes, so near and yet still a stranger, for now he was big and muscular and his voice was harsh and unyielding. The stripling had become a man. To love the Earl was to betray Freddie.

'I accept your apologies, my lord,' she said stiffly. 'And now, with your permission, I shall go home.'

'Let me escort you. There may be danger lurking out there still.'

She forced herself to laugh. 'I do not think so, my lord. After all, I have only to walk down the drive and along the lane. I shall be home in no time.' It seemed incongruous to curtsy when she was in male attire, so she picked up her hat and swept it across her in an exaggerated bow. 'Goodnight, my lord.'

And then she was gone from the room, leaving him wiping the blood from his forehead with his handkerchief and looking at the broken china with a rueful smile on his face.

She was passing through the gate on to the lane when a shadow crept out of the hedge and stood in front of her. Her heart was already pounding from her confrontation with Ralph and the sudden apparition nearly stopped it altogether.

'Lydia, it's only me,' Freddie said.

She relaxed and began to breathe a little more normally. 'Oh, Freddie, you startled me. Have you changed your mind about coming home?'

'No, I have not. What were you doing at the Hall? Why didn't you go home, like I told you to?'

'I was on my way there. His lordship saw me and—'

'You mean Ralph Latimer?'

'Yes, who else? He is the Earl now.'

'Lucky for him. What was he doing out so late? Does he like midnight walks too? Or did you meet him by design?' He sounded angry and bitter, but then she supposed he had every right to be. Until tonight, she would have felt exactly the same. Now she did not know what she felt and her brother's presence was confusing her more than ever.

'No, of course not. Freddie, how can you say such a thing? I have no doubt he was doing the same as I was, looking out for smugglers.'

'What did you tell him?'

'Nothing.'

'Then why go home with him? What did he do to you? If he touched a hair of your head—'

'Freddie, he did nothing,' she lied. If he knew the truth, there was no telling what he would do. 'I agreed to go with him to give you time to get away. If I had known you wouldn't even try to escape, I would not have bothered.'

'I had to make sure of you. I can't have you betraying me.'

'Freddie, I haven't, I promise you.'

'Nor must you. You must not tell anyone you have seen me.'

'Let me tell Mama?'

'No, not yet. Not until I say you may.'

'Why not, Freddie? What are you up to? It's more than just smuggling, isn't it?'

'No, of course not,' he said. But, remembering what Ralph had said about spies, she did not believe him. 'But I am going to have my revenge on Ralph Latimer at last. Ten years I have waited, ten years…'

She was alarmed. He was not the gentle brother she remembered, the boy she had grown up with, who often shared his games with her, found mischief with her; he was a rough, hardened man. She supposed ten years of exile had made him like that. 'Freddie, what are you going to do to him?'

'I can't tell you, not yet. But I may need your help.'

'My help? To do what? Oh, Freddie, I do think you should stop and consider—'

'I have had long enough to consider. He must pay for what he did. Now, I must go.'

They had been walking along the lane as they talked and had almost reached the gate of the dower house. She stopped and put her hand on the latch. 'Freddie, come in and speak to Mama, please.'

'There?' he queried incredulously. 'You live there?'

'Yes. We could hardly stay in the rectory, could we? The old Earl let us live here.' She watched his face contort with anger and put a hand on his sleeve. 'We have so much to tell each other, Freddie, ten years of news. Can't you come in, even if you cannot stay?'

'No,' he said harshly. 'I'll send a message when I want to meet you again. And, Lydia, not a word, or things could turn very nasty, very nasty indeed.' And with that he strode off down the road and did not look back.

She watched him out of sight, trying to still her beating heart, to make sense of the events of the night, to come to terms with the fact that Freddie was no longer the brother she had loved and that Ralph Latimer was no longer the man she had hated. How could she go back indoors and not say a word to anyone? Her mother would guess there was something wrong, she was sure of it. What could she say? And what did Freddie want her to do?

It was almost daylight and she was still in her brother's clothes and if her mother saw her like that, there would be questions and answers and more lies. She had been taught never to lie and, until recently, she had never felt she had to. She hurried up the path and slipped in the house by kitchen door. Janet was already up, raking out the fire, ready to begin another day.

Lydia was hoping to creep past her, but the maid heard her carefully shutting the door behind her and whipped round, a gasp of astonishment on her face. 'Oh, Miss Lydia, you startled me. And whatever are you dressed like that for?'

Lydia put her fingers to her lips. 'Ssh, you'll wake Mama. She must not know I have been out.'

The servant looked her up and down. It was not her place to question her mistress's daughter, but she was obviously eaten up with curiosity and Lydia knew she would have to think of some explanation. 'I've been out for a walk on the beach to see the sunrise over the sea. It was a beautiful sight, all pink and gold, reflected in the water, all the way from the horizon to the beach.'

'Dressed like that?'

'It seemed appropriate. No one would think anything of seeing a boy on the shore, but they might wonder about a girl, don't you think? Besides, it is much easier to walk in breeches.'

Janet giggled. 'Do you know, you look ever so much

like Master Freddie like that. I almost thought it was him
coming through the door. Gave me quite a turn, it did.'

Lydia caught her breath, then said sharply, 'Well, that's
unlikely to happen, isn't it? He's hundreds, perhaps
thousands, of miles away.'

'That's not to say he mightn't come home one day, is
it?'

Lydia sighed. The next few days were going to be very,
very difficult. 'Perhaps he will, one day.'

'You won't be here, will you? You will be Lady
Thomas-Smith and mistress of Sir Arthur's household.'

Lydia had managed for the last few hours to forget all
about that gentleman and she wished Janet had not mentioned him. He was just one more thing to worry about.
'Yes, but I will not be very far away.'

'Miss Lydia, may I ask you something?'

'Yes, but I won't guarantee an answer.'

'When you are married, you will be going to live with
Sir Arthur, won't you?'

'Naturally, I will.' What else could she do?

'And your mother and Miss Annabelle and Master
John, they are all going too?'

'I am not sure. The Earl has said Mama may stay here
if she wishes. Nothing is decided.'

It had been uncertain before, but now, with Freddie
back, everything was in the melting pot again. Except her
marriage. She was a woman, tied to someone she could
not love, could not even *like* and there was no escape. A
man could escape, a man could simply walk away from
an unpleasant situation, just as her brother and Ralph Latimer had done, and everyone would think him no end of
a fine fellow. 'Are you worrying about your position?'

'To tell the truth, yes, I am. I've been with your mama
since I was a little 'un, you know that. I've seen you

through no end of scrapes what your mama don' know about and I'll see you through this one. It's jes' that I ain't ever worked anywhere else and I'm afeared of what will happen to me.'

'There is no need to be, Janet. Mama will still need a maid wherever she lives. And if she lives with me, I am sure Sir Arthur will allow you to stay with her.'

'Oh, you don't know how relieved I am, Miss Lydia. I thought the gentleman being so rich and havin' that grand house, wouldn't want someone like me.'

Lydia smiled at the maid's little attempt at blackmail. 'Janet, you are indispensable and there is no question of you being turned off. My goodness, do you think Mama and I could be so ungrateful after all the years you have worked for us? Now think no more about it and help me get out of these clothes and dress for breakfast.'

Lydia crept through the hall and up to her room, followed by the maid, who helped her out of her brother's clothes and took them back to his room while she washed and dressed. She was exhausted, not only from lack of sleep but spent emotion and shock and the need to deceive so many people. Oh, how she wished she had never thought about catching the smugglers! But if she had not, Freddie might even now be in prison, put there by Ralph Latimer.

Janet brought her a pot of coffee and that served to revive her a little and more rouge brought some colour to her cheeks, but it was all in vain. Nothing could disguise her pallor, nor her listlessness, and her mother was quick to notice it when Lydia joined her at the breakfast table. 'Lydia, you look dreadful. Are you ill?'

'No, Mama, I am tired, that is all.'

'Did you not sleep?'

'No, I couldn't. There is so much to think about. I don't

know how we can be ready for the wedding in two weeks.'

Anne looked at her daughter, knowing there was something more than tiredness troubling her, and wished, with all her heart, she had not promoted this marriage. 'You are right,' she said. 'I think we should ask Sir Arthur if we cannot postpone it for a week or two.'

Lydia brightened perceptibly. 'Do you think he would?'

'I will ask him. If he agrees, I think it would be a good idea if you went to stay with Susan in London for a week or two. You can take Annabelle with you. It will separate her from Peregrine Baverstock for a little while and maybe that will cool his ardour.'

'But what will you say to Sir Arthur? He was so anxious that the wedding should be soon and we have already put him off one date.'

'I'll explain that you need to buy your wedding gown in town because there is nothing suitable to be had in Chelmsford.'

Lydia longed to go, to escape from everything that was oppressing her, but she was worried about her brother. He had said he might need her. He wanted her to help him wreak revenge on Ralph Latimer. Only a week before she would have been pleased to do so, but now she could not. Would he go ahead without her? Could she do anything to stop him? 'But we've already ordered my gown, Mama.'

'Oh, it will be easy to say it is not fine enough. Sir Arthur is so anxious that you should have the very best as befits his wealth and standing, he will agree, I am sure. I will speak to him this morning and then I will write to Susan. We should have a reply by the end of the week. Now, I think you should go back to bed. Janet will bring you something to help you sleep and by this evening, you will be feeling more like yourself.'

Lydia was too exhausted to argue any more. Besides, Freddie had spoken of coming home in a day or two, which meant whatever he was planning would be done by the end of the week before she and Annabelle set off for London. And going to London meant she could have another two weeks of freedom before she was irrevocably tied to Sir Arthur Thomas-Smith.

The draught Janet gave her was a strong one. She slept the whole day and the next night too, waking refreshed the following morning, determined to enjoy her sojourn in the capital when she learned that her mother had managed to persuade Sir Arthur to postpone the wedding until June, though he had been a little reluctant. 'I told him that some of our more illustrious guests cannot come on the date we arranged, due to the short notice,' Mrs Fostyn said, with a smile. 'I think that was what decided him. He wants this wedding to be the social occasion of the year.'

Lydia heaved a sigh of relief, even though it was only a postponement. She began to plan her trip and she and Annabelle went into Chelmsford to buy new clothes for their stay in London.

Annabelle was a little subdued, but Lydia was still too absorbed with her own problems to worry about her sister. Her earlier optimism faded as the day wore on and she began to worry about Freddie. The man who had brought him in on the boat had definitely been French and he had also been expecting a package to be delivered to him. If he found out where it was, would he think Freddie had stolen it and given it to her? Should she tell Freddie about it? But how could she? She had no idea where he was.

And there was the Earl, wandering about the estate

looking for smugglers. He did not know that one of them was Freddie bound on revenge for what had happened ten years before. Was he in danger? Was he in more peril than her brother? Oh, she prayed she would never have to choose between them. She loved them both. In the midst of all this deception, it was time to be honest with herself.

'Shall we call on Caroline Brotherton while we are in town?' Annabelle broke into her thoughts as they made their way back to the carriage, laden with parcels. 'I must tell her of our trip to London. She is going herself, you know. We might arrange to call on her, or she and her mama might call on us while we are there. Susan would not mind, I know.'

'Very well, but we must not stay long. Mama is expecting us home for dinner.'

Lydia was a little disconcerted to discover that Lady Brotherton was having an At Home and half of the county society was there, including Peregrine Baverstock. As soon as they had greeted their hostess, he made his way over to them. Without his parents watching over him, he seemed more confident. He bowed to them both and began talking about the Earl's ball and how grand it had been and how charming Annabelle had looked and how he was going to London the very next morning. Annabelle smiled and smiled, completely besotted by him, and Lydia, looking from one to the other, felt a frisson of unease.

She wondered if she ought to say something to her mother, who had suggested the trip to London to separate them, but it went completely from her head when she arrived home.

'There's a letter for you, Miss Lydia,' Janet said, pulling it from her apron pocket. 'A boy brought it.'

'A boy?'

'Yes, I think he's one of the boys from the village who helps Sir Arthur's gardener. Cheeky little devil, he is too.'

'Oh, Sir Arthur,' she said, wondering why he should choose that unusual mode of communication, but the boy was perhaps coming home and it must have seemed a quick and convenient way to have a letter delivered. She took it and went upstairs to change out of her outdoor clothes, breaking the seal as she did so.

'Meet me at the cottage in the woods as soon as it gets dark tonight. I will wait one hour. And do not forget your promise of secrecy.' It was signed with a flourishing letter *F*, no more.

She sat down on her bed with the missive in her hand. How audacious of Freddie to use one of Sir Arthur's employees to deliver it! But how did he know she was connected with Sir Arthur? Or was it coincidence? Was the boy one of the smugglers? It was very likely, she told herself, wondering how she was going to keep the appointment without telling her mother where she was going.

Being May, it did not grow dark until quite late and, by that time, John was already in bed and Anne, who had been sewing, was herself feeling tired. 'I think helping to arrange that ball must have fatigued me more than I thought,' she said, putting up her hand to stifle a yawn. 'And what with everything else…'

Lydia looked up from the book she had been pretending to read and smiled. 'Go to bed, Mama,' she said. 'I will make sure everything is locked up.'

'I think I will.' She stood up and kissed both her daughters. 'Do not stay up too late, Annabelle.'

Unusually for her, Annabelle decided she would retire too and left Lydia alone. She waited several minutes until she could no longer hear her mother or her sister moving about and Janet had gone up to her own bedroom on the top floor, then she hurried up to Freddie's room and dragged his clothes out once again.

In less than a quarter of an hour, she was hurrying up the lane towards Colston wood, her brother's hat crammed on her curls. She kept a sharp look about her as she plunged into the wood, half expecting to see the tall bulk of the Earl of Blackwater blocking her path. Everywhere was silent except for a slight breeze moving the leaves and the snuffling sounds which could have been rabbits or badgers or game birds.

Just when she thought she must have missed it, she saw a glimmer of light in a window and made out the dark outline of the hovel against the night sky. She set out across the open space, making herself walk firmly, unwilling to let whoever was in the cottage know she was afraid. The door opened and her brother stood outlined against the light behind him.

Until that moment she had wondered if she really had seen him two nights before, that perhaps her dreams had spilled over into her waking hours and it had been wishful thinking. But here he was, as large as life and smiling at her in the wry way he had. She ran and threw herself into his arms. 'Oh, Freddie, it is so good to see you again. I really couldn't believe you weren't a ghost.'

'There is nothing ghost-like about me, Lydia,' he said, hugging her, before drawing her into the room where a single candle glimmered on the table. 'Let me look at you.' He took her hands in his and held them out, arms outstretched. 'My goodness, how you have grown! And in all the right places. My sister has become a beauty.'

'Oh, Freddie, where have you been all these years? One letter when you first left home saying you had enlisted and then nothing. Mama has been so unhappy. We all have. Why did you not write?'

He let her go and turned away, as if the hurt was still too raw and he did not want her to see it. 'I had been sent away, Lydia, sent away like a common criminal. Even Mama had turned her back on me. She did not even argue with the Earl when he said I must go.'

'I think she thought it would be better than having you arrested for duelling.'

'But the duel never took place and I would rather have had the opportunity to plead that in a court of law, than what did happen.'

'Why, what did happen?'

'I cannot tell you the half of it. Having no money for a commission, I enlisted as a common soldier. The life of such a one is harsh in the extreme. Not enough to eat and most of it unpalatable, hard work such as you would never believe and at the end of it, the possibility of being killed. I was sent to Canada. Life on board the troopship was even worse. And when we arrived, not only were we expected to fight the French but also the murderous Indians, who used our scalps as battle trophies.'

'Oh, Freddie,' she said, reaching out to take his hand. 'But you are home now and no longer a soldier.' She paused. 'You are not still a soldier, are you?'

He smiled lopsidedly. 'Are you asking me if I deserted?'

'No, because I do not care. Except that someone might come after you.'

'They won't because I was Trooper Frederick Brown and Trooper Brown was captured by the French and never heard of again, presumably dead at their hands.'

'You escaped?'

'That is one way of putting it. Let us say, they were persuaded to let me go.'

'By whom?'

'It does not matter. I had to agree to do something for them in return.'

'Spy? Oh, Freddie, did you agree to that?'

'No, of course not.' He paused. 'A certain person wanted to bring contraband into this country and smuggling is something almost everyone does, and it seemed a good way to get home. And coming home is what I wanted most.'

'Oh, and I am so glad you are here. But why all the mystery? Now that you have landed the goods, what is to stop you coming home?'

'It is not as simple as that. I have not yet been paid for my services and there is the little matter of Ralph Latimer...'

'Can you not forget him? He cannot harm you now.'

'He owes me. He owes me ten years of my life.'

'It is impossible to repay that, Freddie.'

'No, but I need to see him squirm, I need him to feel my anger. He has inherited his father's title and his wealth—'

'Wealth, Freddie? The old Earl died impoverished. Any wealth there is Ralph brought back with him from India.'

'India. Is that where he's been?'

'I believe so.'

'And while he has been growing rich, you and Mama and the others have suffered too, is that not so? Humiliated, having to accept the Earl's charity...'

'Yes,' she said, wishing she could say it had not been so. She did not want to encourage his anger and resentment, though she could understand it. She had felt it too, but now.... Oh, everything was different now; his return

had made her so happy she felt benevolent towards everyone, including the Earl. 'But it has not been all bad and
if it had not been for not knowing where you were, we
would have been perfectly content.'

'Now I am home and in a day or two I will take my
place as head of the family and you will be able to hold
up your heads again.'

'We were always able to hold up our heads, Freddie,'
she said quietly.

'And I must be able to hold mine up too and that means
coming home wealthy and not belittled by that man at
Colston Hall.'

She smiled a little, remembering that until recently that
was exactly how she referred to him. And her mother had
remonstrated with her. 'He is not at all bad, Freddie. And
we have to live as neighbours. At least until…'

'Until?' he prompted.

'Until I marry. Freddie, you are home just in time to
attend the ceremony.'

'Who is he?'

'You would not know him, he has only lately moved
into the district. He is a widower, but he is very wealthy.
His name is Sir Arthur Thomas-Smith.'

She heard his quick intake of breath before he said,
'When did you become contracted to this man?'

'Less than a month ago. We thought we would have to
move from the dower house when Lord Latimer became
the new Earl but…'

'Is this marriage to be put to the account of the Squire
of Colston too?'

'No, Freddie, not really,' she said, alerted by the anger
in his voice. She did not want to give him any more reason to have his revenge. 'It is an advantageous marriage
and Sir Arthur is very generous.'

'So he should be,' he said enigmatically.

'What do you mean?'

'You are a prize above diamonds. I shall make sure he knows that. As for Ralph Latimer, I have something else in store for him.' He paused and seized her upper arms until she winced. 'I want you to persuade him to come here, tell him you have seen the smugglers, anything, but get him here. I shall be waiting for him.'

'What are you going to do?'

'It is not for you to know. The last time I let you in on a secret, you told Papa.'

'I could not help it, he caught me going out of the house after you.'

'But I sent you back to bed. Lydia, why, oh why, did you not do as you were bid?'

'I had to stop you. I knew you were going to fight a duel and I was afraid one of you would be killed. When Papa caught me and refused to let me go, I had to tell him. Someone had to stop you.'

The candlelight, playing on his face, caught his expression of chagrin and hurt and faint humour. 'He did that and no mistake and paid dearly for it. We all did.'

'But it was an accident, Freddie, you must see that.'

'Then we will stage another little accident.'

'No, Freddie, no! You must not. You really must not. If anything happens to the Earl, you will never be able to come home. You will be lost to us again. Please, please, I beg you…'

'Lydia, while he is here, while he is Squire of Colston, I cannot come home, don't you see that? The place is not big enough for both of us.'

'Then go and live somewhere else,' she snapped. Then regretting it, she added, 'You could live somewhere close at hand where we may visit you from time to time…'

'And have him laughing at me all over again.'

'I am sure he is not laughing at you. Talk to him, let him explain. Try to understand each other.'

He smiled slowly and cupped one of her hands in both his own, stroking it with his thumb before raising it to his lips. 'Dear Lydia, always the peacemaker. I remember when we were children and Ralph and I quarrelled, you always came between us and made us be friends again.'

'Then let me do it once more.'

He sighed. 'Why are you defending him?'

She could not tell him, she could not bring herself to say it aloud, but in her heart the reason was plain enough: because she loved him and he was entirely without malice himself. All these years she thought she hated Ralph Latimer when there was nothing about him to dislike. He was, she had discovered, a good man. 'It is not a question of defending him, Freddie, it is a question of preventing more heartache for all of us.'

'Tell him to meet me here, then. Tomorrow night.'

'I doubt he will come.'

'He will if you tell him he'll catch the smugglers. Now, you must go home.' He smiled and touched her cheek with the back of his forefinger. 'And, Lydia, go straight there and do not come anywhere near the wood in the next two days.'

She left him and walked home in a dream. Freddie was home, but such a different Freddie. Had she expected him not to have changed? Had she expected to see the same boyish grin, the slim figure, the blond tousled hair? How foolish of her!

But could she do as he asked? Could she lure Ralph to a rendezvous, the outcome of which was so uncertain? She did not want him hurt, or even humiliated. She loved him. She loved her brother too. If they met and fought, it would be almost like history repeating itself, but this time her brother had accomplices and the advantage of surprise. Oh, she could not let it happen, she could not.

Chapter Nine

Lydia woke next morning, knowing she could not do as her brother asked and lure Ralph to a rendezvous which might lead to his death. She could not believe Freddie wanted to do anything more than humiliate him, perhaps give him a bloody nose, but the other men might not be so merciful. If she did nothing, Freddie might be angry with her, but he would calm down in the end. But how could she be sure that Ralph would not wander abroad or try to lie in wait for the smugglers, as he had done on other occasions?

She ought to find some way of occupying him so that he could not go out. But what? She could not tell him the truth without involving her brother, and trying to divert him with conversation about anything else would not serve. Everything they had to say to each other had been said the night before and there was nothing left to say which would not increase the hurt in her heart. She could perhaps arrange an impromptu social occasion to which he could be invited, but who was to say he would come? Or anyone else at a moment's notice? Supposing she sent him on a wild goose chase somewhere else? Into Burnham, perhaps, or Chelmsford? But what?

She ought to tell her mother, but she had promised Freddie she would not. She could go to Burnham and alert the revenue officer but that meant that all the smugglers would be rounded up, including her brother. Robert Dent. His name came to her in a flash of inspiration. He had been a friend of both men, was still friendly with Ralph, and though he might be implicated with the smugglers, he was not a violent man. She scrambled from her bed, drank the chocolate Janet had brought her, washed and dressed in her pink muslin and hurried downstairs. Her mother was in the kitchen talking to Cook and Janet about the day's menus.

'Mama, I forgot to buy some yellow ribbon when I was in Chelmsford yesterday. May I ask Partridge to take me back this morning?'

'You can buy ribbon in London, dear, and there will be far more to choose from.'

'Yes, but I want this for my travelling gown and hat. I will not be gone long.'

'Oh, very well.'

When Lydia came in from asking Partridge to harness the horse, she found Annabelle in the hall putting on her blue cloak and bonnet. 'I'm coming with you.'

'Why? I am only going to buy ribbon. It will be very dull for you.'

'And duller still here.'

'Does Mama not want you to help her?'

'No. I have asked her. Lydia, I begin to think you do not want me with you.'

'Nonsense. I was only thinking of you.'

'Then I shall come.' She picked up a bulging carpet bag from the floor at her feet. 'I want to show Caroline the lilac gown we bought yesterday.'

'You could have done that yesterday when we called.'

'I know. I forgot.'

Lydia was too concerned with her own problems to
think this strange and the sisters set out, with Annabelle
chatting happily beside a rather subdued Lydia. How
could she leave Annabelle in order to find Mr Dent without arousing suspicion?

'I think it would save time if you were to call on Caroline while I search for my ribbon,' Lydia said, as they
entered the town. 'Partridge can set us down at the Spread
Eagle and he can enjoy a drink with his brother while we
are gone.' Partridge's brother kept the hostelry in question
and the horse could be looked after there too.

'Oh, that is a splendid idea,' Annabelle said a shade
too enthusiastically.

The orders were given to their old coachman; as soon
as they stopped at the inn, Lydia left her sister and hurried
in the direction of the centre of the town where most of
the shops could be found. Once out of sight of her sister,
she turned sharply left and then right and a few minutes
later arrived outside Robert Dent's house, which stood in
a row facing a small park.

She had not thought what she would do when she arrived, but now she paused, undecided. It was hardly fitting
for an unaccompanied young lady to call on a bachelor,
so how was she going to speak to him? Nor could she
stand outside until he appeared, she did not have the time
and someone she knew might see her.

And then, by a great stroke of luck, she saw him striding towards her, evidently on his way home. 'Mr Dent,
good morning,' she said with a smile, as he reached her.

'Miss Fostyn.' He lifted his tall buckled hat and smiled.
'This is an unexpected pleasure. What brings you here?'

'I am shopping for ribbon.' She paused. 'And hoping
for some conversation with you.'

'With me?' he queried. 'Miss Fostyn, you are full of surprises. First I find you on the marshes at dead of night and now you arrive at my door unaccompanied and say you must speak to me. Could the two be connected, I ask myself.'

'Yes, you could say they are. I have some information for you.'

He smiled and offered her his arm. 'Let us walk.'

They strolled into the park, with the breeze blowing her skirts round her ankles and lifting her hat so that she was obliged to hold it on with one hand. 'It is about the smugglers,' she said.

'What about them?'

'Do you know who they are?'

'I have a fair idea. Local men.' He paused and turned his head to look at her. 'Am I to understand you know more than that?'

'Yes. My brother is with them.'

'John? He is only a schoolboy. Oh, I see, you are appealing to me to fetch him out of the scrape he has got himself into.'

'No, not John. Freddie.'

He whistled. 'Freddie is back? My eye, that is extraordinary news.'

'You did not know?'

'No, why should I?'

'I thought that with you being one of the smugglers, you might have met with him.'

'Did you, now?' He smiled enigmatically. 'But that is by the by. Why is your brother with the lawbreakers when he could be home with you? Just in time for your wedding too. It should be a happy time for everyone.'

'It would be, but...' She paused, not wishing to think about the wedding. 'I am afraid he means to revenge himself on Ralph—I mean the Earl of Blackwater—for what he did all those years ago. I think he only means to knock him down, but I think the smugglers might take the opportunity to rid themselves of someone who is a thorn in their side.'

'Oh, surely you are jesting?'

'No, I am not. I am in deadly earnest.'

'But if I am one of the smugglers, as you say I am…' He paused to raise his hat to a gentleman they were passing. 'You do not suppose I am about to put a bullet or a knife into him, surely?' he went on, when the man was out of earshot.

'No.' Put like that it did seem fanciful. 'You would not condone murder, would you? Lord Latimer was your friend and I believe he still is.'

'True, but I thought you had no love for him.'

'I didn't. I don't.' She felt the colour flare into her cheeks and hoped he had not noticed her slip. 'But I could not live with myself if I was party to him being…' She shuddered and could not go on.

'What do you want me to do, Miss Fostyn?'

'Why, prevent it, of course.'

'Not easy,' he murmured. 'Not easy.'

'But you will try? Oh, please say you will try.'

'When and where is this to take place?'

'Tonight. In his lordship's wood. There is a cottage in a clearing. I am supposed to lure his lordship there by telling him I know the smugglers will be moving the contraband from there at midnight.'

'Can you not simply warn his lordship?'

'No. He might call the revenue men in and Freddie might be arrested. Don't you see, I cannot betray the men, not even the Frenchman, because they will guess it was

Freddie who gave their hiding place away. It has to be you.'

'Frenchman?'

'Yes, he came in on the boat with the contraband.'

'My, you have been busy. What else do you know?'

'I know there was also one called Gaston who has disappeared and they think the revenue men have taken him.' She paused, wondering whether to tell him of the package she had found, but decided against it; it might come in useful to bargain with, but on whose behalf she was not at all sure. 'Have you heard of such a man being arrested?'

'No. This Frenchman, did he return to the ship?'

'I don't know.'

'A dilemma, all round,' he said.

'Will you help me, please, Mr Dent?'

'Why did you not go to Sir Arthur? After all, he should be your protector. And he is nearer.'

'He would not understand.'

He chuckled suddenly. 'I'll wager he would not.'

'Then I can rely on you?'

He patted the hand that lay on his sleeve, before detaching it. 'Leave it to me, Miss Fostyn. Now, I think you should go home and put it from your mind. I believe you are leaving tomorrow to stay with your sister in London?'

'Yes, Annabelle is coming with me. How did you know?'

'Oh, I believe Sir Arthur mentioned it,' he said airily. 'Give Lady Mallard my respects, will you?'

'Yes, of course.'

'We shall see her for the wedding, I expect.'

'Yes.'

He doffed his hat and bowed to her, then turned on his heel and went back the way they had come. She set off for the Spread Eagle, fully expecting Annabelle to have returned before her. But there was no sign of her sister, nor had Partridge, ensconced in the parlour with a pot of ale in front of him, seen her.

Lydia waited twenty minutes and then with a sigh of annoyance went to the Brotherton mansion, meaning to winkle her sister out. She was shocked to learn Annabelle had not been there and everyone was busy preparing to leave for London; the hallway was stacked with bags and boxes and two coaches stood at the door. Lydia turned away, wondering where her sister could have gone. If Caroline Brotherton had had no time to entertain her, she would have left and gone in search of her sister, supposedly buying ribbon.

Lydia had forgotten all about the purchase which had been her excuse for coming to Chelmsford and hurried back into the centre of town to make good the omission, expecting to see Annabelle on the way. But there was no sign of her. She had not returned to the inn either.

'We'll help look for her,' Partridge said, indicating his brother. 'We'll all look.'

In a growing panic, Lydia dashed up and down the streets, poking her head into shops, peering down alleyways, calling on everyone her sister might have visited, but no one had seen Annabelle. After two hours of fruitless searching, they were forced to conclude Annabelle was not going to be easily found.

Slowly it began to dawn on Lydia that Annabelle had meant to disappear. She had been too eager to accompany her to town and she had that carpet bag with her and there was only her word that it contained a gown she wanted to show Caroline. It probably did hold a gown and other things as well, Lydia decided, underclothes and night clothes and the little jewellery she owned. Peregrine Baverstock had been very voluble the day before, talking of leaving by the flying stage. But why would Annabelle travel with him when she was going to London next day in any case? The answer arrived in a flash. Because they were not going to London.

She rushed round to the inn in the market place from which the stagecoaches left and, after questioning several people who worked there, was told that yes, a young lady in a blue cloak and a velvet bonnet had boarded a coach, but it was a north-bound one and she had been alone. On being pressed, her informant insisted there was no young man. Lydia was tempted to give chase, but she knew that would be a foolish thing to do. The coach, with four fresh horses, had left over an hour before and the old Fostyn horse and carriage would never stand the pace of a chase. She could buy a ticket for the next stagecoach, but that did not leave for another four hours and her mother must be told as soon as possible. Lydia went back to Partridge and ordered him to get her home as fast as the old horse would take them.

Anne had been pacing the floor, wondering what had become of her daughters when Lydia finally returned home, hours later than she should have been, and told her the reason. She sank back into a chair, her face paper-white. She seemed not to be able to take in what Lydia was saying, she simply sat with her head in her hands, rocking herself to and fro, too overcome to think rationally. Lydia sat beside her and put her arms round her. 'Don't cry, Mama, we'll find her, we'll fetch her back.'

'Are you sure she is with Peregrine Baverstock? You don't think she might have visited someone else?'

'I thought of that and tried everyone I knew. No one had seen her.'

'She could have met with an accident or been abducted, she might be lying dead somewhere—'

'No, I am sure she is not dead, Mama.' She tried to sound confident, but it was an effort when she wanted to weep as her mother was weeping. One of them must be strong. 'And who else could she be with? You know how she has been behaving lately.'

'Where have they gone?'

'The coach was going to Norwich, but she could have left it at any of the stops on the way.'

'It does not bear thinking of. Anything could happen. Oh, my poor baby! We have all been so busy with your wedding plans—'

'And the Earl of Blackwater's ball.'

'As you say, the Earl's ball.' She sat up suddenly. 'Lydia, you must go up to the Hall and enlist the help of his lordship. He will know what to do.'

'Oh, Mama, we can't ask him to help us.'

'We need help and we certainly cannot appeal to Sir Arthur or any of our friends' husbands, it will only fuel the gossip about us. The Earl is the only one I would trust to be discreet. I would go myself, but I fear I am in such a shake of nerves my feet would not carry me. And you can tell him exactly what happened. Now, put your hat back on and go to him at once.' And, as Lydia was going out of the door to obey, added incongruously, 'Take his umbrella back to him.'

How funny Mama was, Lydia thought as she hurried from the room, to remember the umbrella in the midst of her distress. Nevertheless she picked it up and hurried up to the Hall, wondering how she was going to bring herself to beg for the Earl's help after what had happened between them. Even thinking about it made her go hot all over. He might even laugh at her and send her away,

telling her to sort out her own muddle. Half of her wished
he would be away from home, but then who could they
ask to help them? Annabelle was far more important than
a few moments' embarrassment.

He was busy talking to a plasterer in one of the back
rooms which had yet to be refurbished, but he stopped
what he was doing and came forward to greet her when
she followed the footman without waiting to be fetched.
'Why, Miss Fostyn, I had not expected the pleasure of
your company again so soon. You have brought me my
umbrella. How kind of you.' He took it from her and
handed it to the footman. 'Tea? Cordial? Madeira wine?'

'No, thank you. I cannot stay, I must go back to
Mama…'

She looked almost distraught, her hat was awry and her
big hazel eyes troubled. There were red spots of colour
on each cheek and her breath was ragged as if she had
been running. 'Is something amiss?'

'Yes, we need your help. You see…' She paused and
took a deep breath. 'Annabelle has disappeared.'

'Disappeared? Surely not. She is probably playing hide
and seek.' He paused, suddenly serious. 'She hasn't gone
into the wood, has she?'

Fleetingly she remembered the smugglers and Freddie.
He was the one who should be looking after the family,
but he could not be reached and she wondered if he would
come out of hiding even to find his sister. 'No, no, I left
her in Chelmsford.'

'Mayhap she has met with a friend—'

'No, we asked everywhere and searched the town very
thoroughly. You see, someone very like her was seen
boarding a coach. I am sure it was her.'

'You mean she has run away?'

'I fear so. You see—oh, dear, it is such a shameful

thing to say. I think she might have gone with…with Peregrine Baverstock. They wanted to marry and his parents would not allow it…'

'No, I do not suppose they would,' he murmured. 'Have you any idea where they would go?'

'No, but the coach was going to Norwich. I am sure they would marry as soon as they could…'

'Then it must be Scotland.'

'Scotland! But that's hundreds of miles away. Why would they need to go so far?'

'It would be necessary if they want to do it legally.' He shouted for the footman, who appeared almost at once. 'Hardy, tell Garrard to harness the four best horses to the big coach and bring it to the front door and put your best rider on a good mount. I shall need him to ride ahead and arrange for fresh horses.'

'Yes, my lord.'

'And send my valet to me.'

The man disappeared and his lordship turned back to Lydia. 'Have you heard of Lord Hardwicke's Marriage Act?'

'No.'

'It became law ten years ago, just before…well, we won't go into that again. One of its clauses outlawed Fleet marriages. They were called Fleet marriages because they were performed without banns or licences in the inns and taverns of the Fleet, especially popular among young people whose parents disapproved of their choice. But they occurred in other places too, wherever a cleric could be persuaded to perform them. The consequence of making them unlawful is that anyone wanting to marry without parental consent is now obliged to make the long journey to Scotland, where it is possible to be wed at Gretna Green by making a simple declaration.'

'And that is legally binding?'

'Yes.' His valet appeared in answer to his summons and he turned from Lydia to order him to pack a few clothes for a few days from home. 'Nothing lavish,' he said. 'I shall be travelling light. And fast.'

'You are going after them?' Lydia asked as the man went off to do his master's bidding.

'Yes, after I have checked with Lord and Lady Baverstock that their son is also missing.'

'You think he might not be?'

'It would be foolish to make assumptions. You did say your sister was alone when she boarded the coach?'

'Yes, but I have been thinking. The coach calls at Malden and that is the nearest staging post to the Baverstock home. He might have joined her there.'

'We shall soon find out. Now go back to your mother and bear her company. Do not let her become dispirited, and, please God, I shall be back in no time with your sister safe and sound.' If his guess as to the runaways' destination was correct, they would change from the Norwich coach to one going to Cambridge and thence to Peterborough and the Great North Road. He might, if he left immediately and if his equipage did not let him down, stop them before they managed to go any further.

'Oh, thank you, my lord.'

He regarded her with his head on one side and smiled crookedly. 'You may thank me when I bring her back.'

He could not refuse her plea for help, he told himself, as he hurried out to his coach, could not refuse her anything, but this latest crisis could not have come at a worse time. He had, only that morning, been to the cottage in the wood and seen the evidence of a new cargo of contraband. Brandy and wine, silks and tea, all had to be distributed and paid for and he had meant to be there when they moved it and then he would apprehend them all. Being a magistrate he could, within limits, choose how to deal with them after that: leniency for some, the Assizes for the hardened criminals. With luck he might fetch the runaways back in time but they had had several hours' start and he was not hopeful.

He smiled wryly as the coach passed Lydia as she went out of the gate and turned down the lane towards the dower house. At least if she was safe at home, comforting her mother, she would not be out on the marshes or blundering through the wood, where anything could happen to her.

Lydia let herself into the house. There was only one consolation to Annabelle's disappearance that she could see; Ralph Latimer would not be able to keep that rendezvous with Freddie. Freddie. He would wonder why she had not obeyed him. Would he be angry enough to come to the house? In her present state, how would her mother react to his sudden reappearance?

She could not tell her about the smugglers. Her mama would be horrified if she knew her son was mixed up with lawbreakers and planning some dark deed. And then her heart jumped into her throat. Supposing it had not been Annabelle getting on that coach? Supposing she was not with Perry at all? Supposing her sister had met Freddie and Freddie had involved her in his scheme because Lydia herself had been reluctant to cooperate? Supposing Freddie had gone off to do something else and was not with the smugglers and they had got Annabelle? All supposition, but all very frightening.

She could not sit still and paced the drawing room from window to door and back again while her mother sat on a sofa, watching her, doing nothing except knead her hands in her lap and sigh softly. Hour after hour.

'Mama, you must go to bed,' Lydia said at last. 'They cannot possibly be back tonight and you will need all your strength tomorrow. Take some laudanum, that will help you sleep.'

'What will you do?'

'I shall come and sit with you until you fall asleep, then I shall go to bed too. We must put our trust in his lord-ship.'

'You do trust him, don't you, Lydia?'

'Yes, I do.'

'Then perhaps I will lie down.'

Even under the influence of the drug her mother took a long time to fall asleep, but once she had done so, Lydia dressed in Freddie's clothes, fetched the package from her clothes chest, hurried downstairs and into the night. She would use what she had to buy Annabelle's release.

She had spent so much time walking in the dark lately, she found the way with no trouble at all. There was no one at the hovel in the wood, though the contraband was still stacked on the floor, covered with an old sail. She sat down and leaned against a tree trunk on the other side of the clearing where she could see anyone who came and prepared to wait. What she had not bargained for was that she would fall asleep.

She woke suddenly to the sound of a horse snuffling. It was very dark and, for a moment, she wondered where she was, but then she saw a pinpoint of light which grad-ually became a lantern on the cart to which the horse was harnessed. She sat up cautiously. There were men there, two she knew for villagers, two she did not know and the fifth was her brother. There was no sign of Annabelle or Robert Dent.

While she watched, they finished loading the cart and

covered it with the sail. 'We'll come back for the rest later,' one of them said. 'Daniel, you keep watch.'

Daniel, Lydia realised, was the gardener's assistant who had brought her the letter from Freddie. She wondered if Sir Arthur knew what his employee was up to.

'No, I'll wait,' Freddie said. 'You take the boy with you.'

'What are you up to, Fostyn?' the first man said. He seemed to be the one in charge.

'Tell him I'm waiting to see if Gaston turns up.'

'He won't. Either he drowned or the revenue men have got him.'

'You can't be sure of that. I'll wait anyway. You tell him I'll come with the second load. I might have other good news for him.'

'What other good news?'

'He'll know. Now get going, or you'll not be finished by dawn.'

They all left, except Freddie, who watched them take the rutted track through the trees to the old Roman road, then turned back into the hovel.

Lydia waited a few moments, then left her hiding place and crept towards the tiny building, but in spite of her care, his senses were alert and he heard a twig snap under her foot. It sounded like a pistol shot. He was up in an instant and at the door, a pistol in his hand.

'Don't shoot, Freddie, it's me.'

'Lydia! What are you doing here? I told you to keep away.'

'I had to come.'

'Why? Did you want to see the fun?'

'I do not think it would be much fun, Freddie. You would have shot me, if I had not called out, wouldn't you?'

'You foolish girl, that is just why I told you to stay away. Not that I would have shot you, but someone else might.'

'And Ralph Latimer? Were you planning to shoot him?'

He grabbed hold of her arms in a grip that hurt, making her cry out, but he did not release her. 'You told him. You told him I was here and the coward has sent you to say he is not coming...'

'No, Freddie, I have said nothing to him, but Annabelle has disappeared...'

'Annabelle? My baby sister?'

'Yes, but she is no longer a baby, Freddie. She is sixteen. She thinks she is in love and at first we thought she might have eloped. Mama still believes it, but I was afraid...'

'Afraid of what?'

'I thought she might have been abducted by...by...' She stopped, frightened by the steely look in his eye. 'The smugglers.'

He gave a cracked laugh. 'Why should smugglers be interested in Annabelle?'

'I do not know. Perhaps, like me, she stumbled upon something she shouldn't have. There is more going on here than shipping contraband, isn't there?'

'What else?'

'I don't know. But I heard a Frenchman talking and something about a man called Gaston who has disappeared—' She stopped suddenly because his grip had tightened. 'You are hurting me, Freddie.'

'Sorry.' He released her and she stood facing him, breathing quickly. 'I did not mean to hurt you. I am afraid, being so long out of society, I have forgotten what a tender flower is.'

'I am not so tender, Freddie. I am tough because I have

had to be to help Mama, but I am also very worried about Annabelle.'

'Lydia, I promise she is not with us. Oh, I wish I could come home and help you look for her.'

'Why can't you?'

'Lydia, I cannot.'

'Then you cannot complain if Ralph Latimer is gone in your place. Mama trusts him and he has promised to find her and bring her back.'

'So, he is not coming here tonight?'

'He cannot. He is miles away, chasing after Annabelle.'

'Damnation!'

'If he does bring Annabelle back to us, then you will owe him a great debt, Freddie, and I hope that means you will forget your hate and anger and learn to live with him as a neighbour, as I have had to do.' It hurt her to say it, not because she had been wrong all these years, which she freely acknowledged she had been, but because she loved the Earl and living with him as no more than a neighbour would be even harder to bear, especially when she was married to Sir Arthur.

'I cannot.'

'Then you are no brother of mine,' she said angrily.

'Lydia, dearest Lydia, it is entirely out of my hands now…'

'What do you mean?'

'I cannot tell you. Oh, I am in worse straits than I was when I left here ten years ago. But I wanted to come home, it is all I ever dreamed of, and so I agreed—'

'Agreed to what?'

'Lydia, go home,' he said suddenly. 'Those men will be back shortly and you must not be here when they come. Go, please.' He gave her a little push and reluctantly she went, head bowed, brain whirling. She no longer thought

Annabelle was in danger from the smugglers, but what of Ralph? What had they got against him? And Robert Dent, where was he?

'Got you!' She was suddenly enveloped in something thick and sour smelling. She could see nothing, could hardly breathe. She struggled, trying to cry out, but her voice was muffled by the coat or blanket or whatever it was that had been thrown over her head. A rope was flung round her, pinioning her hands to her sides. Then she was lifted up and thrown, none too gently, into what she took to be a cart, for it started to move off.

She kicked and wriggled but she could not free herself and gave up trying. If her captors were the smugglers, they were probably going back to the hovel for the next load and Freddie would be there and would make sure she was freed. She could not see, but she could hear well enough.

'He says he sent a message to the Earl, telling him the smugglers are at the cottage in the wood, and if he wants to catch them he must move immediately.'

'Good,' said another voice. 'I hope he makes a good job of it. Sometimes I wonder if his heart is in it.'

The first man laughed. 'Never mind his heart, I am only concerned that he keeps his head. I think we should stay around and make sure. Wouldn't want him to turn lily-livered.'

'Do you reckon he will? According to him, he's going to throw the body in the marsh where it will never be found... No body, no one to blame and everyone to think he's gone back where he came from on account of the rumours.'

'Our lord and master ain't interested in old feuds, he wants the man dead for other reasons.'

So, they did mean to kill Ralph and her brother was

supposed to be the one to do it. How thankful she was
that Ralph was miles away on another errand entirely. But
what of her? Failing to deal with their first target, would
they take her instead? Freddie would never allow that. Nor
would Robert. But where was he? She had trusted him,
but perhaps he never meant to help.

The cart drew to a stop and then there was Freddie's
voice, strong and reassuring. 'You took your time.'

'Did he come?' The man who spoke was jumping down
from the cross seat of the cart.

'Gaston? No. I reckon you can kiss that parcel goodbye.
It'll be at the bottom of the sea.'

'Which is where you'll be, if you don't keep your part
of the bargain.'

'I will, never fear. Come and give me a hand with the
rest of the load. It'll take all night if I have to do it alone.'
He was very near the back of the cart now. 'What have
you got there?'

The man laughed and grabbed Lydia's shoulder to
make her sit up. 'A prisoner. Found him spying...' He
whipped the covering off Lydia's head and with it went
her hat. 'My, my, what have we here? A pretty little fe-
male, to be sure.' The man was big and broad-shouldered.
His hands were massive and his grip as strong as steel.
'Who are you, girl?'

Lydia stared at her brother, not daring to speak, and he
stared back. Then he laughed. 'My sister, poking her nose
in where it's not wanted.' He sighed heavily. 'She was
always the same, even when she was little...'

'Thought you said you weren't going home, said you'd
stay here until he came...'

'So I did, so I have. She came here this afternoon, exercising the dog. I had to speak to her, sent her home.
Had no idea she would come back.'

'What are we going to do with her, Joe?' This was the second man who had jumped down from the cart and joined them.

'Let her go home,' Freddie said. 'She won't tell, she wants him out of the way as much as I do. That right, little sister?'

Lydia nodded; she dare not trust herself to speak.

'Well, I ain't so sure,' the man called Joe said. 'We'd better keep her until it's all over.'

'No, let her go. Can't you see she's terrified?' This was patently true, she was shaking with a cold sweat.

'Can't do that. Need to ask Sir. He might have other ideas.'

Freddie, who had obviously been trying very hard to remain cool, suddenly lost his nerve and grabbed Lydia, manhandling her out from the back of the cart. She tried to stand but her legs had become numb and she felt herself sinking to the ground. He hauled her upright. 'Let her go, can't you? She won't say a word. She wants me home and she knows it cannot be done any other way. And she's only a child.'

'Old enough to dress herself in boy's clothes and go spying.' The man took hold of her shoulder and pulled her from Freddie's grasp. She felt like a toy being fought over by fractious children. 'Ain't that right, miss?'

'Not spying,' she whispered. 'Wanted to join in…'

Joe laughed and began to untie her bonds. She stood facing them, rubbing her wrists, but otherwise not daring to move. He continued winding the rope round his hand and elbow as he did so. His hand moved over the bulge in her pocket. 'What have we here? A gun, is it?' Before Lydia could deny it, he had his hand in her pocket and had withdrawn the package. 'Not a gun. Something far more interesting.'

She looked about her, wondering if she could make a run for it while he was busy untying it, but the other man anticipated her and grabbed her.

The map, the water-stained documents and the stones, white in the moonlight, lay open in his hands. He looked up and his expression terrified her even more, if that were possible. 'Where did you get this?'

'I found it.'

'You lie.'

'No, it's the truth.' She looked to Freddie for support, but he was looking at the contents of the package as if mesmerised.

'Where's Gaston?' the big man demanded.

'I don't know who you are talking about.'

'Let her go,' Freddie said desperately. 'I'll stand buff for her.'

'And who'll stand buff for you?'

'What do you mean?' Even in the poor light, Lydia could see him pale. Unless he could remain in control they were lost.

'I mean it looks as if you did away with Gaston to take possession of these.' He picked up one of the stones between finger and thumb and held it up to the moon. It seemed to glow with a light of its own. 'Worth a fortune and well worth killing for. Passed them on to the little sister, did you? Told her to keep them safe for you.'

'No. I didn't know she had them. Lydia, you did find them, didn't you?'

'Yes, on the beach.'

'Well, it puts a different complexion on things, to be sure. Get in the cart, both of you.'

'No, let her go,' Freddie said. 'I'll come, if you let her go.'

'You'll come in any event.' He suddenly shot out a fist

and Freddie went down like a stone. Then he turned to
the other man. 'Put him in the cart. And her. We'll come
back for the rest of the stuff and see to that other business
ourselves.'

Once more she was tied, this time with her hands behind her back, and manhandled into the cart beside her
unconscious brother and they set off again. Where were
they going? What was to become of them? If they were
killed, what would become of her mama? And Annabelle
and John? If only Ralph would come. She needed him,
she needed his strength, his protection. But he was on
another mission on her behalf and could not come.

The horse plodded on. The two men were silent. She
looked down at Freddie, lying in the bottom of the cart.
He seemed to be still unconscious, but then she saw his
eyes open and he winked at her. Reassured, she turned
away and looked about her. They were passing Mistress
Grey's cottage, but she did not think there would be any
help from that quarter. When the smugglers were abroad,
it did not pay to be too inquisitive. She would be in bed
with all the lights out and the door locked and perhaps
tomorrow, there would be a bottle or two of wine on her
doorstep, payment for her silence.

They could not be going far, she calculated, because of
the time the men with the cart had taken to return on the
previous occasion. Where? They were moving inland in
a north-westerly direction. Southminster. The road to
Southminster had been marked on that map. The big man
looked back at her from his perch on the cross seat beside
the driver.

'Did you think I might try and escape?' she asked.

'No hope of that.'

'But why should I want to? I have no interest in what

you do, what any of you do except my brother. I want
him home safe and sound. At any price.'

He seemed to find this statement extremely amusing
and laughed aloud, nudging his accomplice. 'Did you hear
that, Martin? At any price, she says. Sir will be pleased
to hear that.'

'You have the map and the stones, what more do you
want?'

'Me? Nothing at all, my dear.'

He turned his back on her and they plodded on, the
cartwheel creaking over the rutted road. 'You'll have to
do something about that hub,' the big man said to his
companion. 'We can be heard for miles.'

'Aye. I'll see to it before I go back.'

They turned off the track onto the Southminster road.
Lydia recognised it easily; she had walked it many a time,
most recently the day she had ventured through the gates
of Sir Arthur's mansion uninvited, the day Ralph had
taken her up in his coach and lent her his umbrella. He
was her umbrella man then and this nightmare undreamed
of. Nor the exquisite torment of knowing that she loved
the man who had been the object of her loathing for ten
long years. And for what? Was her brother worthy of her
loyalty? For the first time she began to doubt it.

She was not allowed to dwell on this unpleasant
thought because the cart turned in the gates of Sir Arthur's
house and she gasped aloud. 'Why are we coming here?'

'You'll see.'

They went on past the front of the house and drove
straight into the stables. It was dark inside, the only light
the lantern on the cart, but even by its poor light, she
could see that this was no stable, but a great warehouse
stacked with contraband. Surely Sir Arthur could not be
unaware of what was happening on his own property?

Daniel and the other man came out of the gloom as the two men on the cart, jumped down and spoke to them, explaining why they had not brought everything from the cottage. 'But we've got something more interesting,' the big man was saying.

Lydia felt Freddie nudge her and looked round to find him sitting close beside her, untying her hands. 'Now,' he mouthed. 'Get out and run for it while they're busy.'

'What about you?'

'I'll be right behind you.' He almost pushed her off the back of the cart.

She ran towards the open door and straight into the arms of Sir Arthur Thomas-Smith.

'Why, Miss Fostyn,' he said. 'What an unexpected pleasure.'

'They forced me…' She jerked her head backwards in the direction of the men behind her who were struggling with her brother. She dare not look back, but she knew he was no match for four men.

'You utter fools!' He was very angry; his usual urbane manner had completely disappeared. 'What did you bring her here for?'

'Found her snooping in the woods,' the big man said, having felled Freddie with another blow of his massive fist. 'She had Gaston's package. We reckon Fostyn killed him and gave it to her to mind.'

'Then give it to me.' He held out his hand. Reluctantly the man produced it from his coat pocket and handed it over. Sir Arthur slipped it into his own pocket and turned to Lydia. 'Now, my dear, I think we should go inside and have a little talk, don't you?'

'What about?' She did not want to go into his house, it would be harder to escape from there.

'About what is to be done.'

'What about him?' the big man asked, as Freddie sat up and rubbed his chin.

'Keep him safe until I decide matters. Now come along, my dear.' He took Lydia's arm in a vicious grip and propelled her out of the building across the yard and in at a side door.

Chapter Ten

The bright light of the room they entered dazzled her for a moment, but he pushed her on to an upright chair. 'Look what we've found,' he said.

It was only then that she realised they were not alone in the room. The Comte de Carlemont, in pale pink and primrose satin, was sprawled in an armchair in front of the hearth.

The Comte scrambled to his feet and executed a flourishing bow. 'Your obedient, Miss Fostyn.'

She pulled herself upright. 'Good evening, Monsieur le Comte.'

'You have been to a masquerade ball, I see.' He held a quizzing glass to his eye and surveyed her minutely. 'A remarkable transformation. But impossible to disguise such a pretty figure.'

She opened her mouth and shut it again, deciding not to comment. She did not think for a minute he believed what he was saying; it was all a tease, but a deadly one. Looking about her, she realised they were in a small parlour. There were two comfortable armchairs and several upright ones round a refectory table, and a sideboard upon which stood decanters and glasses. There was one window over which the curtains were drawn, and the door by which they had entered. Not an easy room to escape from.

'But where is your escort?' the Comte went on. 'Arthur, my friend, you have been very remiss in not taking better care of your bride-to-be.'

'Indeed, I have.' He smiled, but instead of making Lydia feel better, it made her shiver with apprehension. 'I must make amends.' He went to the sideboard and poured wine from a decanter into a glass, which he held out to her. 'Drink this, my dear, it will revive you.'

She took it, but did not drink; she needed all her wits about her.

'I think we had better have a little talk,' he said, drawing up a chair opposite her and sitting down.

'What about?' Her voice was no more than a croak and she coughed to clear her throat.

'All manner of things. Mainly why you should be so foolish as to walk in the woods at night.'

'It was foolish and I am sorry for it,' she said. 'So, will you please release me?'

'Am I holding you? Have I tied you up? Have I locked the door?'

'No,' she said doubtfully, setting the full glass down on the table beside her. 'Do you mean I am free to go?'

'Naturally.'

'And Freddie, my brother?'

'Ah, Mr Frederick Fostyn, such a disappointment to me. I am afraid he has work still to do.'

'You mean…' She could not bring herself to say it.

His smile became even broader and more oily. 'There are goods not yet delivered, deeds not done. When all has been accomplished to my satisfaction, he may return to the bosom of his family…' He paused, watching her face. 'But I must have safeguards, you understand.'

'Safeguards?'

'Guarantees.'

'About the smuggling,' she said, trying to make light of it. 'What of it? It is nothing. Everybody does it round here. You may be sure neither my brother or I will say anything of it to anyone, you have my word.'

'I am glad you are being sensible about it, but I need more than your word. I need your binding oath in a marriage ceremony. If you had been a little less independent and contrary, we would have been married already.'

She thanked God they were not, because whatever the scandal, she could not marry him now, not even her mother would expect it of her. She refrained from telling him so, guessing it would not help her. 'But why do you want to marry me?' she asked. 'You do not love me.'

'Love, now there's a strange thing,' he said. 'It comes and it goes according to the weather.'

'No, it does not,' she retorted. 'Love is constant, it does not waver.'

'Oh, I am very relieved to hear that. I should be concerned if my bride's constancy were to be in doubt.'

She felt as though he was playing with her like a fish on the end of the line and, however much she struggled, he would reel her in in the end. She remained silent, thinking of Ralph. Please God, she prayed, let him stay away from the wood, I don't want him killed, not by Freddie, not by anyone. I would rather die myself.

He smiled again and took her hand. She did not struggle, though she was repulsed by his touch. Better to appear passive, to hear him out, then she would know the extent of the coil she was in. 'Now, Lydia, my dear, let us stop bandying words and come to the crux of the matter. You are engaged to marry me—'

'Still?' she queried.

'I do not remember breaking it off, my dear, and I am sure you will not do so, because if this little visit to me all alone in the middle of the night, dressed like that, were to be noised abroad, it will do your reputation no good at all.'

'But if it is also noised abroad that you are a smuggler and goodness knows what else besides, you will be arrested and I shall not be blamed for calling off the wedding.'

'Ah, but who will do the talking? Not you, I know, because if you do, Master Frederick Fostyn will hang.'

She gasped aloud. 'No.'

'Oh, yes, my dear.'

She hear the Comte chuckle and whirled round to face him. 'And I cannot think why you should find that a subject for amusement.'

'Oh, Miss Fostyn, you are such an innocent,' he said. 'It is a pity you 'ave to learn the 'arsh truths of the real world, but learn them you must.'

'Do shut up, Antoine, there's a good fellow,' Sir Arthur said mildly, then, turning to Lydia. 'He is right, you know. The truth is often unpalatable, but it is still the truth and must be swallowed. Your brother is a murderer.'

'No, he is not.'

'Then what is this?' He produced the package from his pocket and waved it under her nose, before tossing it into the Comte's lap.

'That has nothing to do with Freddie,' she said. 'I found it. I found it in a coat on the beach.'

Sir Arthur turned towards her. 'Just a coat? No body?'

'Just a coat. And I found it before Freddie landed, so you see Freddie had nothing to do with it…'

He laughed. 'Oh, that is the least of it. I could give you chapter and verse of how he was captured by the French and how he bought his freedom, how he had nursed a resentment against a certain person for ten long years and that he was prepared to do anything to come home to settle old scores...'

'Not murder! I will never believe that of him.'

'Nevertheless, he wanted to return home. To do that he had to be brought from Canada to France and from France to England, an undertaking which took a great deal of time, money and risk for which there was a price.'

'Turn informer, you mean? But what could he tell you that was of any importance? He has been away from these shores for ten years and in that time the war has ended. We are at peace with France.'

'Indeed, yes, which was a great disappointment to those who employed him, after all the trouble they had taken, but there were other things he could do. A certain person had to disappear...'

She knew they were talking about Ralph. 'But why?'

'You do not need to know that, my dear. But young Mr Fostyn expressed himself willing to arrange it.'

'He won't do it. I know him. He may be headstrong and foolish, but he would never deliberately kill anyone.'

'Oh, yes, he will, my dear. You see, I have got you and he knows that if you are to live a long and happy life, he must keep his word.'

She slumped back in the chair and closed her eyes. She could not bear to see the look of satisfaction on his face. She had to marry him to keep Freddie safe, and Freddie had to kill Ralph to keep her safe. The man was evil, a devil...

'I should marry her tonight, if I were you,' the Comte put in. 'Make sure of her.'

'I think perhaps you are right, Antoine. Will you stand witness?'

'*Mais oui.* It will be my pleasure.'

'You can't,' she said, almost triumphantly. 'Fleet marriages are banned. Nowadays, you have to have a licence and banns read…'

'But, my dear Lydia, the banns have already been read, or had you forgot we were to have wed two days hence, if you had not postponed it to go to London? I am only bringing the nuptials forward.'

'Everyone will think that very strange. What will you tell them? Mama particularly.'

'Nothing, we will have two weddings; a secret one tonight, another in June in public which your mama shall have the pleasure of arranging.'

'No! No! No!'

'Oh, yes, my dear. Antoine, go and send Daniel to fetch the parson, will you? I would go myself, but I cannot drag myself away from my bride. And while you are there, make sure Fostyn goes back to the rendezvous. Tell Joe to go with him, he might need a little prodding.' He turned back to Lydia. 'I should take that drink now, if I were you. You look as though you might faint.'

Ralph hung on to the strap in the swaying coach. Opposite him sat a very subdued Annabelle and a resentful Peregrine Baverstock. No one had spoken for some time, although it would have been difficult to hold a normal conversation in any case, the coach was rattling at breakneck speed and buffeting all three against the sides and the roof as it slid in and out of potholes and round bends which should have been taken at a walk.

He had found them in the waiting room of the Crown in Colchester, sitting side by side and looking anything but happy. The young man looked sheepish and Annabelle pale and frightened. He surmised she was having second thoughts about the journey they had undertaken, having only just been told how far it was and how long it would take. And the lad, unused himself to public travel, had badly miscalculated how far they would manage to go before night fell and they would have to find somewhere to sleep.

It was past ten o'clock when he found them and they had, so he discovered, been arguing as to whether to put up at the inn or go on and snatch what sleep they could on the overnight coach. Peregrine was all for going on in case anyone was in pursuit, while she had been accusing him of being too mean to procure a bedroom for her. The sudden appearance of the Earl had naturally put an end to the debate.

With some resistance from Perry, who told him it was none of his business, and no opposition at all from Annabelle, he had bundled them both into his carriage, now with the fresh horses, and set off back the way he had come. His groom was left behind to bring his own horses back the next day with the help of one of the ostlers, who would take back the horses belonging to the Crown.

They had almost reached Malden when Annabelle spoke for the first time. 'What do you think Mama will say?'

'I do not know,' he said curtly. 'You should have thought of that before you left.'

He was in no mood to be sympathetic. Thanks to these two silly children, he had probably missed the chance to catch those smugglers or to find out what else was going on. If it was anything more serious than smuggling a little wine and cognac, he wanted it stopped. He felt responsible for the Colston men caught up in it and he did not want to see them hanged if they were ignorant of wider implications.

'I am sorry.' She began to weep and Perry took her hand and squeezed it but he did not speak.

'Say that to your mama and your sister. You know Lydia should not have to worry about you, she has enough to occupy her without having to spend hours searching for you.'

'I know,' she said miserably. 'It was because of me she agreed to marry Sir Arthur Thomas-Smith.'

'You?' he queried in surprise. 'How so?'

'He promised me a dowry.'

'Then why did you run away instead of waiting for it?'

'Because Lord and Lady Baverstock would never allow us to marry, whether I have a dowry or not. They said so. They think we are too much the subject of gossip.'

'And so you subject the family to even more of it,' he said grimly. 'If it was left to me, I should put you over my knee and spank you.'

'I am truly sorry. I thought if we ran away and married without a dowry, Lydia would not have to go on with the wedding.'

'Do you mean that was your sister's only reason for agreeing to marry Sir Arthur?' He could not believe it. He knew Lydia was selfless, but surely that was more than anyone had a right to ask of her?

'Not all,' she said. 'He said he would pay John's school fees. And…'

'And what?'

She hesitated. 'I am not sure she would like me to tell you.'

'You will tell me,' he said, almost grinding his teeth in frustration.

'Sir, you are frightening her,' Peregrine protested.

'I shall frighten her a deal more if I do not hear the truth.'

'The truth,' she said, suddenly blazing with anger, 'is that you were going to turn us out of the dower house and we had nowhere to go and no money either and Sir Arthur offered to provide for us. Lydia had no choice.'

'Are you certain of this?'

'Yes. You do not imagine Lydia wanted to be married to him, do you? She hates him. And you made it worse, offering to let Mama stay in the dower house when it was too late. And now I do not know what will happen.'

He did not either, but whatever she thought of him, he had to do something, he had to stop Lydia throwing herself away on that middle-aged rake who called himself Sir Arthur Thomas-Smith. Why did he think that wasn't the man's real name? Or perhaps it was and he had known him by another. India. A picture formed in his mind of a busy Bengali bazaar and an Indian spice seller in a dirty turban. But the spice seller hadn't been an Indian. He had been French. Gaston Marillaud. But where was the connection?

Gaston Marillaud was a French spy and a very clever man. At a time when Britain and France were in conflict over who should reign supreme in the subcontinent, he had darkened his already tanned skin to make him look like a native and passed himself off as a street vendor. Thus disguised, he had learned the British East Indian Company's plans and passed them on wrapped in packets of spice. The authorities had their suspicions, but he was a clever one and knew everyone who might be sent to track him down, except Ralph himself, who had not been in the country above a few months. The Governor, hearing about other daring exploits in Europe and the Middle East with which Ralph had been credited, had summoned him and given him the job of watching the man.

That was how he came to witness the transaction be-

tween the Indian and the overweight European and realised the Indian was not passing on information, but receiving it. Soon afterwards, he packed up his stall and set
off at a fast lope, followed by Ralph, determined to see
where he was taking the information. It was due to Ralph
the man had been arrested with the information on him.
Only then was his nationality discovered. He had been
locked up, but before his trial someone had engineered
his escape. It was supposed he had gone back to the
French lines and from there, because he was no longer
useful, back to France.

His European accomplice, the one who was passing on
the secrets, had never been apprehended. Everyone was
suspect, except perhaps the Governor himself and his immediate staff, among whom was an Englishman called
Thomas Ballard. Now, suddenly Ralph knew the connection. Thomas Ballard had been the oversized European,
padded out with extra clothes, hair died black and a false
black beard. Thomas Ballard. Sir Arthur Thomas-Smith,
fatter, older, richer, but the same man, he was sure of it.
And Lydia was engaged to marry him!

Did she really hate him? Did she wish herself free? He
could free her simply by reporting what he knew; he believed the man was still a wanted traitor. Did he have
anything to do with the smuggling? This new thought was
more than worrying, it was terrifying. If Thomas Ballard—Sir Arthur—or whatever he called himself, was using the smugglers to cover other activities, then Lydia was
deeply involved. He had done enough harm to the Fostyn
family in the past, he had to see them all safe before he
confronted the traitor. Besides, he loved her more than
life and that counted for more than all the other arguments
put together.

If he had been on horseback instead of in a carriage,

he could have ridden across country and forded the dozens of inlets and creeks which made building roads over that terrain impossible; he could have been in Colston in less than an hour. Instead he had to endure this coach ride and stop at Malden to deliver Peregrine back to his parents.

Leaving Annabelle in the coach, they were received by Lord Baverstock in the drawing room. Sending Peregrine to his bed, saying he would deal with him the following day, his lordship turned back to Ralph. 'My dear Blackwater, I cannot tell you how relieved I am that the young rascal is home safe and no damage done.' He picked up a decanter. 'You'll take a glass?'

'No, thank you. I must deliver the young lady to her mama.'

'Oh, yes, quite. You don't know what a relief it is to know that we shall not find ourselves connected to that family.'

'I should be proud to be connected to it, sir,' Ralph said sharply. 'They have been ill used by those who should have known better...'

'But it was you they wronged.'

'No, I never said that, nor ever will. Mrs Fostyn is the epitome of good sense, of courage in adversity and compassion to those who have ill used her, and she has brought up her family to be the same. Now, I bid you goodnight.'

As he left the room, he heard his lordship say, 'Well, I'm dashed!'

'What are you smiling at?' Annabelle asked as he climbed back into the coach and told his driver to set to and not spare the horses. 'Was he very angry?'

'Oh, he will recover, I do not doubt, but if you still want to marry that young man—'

'I don't. At least, not yet. I have decided I am not ready for marriage.'

'It is a pity you did not make that decision before to-night. You have worried your mother half to death, made your sister feel guilty that she allowed you to go off alone and inconvenienced me.'

'I am sorry for that, indeed I am.'

'I shall say nothing of my own inconvenience, but I shall expect you to make amends to your family.'

'Oh, I will. But, my lord…' She paused. 'You will not tell Lydia what I told you, about…'

He smiled. 'About why she agreed to marry Sir Arthur?'

'Yes. She would be even more angry with me.'

'Why?'

'Because I believe she cares for you.' She giggled suddenly. 'She calls you her umbrella man, did you know that?'

'No, I did not.' He spoke sharply to cover the sudden surge of hope that spread through him.

'She is very good at hiding her true feelings and you are the last person she would wish to know about it.'

'Is that so?' He was smiling, unable to maintain his anger towards her.

'Yes, which I own I find difficult to understand,' she said. 'Me? I would not be able to keep such a thing secret, so perhaps she is not in love with you, after all.' And she heaved a huge sigh.

He smiled but said nothing. What did she really know about her sister's true feelings if, as she said, Lydia was clever at concealing them? Annabelle was an empty-headed child only just out of school. She must like weaving fantasies. Umbrella man, indeed! But could there be anything in what she said, just a grain of truth, enough

for him to dare to hope? Always supposing Thomas Ballard could be dealt with. His impatience was becoming
almost unbearable.

Annabelle, after all the excitement, had fallen asleep
with her tousled head against his arm and thus they arrived at the dower house at two o'clock in the morning.

Everywhere was in darkness, which surprised him; late
though it was, he had expected either Mrs Fostyn or Lydia
to be keeping vigil. He knocked loudly and when no one
came, tried the door. It was unlocked. 'Perhaps we should
not disturb them,' Annabelle whispered, leading the way
into the hall, where a lamp burned very low. 'I could creep
up to bed and talk to them in the morning.'

'No. I cannot simply dump you on the doorstep like a
cask of contraband cognac. Go, wake you sister.'

Annabelle turned up the lamp and took it upstairs with
her, dragging her feet a little, because she knew she was
in for a scold. Ralph watched her go. His heart was
pounding with anticipation. Soon he would see his love
again and he would insist on the truth. And then he would
deal with Thomas Ballard.

Annabelle came rushing down the stairs, almost tum-
bling in her haste. 'She isn't there! She was never in her
bed.'

'Oh, my God, surely she hasn't—' He stopped. 'Annabelle, wake your mother, gently though, let her know
you are home and then go to bed. Both of you. Do not
let her know your sister is gone out. If she asks, say Lydia
is sleeping and you do not want to wake her. I will be
back with her before she is missed.'

He turned on his heel, climbed back into the coach and
directed the coachman to take him home. Foolish, foolish
Lydia! Why was she so obsessed with those smugglers?

Did she know something he did not? He felt like shaking her until her teeth rattled; she was risking her life by falling in with them and their nefarious activities, but though he had tried to tell her so, she had evidently not been listening.

He would have expected them to have completed their night's work long before now. So why had she not returned home? If they had discovered her, what would they do to her? Ordinary smugglers might very well frighten her and send her home but these... Were they ordinary smugglers? Had Ballard drawn her into his web? Did she know anything at all about him?

Back at the Hall, he left the coach, almost before the wheels stopped turning and rushed upstairs to change into his old, dark clothes, tuck a pistol into his belt and set off for the clearing in the wood. He did not doubt that was where she had gone. It would soon be dawn and the smugglers would not want to be abroad in daylight.

He stopped his headlong dash as he reached the edge of the trees. Now, for all the need of haste, he must go silently. He crept forward, testing each footfall before putting his weight on it, looking about him, watchful, trying to penetrate each bush, each dark shape, ready to defend himself. The trees thinned and he was on the edge of the clearing. And there she was, dressed as a boy, talking to a huge man. Even her stance and the way she held her head was boyish as if she had taken great pains to master her role.

She had her back to him, so he could not see her face and could not tell if she was being held against her will, but it did not look like it. There was a pistol tucked into her belt, which would surely have been taken from her, if they did not trust her. His mind was in turmoil. She looked so easy with the big man, as if they were waiting for something or someone. Did she know what she had got herself into? He ought to creep nearer so as to hear what they were saying.

Before he could move, a hand shot out and covered his mouth and a voice whispered, 'Don't make a sound,' so close to his ear he could feel the man's warm breath on his neck.

He froze and the whisperer went on. 'It's Robert, Ralph. I'm here to help. Do you understand?' He nodded and the hand was removed. 'Come, where we can talk.'

Reluctantly he turned his back on Lydia and followed the other man until they were far enough away to speak, though still in whispers. 'What are you doing here?' Ralph demanded.

'A little bird told me that if you came into the wood tonight, you would not leave it alive...'

'You mean it is an ambush?'

'I believe so.'

'But why? Who wants me dead? Not... No, I will not believe she would...'

Robert gave a low chuckle. 'If you mean Miss Lydia Fostyn, she is intent on saving you. She enlisted my help, which was fortuitous because I am already fully invo—'

'In the smuggling?' Ralph was astonished.

'No, but Miss Fostyn thinks I am.' His teeth showed white in the darkness as he smiled. 'She feels I have some influence over those who would harm you. Nothing could be further from the truth. I have other fish to fry but, since one is connected with the other, I am here to offer you my assistance.'

'Thank you, but we must fetch Lydia out first.'

'She is there? Oh, my God, I had thought she was safe in bed. Then we had better be extra careful. Are you armed?'

'Yes.'

'Then you go that way and I will go this and come upon them from two sides. There is help on the way, but we cannot wait for it.'

'What help?'

'From London. I sent word.'

'I want Lydia out before they arrive. I do not want her implicated.'

'Then let us go.'

They parted and, using the trees for cover, flanked the two men at the cottage. Ralph waited in position for Robert to give the signal. The big man and Lydia were standing together at the door. Ralph was almost certain Lydia would never use the pistol she wore so bravely in her belt and decided to concentrate on the big man. He saw Robert raise his hand and sprang into the opening, pistol raised.

'Drop your weapons!' he commanded.

The big man hesitated, made as if he was going to obey, then his pistol cracked loudly in the clearing. Fortunately he had not given himself time to aim properly and his shot went wide and landed in a tree beside Ralph's head. He cursed loudly.

Robert dashed over to relieve the big man of the gun before he could reload and make him lie face down. 'You get the other one.'

Ralph turned, fully expecting to see a frightened Lydia. Instead he found himself facing Freddie, whose gun was aimed at his chest. For a moment his astonishment was so great, he simply gaped. 'Freddie!' he said at last. 'It is you, isn't it? I thought it was—' He stopped. Did Freddie know Lydia went out in his coat and breeches? Was that why she was so involved and determined to thwart him?

'Lydia.' Freddie finished for him. He was grinning,

though he kept the pistol aimed at Ralph. 'She looks good in my clothes, don't she?'

'How long have you been back?'

'Cut the cackle,' Joe grunted, as Robert sat astride him to stop him struggling. 'Now's your chance, shoot the devil.'

Freddie glanced at his accomplice and back at Ralph. Ralph tensed. The gun his erstwhile friend was aiming at him was far from steady, which gave Ralph no relief; a pistol held by a man half-crazed with fear was no less deadly than one in the hands of a cool man. 'Where's Lydia?' he demanded playing for time.

'With her husband,' Joe put in and laughed.

'Husband?' he echoed, momentarily taking his eyes off Freddie.

'Yes.' The big man went on. 'A wife cannot give evidence against her husband, can she? Sworn to love, honour and obey him, ain't she? The boy was going for the parson when we left. Pity we had to miss the ceremony...' He stopped abruptly because Robert had knocked him out with a well-aimed blow and pulled a coil of rope from his belt with which he proceeded to tie the man's hands and feet together.

'Is this true?' Ralph asked Freddie, who had dropped the hand holding the pistol to his side. 'Have you sold your sister for your petty revenge? My God, I could kill you...' He stepped forward but Freddie jerked the pistol up again.

'Steady,' Robert said, coming to stand beside Ralph. 'He's mine.'

'No. If you take him in, it will kill Mrs Fostyn. Poor lady, she has had enough to bear and Lydia would never forgive me, not a second time.' He took a step forward, careless of his own life, and held out his hand. 'Freddie, if you love your mother and your sisters and brother, give me your gun. I will not harm you.'

Freddie looked wildly about him. Joe lay trussed and unconscious on the ground. How many others were in the trees, lying in wait for him? He threw down his gun. 'Kill me,' he shouted. 'Go on. Kill me. You should have done it ten years ago.'

'No, I could not do it then, nor can I do it now.'

'You can't mean to let him go,' Robert said, picking up the discarded pistol.

'No. He's going to take us to Lydia, aren't you, Freddie?' He forced himself to sound calm, but inside he was bubbling with anger and impatience. Was it too late to stop the wedding? And if it had already taken place, what could he do about it? 'You are going to take me to the traitor and, on the way, you will tell me everything you know, every last thing. Is that not so?'

Freddie shrugged, but Ralph's sharp prod in the small of his back propelled him forward.

How long had they been sitting there? Lydia asked herself. He had not taken his currant eyes off her the whole time and he was smiling to himself. She decided he was mad. When she complained she could not possibly be married in man's attire, the Comte, returning from his earlier errand, had been despatched again to rouse Mrs Sutton and request her to find lady's clothes which would fit his bride. She hoped the woman would take a long time, a very long time. She had to find a way out of this room and this house before the clothes and the parson arrived.

Even then it would not be the end of her troubles. Freddie was still out there somewhere, and Ralph, all unknowing, would return from his selfless errand on her behalf and straight into danger. If she could only talk to Freddie, make him see sense, tragedy might yet be averted. And if she had to marry Sir Arthur Thomas-Smith to keep them both safe, then she would do it.

'Why?' she asked him now. 'Why me? Why Freddie?'

'Oh, you were simply instruments of my revenge, Miss Fostyn.'

'On whom?'

'Lord Latimer.'

'You mean, the Earl of Blackwater?'

'Yes, but he was Lord Latimer when I knew him out in India. Little more than a stripling, he was, but cleverer than I thought. He was instrumental in my having to leave India in a hurry. I lost my position, lost credibility with those I served, most of my wealth and my wife was never the same…'

'He never gave the slightest indication he had met you before,' she said. 'Are you sure you have not mistaken him for someone else?'

He smiled. 'No, how could I? I was in a position of trust, I knew who had been given the credit for Gaston's arrest, who had pointed the finger at me, though nothing was proved. He did not know I knew.'

'Gaston?' she repeated. 'I have heard his name several times. Who is he?'

He sighed. 'My late wife's brother. He is a loyal Frenchman.'

'A spy?'

'He was.'

'So you were a spy too?'

'Yes.'

She was beginning to understand. 'And Freddie?'

'Freddie is a foolish boy who never grew up,' he said. 'Homesick, easily persuaded.'

'And me?'

He laughed. 'Oh, you are the plum in the pie. Married to me, you cannot give evidence against me, nor will you want to, knowing your brother has wreaked his revenge along with mine. You will restore my credibility and we will be one big happy family.'

She was silent. She longed to tell him that nothing would persuade her marry him, but to say so would anger him and he might tie her up or lock her up or both and she must retain at least a semblance of freedom. But she was shaking with a mixture of fear and fury and at that moment was not sure which was in the ascendancy. She had never felt so alone.

'And will you keep your word and give Annabelle a dowry and look after Mama and my brother John?'

'Of course. And with the Earl of Blackwater no more and no known heir, I shall purchase the Colston estate and, in the fullness of time, I will become the new Squire and you will be mistress of Colston Hall.' He laughed a little crazily and she realised that he really believed she would acquiesce. 'You will like that, will you not, my little dove? That will be your revenge too, for I know you have always longed for it.'

'Yes,' she agreed, hearing footsteps outside the room. A moment later Mrs Sutton entered with a red silk gown over her arm.

'Ah, there you are my dear,' he said. 'Have you found something?'

'Yes, though I doubt it will fit.'

'Then make it fit.'

'I can't see why you don't send her home as she is. Strumpet—'

'She is to be my wife, Martha, please do not speak of her in that vulgar way. Take her upstairs and help her dress. And please make sure you stay with her the whole time. When I send for her, bring her down. You shall stand as a second witness.'

He was not so confident that he was prepared to let her change in privacy, Lydia realised, as she was pushed out of the room, prodded along the corridor and up the back stairs.

'In here,' Mrs Sutton said, opening a door to a bedroom. 'Get those breeches off. You are an offence to the eye. If I had my way, you'd be horsewhipped and stood in the stocks, never mind marry my brother. You don't deserve him. And he don't deserve the likes of you.'

'True,' Lydia murmured, looking about her. There was a bed, a wash stand with washing water in a jug, a table with a vase on it and a chair. There was one window and one door and, as she knew there was no creeper on the outside walls, the door it would have to be.

'As soon as I heard that gossip, I said to him, "Tom," I said, "you must draw back, draw back now, before you are tainted by it", but would he listen? He would not.'

'Tom?' Lydia queried, pretending to fumble with the buttons of her coat. 'You called him Tom?'

'It is another of his names,' she said quickly. 'We always used it as children. Now make haste or you will not be ready before he sends for you.' She grabbed Lydia's coat and began undoing the buttons for her.

Five minutes later Lydia stood in the voluminous sack gown while Mrs Sutton pinched and pinned the front of the bodice to make it fit. It had been made for someone very much bigger than she was and Lydia came to the conclusion it had belonged to the late Lady Thomas-Smith. Would Sir Arthur remember that?

It was of no consequence if he did, she thought, she had no intention of returning to that room to be married.

Mrs Sutton, her mouth full of pins, knelt at her feet to pin up the hem. Lydia reached over her, picked up the jug of water and crashed it down on the woman's head. She crumpled in a heap at Lydia's feet among shards of pottery, scattered pins and a pool of water. Almost mesmerised by what she had done, it was a moment or two before Lydia could move. All her instincts were to render aid, but that was foolish. She lifted the skirts and left the room, locking it behind her.

She crept quietly down the stairs and paused at the bottom to get her bearings. And then she was speeding down the corridor to the front door. There was a footman on duty, sitting on a stool with his back to the wall. She stopped, wondering how to pass him. And then she realised he had fallen asleep at his post, which was hardly to be wondered at; it was almost day and he had probably been there all night. Step by silent step, she tiptoed past him towards the door.

Chapter Eleven

'Do you know who Sir Arthur Thomas-Smith is?' Ralph asked Freddie as they walked swiftly along the old Roman road towards the spot where it joined the Southminster road. Robert had been left behind to drag Joe into the cottage and lock him in.

'A nabob. Grown fat and rich in India, just as you did,' Freddie said resentfully. 'While I slaved as a common soldier, frozen with cold, half-starved, you were enjoying a warm climate and opulence, able to come and go as you pleased.'

'I could not come home, any more than you could. And that warm climate was more than warm, it was damned hot, like a furnace. The fevers that went with it were the equal to anything you had to endure, believe me. But now is not the time to speak of that. Where did you meet Sir Arthur, if not in India?'

'I was introduced to him in Paris at the end of last year. I had been taken prisoner in Canada and they shipped me back to France. He was what was called an intelligence officer; he questioned nearly all the prisoners, those that were half-educated, that is. He wanted to know why I,

who was obviously a gentleman, was serving as a private
soldier, so I told him. It seemed to amuse him...'

'I'll wager it did,' Ralph said grimly.

'He told me I could earn my release by smuggling.' He
gave a cracked laugh. 'Smuggling has been going on in
these parts for centuries. Nobody thinks anything of it.'

'So you agreed?'

'Wouldn't you? I was going to be brought ashore not
five miles from my own home and all I had to do was
bring in some diamonds. He explained that he had
amassed a fortune in India, but employees of the Company are not allowed to bring the profits of their trade
back to Europe, it has to be done in a roundabout fashion,
through Turkey and France. He had converted most of his
wealth to precious stones and got most of them out as far
as Paris. He wanted me to take them the rest of the way.
Of course, there would also be brandy and wine as a sop
to the locals who would be needed to get the boat in. His
brother-in-law, Gaston, was sent in ahead to recruit those.'

'And that was all? He did not ask you to spy?'

'No, he did not and I would not have done it.'

'But you did agree to kill me.'

'I agreed, but I couldn't do it. I've had any number of
opportunities since I returned, but I could not bring myself
to it. I kept thinking what good friends we had once
been...'

'Not such good friends if you could call me out over a
chère amie who meant nothing.'

Freddie was breathing heavily because of the speed
they were going. 'I was an ignorant fool. But you made
me so angry with your arrogance, making me feel insig-
nificant...'

'I am sorry for that. It was not intentional. It was simply
that I was older than you and considerably bigger.'

'Oh, you were undoubtedly that. I could not beat you at fisticuffs, or with a rapier, but with my father's pistols I stood a chance.'

'Would you have killed me, then?'

'Would you have killed me?'

'No. How could I? You were my friend.'

'Then you have your answer. I told Lydia not to interfere. I told her to go back to bed and say nothing, but the silly child decided to creep out after me and try to stop us herself.'

'Lydia,' Ralph said, conjuring up a picture of her as she had been when he met her in the clearing the first time. So desirable. And so angry. He had been angry too and stupid. He wished he could expunge that memory, but it continued to haunt him. 'She always wanted to join in our games.' He laughed suddenly though it had a hollow ring. 'She still does.'

'The last thing I wanted was to involve her,' Freddie said. 'But there she was, out on the beach, watching us. And she had picked up Gaston's coat and retrieved the package which was meant to be used to pay the local contact.'

'What happened to him?'

'I do not know. I assume he drowned. You know what the marshes are like. It's easy enough to fall into deep water. He may have thrown his coat off in an effort to save himself and the coat drifted down to the beach where Lydia found it. Makes no odds, it's back with its owner. Along with Lydia.'

'If he has harmed a hair of her head—' He stopped speaking, but his pace quickened until he was running. 'She won't marry him, will she?'

'I don't know.' Freddie was running too. They left the

old road and followed a path which led to the back of Sir
Arthur's mansion. 'She might think she has no choice.'

'Then pray we are in time.'

'What are you going to do?'

'Stop it, what did you think? I can't let her throw herself away on that fiend to save my neck or yours. I would
rather die.'

'You are in love with her yourself,' Freddie said, suddenly realising why Ralph was in such a hurry.

'Yes. We have to stop that wedding.'

'If it ain't too late,' Freddie said morosely.

'You had better pray it is not,' Ralph muttered grimly.
'Or I might be tempted to hand you over with the others
for trial. So, are you with me or against me?'

'With you. You do not need to ask. But we could do
with more help.'

'I believe there is some on the way.'

Sir Arthur's mansion loomed in front of them and
Ralph stopped, breathing heavily. 'Where would he be
holding her? Which room?'

'Somewhere in the back wing, I think. He keeps the
front of the house for his public face, the solid worthy
citizen. And he would not want his daughters upset.'

'How many men does he have?'

'The servants, of course, though how loyal they are I
do not know. There's young Daniel and Joe, but Joe is
safe in the hands of Robert Dent, I hope. And the Comte
de Carlemont. I think he's really the one in charge. He
was Gaston's contact, the man who arranged for the goods
to be moved and paid for.'

Ralph had forgotten about Robert and his promise of
men from London, secret service men, no doubt, and
though he would value any help, he wanted Lydia out and
sent home with her brother before they arrived. His only

interest was in seeing that Thomas Ballard was put away. 'Lead the way,' he said.

There was a glimmer of light in one of the downstairs rooms, but the thick curtains were drawn and they could see nothing of the interior. 'It's a small parlour,' Freddie whispered. 'It's where I was given my meals while I was a guest of Sir Arthur these last two days and where we sat and talked. I reckon that's where they are. That door leads into a corridor and the room is off that.' He pointed to a door a little further along the building.

'Will there be a guard?'

'There hasn't been before. He's seems completely confident of his position in the county, able to fend off awkward enquiries with a well-turned phrase.'

They froze as the sound of a horse and carriage came to them from the front of the house. 'Who's that at this time of the morning?' Ralph demanded, more to himself than to Freddie. 'Go and have a look. I'm going to see if I can get in the house.'

'Aren't you afraid I'll bolt? Or warn them?'

'You love your sister, don't you?'

'Naturally I do.'

'Then go.'

Freddie disappeared, leaving him to creep stealthily towards the door. Silently he turned the handle. It was unlocked. He was inside in a flash and feeling his way along the corridor which was lit by a lamp turned low. Let her be safe, he prayed, as he put one foot carefully in front of the other. He stopped suddenly when he heard voices on the other side of the door he was making for.

'You took your time.'

'I am not accustomed to being dragged out of bed at some ungodly hour, unless for a death, but I am assured by your boy that no one is dead, or like to die...'

'No, it is a happier task I have for you. I wish you to perform a marriage ceremony.'

'At five o'clock in the morning! Sir Arthur, are you run mad?'

Ralph let out his breath slowly and silently. It had not happened yet. The parson had not liked being brought from his bed and had taken his time. Oh, blessed, blessed relief.

'Not at all. I have my reasons.'

'I should be interested to hear them.'

'I hardly dare tell you, sir, but I know I can rely on your discretion. The young lady in question took it into her head to visit me alone and late at night, so foolish, so indiscreet, but understandable, don't you think? Her mama was intent on sending her to London for a few weeks and she did not want to delay the wedding. To save her reputation, I hit upon the idea of sending for you—'

'Quite.' The tone was clipped as if he did not quite believe it, but was not going to argue. 'Where is the young lady?'

Ralph, listening outside the door, caught his breath again. Lydia was obviously not in the room with them, but where was she?

'She has gone upstairs with my sister, to pretty herself up. She was rather dishevelled, you understand. I will send up for her.'

Ralph just had time to dodge back down the corridor and slip into another room before the door was opened and Sir Arthur himself emerged, shouting for Daniel who ran to him from the front of the house. 'Go and tell Mrs Sutton to bring Miss Fostyn down,' he instructed the boy.

Ralph waited. When Lydia came down the corridor towards him, he would grab her and bring her in here out of harm's way while he tackled Sir Arthur. How many other people were in that room beside Sir Arthur and the parson? There would be Mrs Sutton and the boy, Daniel, and that was more than enough for one man to take on. Where was Freddie? He should have joined him by now. Dare he wait? Dare he allow Lydia to go into that room and let the proceedings begin?

Daniel came rushing headlong down the corridor, skittering on the polished marble. 'Sir Arthur! Sir Arthur! She's gone and Mrs Sutton knocked on the head and locked in.'

In the pandemonium that followed, Freddie arrived from the front hall and Robert with him and, behind him, several burly strangers. While the parson looked on in utter astonishment, they proceeded to round up Sir Arthur, the Comte and the protesting Daniel.

'Lydia,' Ralph said. 'I've got to find her.'

Leaving Robert and his men to deal with the practicalities of transporting the criminals to prison, Ralph dashed out of the front door, his only thought to find the woman he loved and never let her out of his sight again. If she would have him. Just because she did not want to marry that murderous traitor, did not mean she would accept him.

There were no large trees in the grounds and the open parkland stood deserted in the rosy light of a new dawn. He ran round the house to the back. Here the path led to the old Roman road and on along the edge of his wood, past Mistress Grey's cottage and on to the home park of Colston Hall and thence to the dower house. With all the activity going on, with secret service men and smugglers blundering about, had she made it safely back home? Oh, how clever of her if she had!

But he had to know. He could not go another hour without speaking to her. He set off at a run. He was just

passing Mistress Grey's cottage when the door opened
and the old lady stood there. She must have dressed hurriedly, for the top button of her bodice was undone and
her white cap on askew. 'My lord, if you are looking for
Miss Fostyn, she is here with me.'

He halted, turned and followed her back into the tiny
living room of the cottage. 'Where?'

'Upstairs, asleep. She was distraught and exhausted,
crying out that the woods were full of evil men intent on
murder. It was some time before I could winkle the story
out of her, but she told it in the end. All of it. She was
so exhausted I persuaded her that she should rest. I told
her you would not be such a goose as to let yourself be
murdered and I would watch out for you and warn you.'

'Thank you, Mistress Grey, you have my heartfelt
thanks,' he said. 'But you will be pleased to know that
the criminals have all been apprehended.'

She looked worried. 'Master Frederick too?'

'No, I think he might be on his way home now.'

'Oh, the relief! Now I think it is time Lydia went home
herself. Will you take her? She is convinced there is a
killer behind every tree.'

'Of course. I have been out of my mind worrying about
her.'

'I thought you might,' the old lady said, with a knowing
smile. 'She is upstairs.' And she nodded her head in the
direction of a door which led to the tiny curving staircase.

He bounded up it and tapped on the door at the top.
There was no reply. Fearing that she had once again
slipped out on her own, he lifted the latch and opened the
door a crack.

Lydia had heard the stairs creak and sat up, drawing
her knees to her chin and pulling the bed covers up round
her so that nothing showed but a pale white face and huge

luminous eyes. Had they found her? Even here, where she thought she was safe, had they overcome her dear friend and were even now coming to take her back to Sir Arthur? She would fight, she would fight tooth and nail to prevent it. She watched, mesmerised, as the door opened slowly.

'Lydia. Oh, my love.' He was across the room in two long strides and gathered her into his arms. 'I've been out of my mind, worrying about you. When I brought Annabelle back and she told me you were not in your bed—'

'You found Annabelle? How is she?'

He smiled ruefully. 'Somewhat chagrined. But we are not talking of that naughty miss, but you. I thought I'd lost you. Why could you not have stayed at home, as I told you to? Anything could have happened…'

'Oh, it was terrible. Sir Arthur…' She shuddered. 'Ralph, you must not go out again, he is determined to see you dead. It has something to do with India, though I did not understand the half of it.'

He smiled. 'One day, I will tell you. But there is nothing at all to be afraid of, not any more. Sir Arthur and his accomplices have all been arrested for treason. Robert and his agents are taking them to London, even now.'

'All of them? Oh, Ralph, Freddie was with them. Oh, I cannot bear it. Poor Mama.'

'Calm yourself, sweetheart, he helped to round them all up and is on his way home.'

'Truly?' Her lovely eyes were alight with joy and his breath caught in his throat so that he could only nod his assent. 'Oh, I am so relieved. How can I thank you?'

'Oh, I can think of a number of ways,' he said, recovering his composure. 'First, will you ever forgive me for that kiss?'

'Which kiss?'

'The one in the wood, when I hurt you. I was angry

and… Oh, you cannot know how I castigated myself for that. But I was profoundly sorry as soon as I had done it. If you could forgive that…'

'I forgive you,' she said, smiling shyly.

He felt the tight knot inside his chest begin slowly to unravel and for the first time in hours—no, days—he allowed himself to relax a little. 'Thank you. I thought I had lost any chance I might have had with that.'

'Chance?'

'That we might end our enmity.'

'Oh, that. But I need forgiveness too, you know,' she went on. 'I wanted to hate you, I had taught myself to hate you, because, to me, you were all wrong and Freddie completely in the right. How could I have been so foolish? It took me until two days ago to admit how mistaken I was. And by then I realised I was in love with you and Freddie was back and mixed up with those men and—' She stopped, suddenly realising what she had said, and he was grinning from ear to ear.

'What did you say?'

'I said Freddie—'

'No, not about Freddie, about loving me. Did you mean it?'

'Yes.' She felt her cheeks colour at her admission, but she could not deny her true feelings. 'I thought it was the umbrella man I loved, I told myself he was kind and gentle and amusing, and the Earl of Blackwater could not possibly be any of those things and… Oh, say you do forgive me for all those years when I nursed my hatred. It hurt nobody more than myself.'

'If you insist, I forgive you, but I do not think there is anything to castigate yourself for.' She had said she loved him; his heart soared with joy. 'Now, though I could continue this conversation for hours, there are other things to discuss. Sir Arthur, whose real name is Thomas Ballard, is in disgrace and may even hang for his crimes. No one will expect you to honour your engagement.'

'I am free?'

'Yes. There will be no wedding, not to him at all events.'

'Oh.' She heaved a great sigh of relief. 'But what about Annabelle and Mama and—?'

'They will be looked after.' He smiled and kissed the top of her head. 'If you marry me.'

'You?'

'Yes. Will that be such a sacrifice?'

'You know it will not. But, Ralph, you do not have to... You have been punished enough...'

'Then you must marry me, for to turn me down would be the worst punishment of all. I love you. I think I have loved you since I first saw you in Chelmsford sheltering from the rain in that doorway.'

'Oh, Ralph!' She put her arms about his neck and kissed him. He smiled and ran his finger round her face, so gently, so tenderly, she knew that the umbrella man and the Earl of Blackwater had always been the same man, though she had been too blinded by her animosity to see it.

'Is that a yes?'

'Oh, yes, yes, please.'

He lowered his mouth to hers, tasting her lips, sweetly and lovingly, and her response was all he could wish for. It was some minutes before he gently disengaged himself.

'Now, my love, I am going to take you home. Your mama will be worried about you and you need to sleep. Later, there will be plenty of time to talk about the future. Our future together.'

'Yes,' she murmured. 'All the time in the world.'

*   *   *   *   *

MILLS & BOON®

Makes any time special™

Mills & Boon publish 29 new titles every month. Select from...

Modern Romance™   Tender Romance™

Sensual Romance™

Medical Romance™   Historical Romance™

MAT

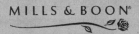

2 FREE

books and a surprise gift!

We would like to take this opportunity to thank you for reading this Mills & Boon® book by offering you the chance to take TWO more specially selected titles from the Historical Romance™ series absolutely FREE! We're also making this offer to introduce you to the benefits of the Reader Service™—

- ★ FREE home delivery
- ★ FREE gifts and competitions
- ★ FREE monthly Newsletter
- ★ Exclusive Reader Service discounts
- ★ Books available before they're in the shops

Accepting these FREE books and gift places you under no obligation to buy, you may cancel at any time, even after receiving your free shipment. Simply complete your details below and return the entire page to the address below. *You don't even need a stamp!*

YES! Please send me 2 free Historical Romance books and a surprise gift. I understand that unless you hear from me, I will receive 4 superb new titles every month for just £2.99 each postage and packing free. I am under no obligation to purchase any books and may cancel my subscription at any time. The free books and gift will be mine to keep in any case.

H1ZEA

Ms/Mrs/Miss/Mr ....Initials.....................................
                                                                BLOCK CAPITALS PLEASE
Surname ....
Address ....

....

....Postcode ....

Send this whole page to:
UK: FREEPOST CN81, Croydon, CR9 3WZ
EIRE: PO Box 4546, Kilcock, County Kildare (stamp required)

Offer valid in UK and Eire only and not available to current Reader Service subscribers to this series. We reserve the right to refuse an application and applicants must be aged 18 years or over. Only one application per household. Terms and prices subject to change without notice. Offer expires 31st January 2002. As a result of this application, you may receive offers from other carefully selected companies. If you would prefer not to share in this opportunity please write to The Data Manager at the address above.

Mills & Boon® is a registered trademark owned by Harlequin Mills & Boon Limited.
Historical Romance™ is being used as a trademark.